Never
Too

D0431007

Novels by Carmen Rita

Never Too Real

Never Too Late

Published by Kensington Publishing Corporation

Never Too Late

Carmen Rita

KENSINGTON BOOKS
www.kensingtonbooks.com

KENSINGTON BOOKS are published by

Kensington Publishing Corp.
119 West 40th Street
New York, NY 10018

All Kensington titles, imprints, and distributed lines are available at special quantity discounts for bulk purchases for sales promotion, premiums, fund-raising, educational, or institutional use.

Special book excerpts or customized printings can also be created to fit specific needs. For details, write or phone the office of the Kensington Sales Manager: Kensington Publishing Corp., 119 West 40th Street, New York, NY 10018. Attn. Sales Department. Phone: 1-800-221-2647.

Kensington and the K logo Reg. U.S. Pat. & TM Off.

eISBN-13: 978-1-4967-0133-6
eISBN-10: 1-4967-0133-X
First Kensington Electronic Edition: April 2017

ISBN-13: 978-1-4967-0132-9
ISBN-10: 1-4967-0132-1
First Kensington Trade Paperback Printing: April 2017

10 9 8 7 6 5 4 3 2 1

Printed in the United States of America

Well-behaved women seldom make history.

—Laurel Thatcher Ulrich

For the sisterhood . . .

Chapter 1

"You haven't spoken to your mom, still?" The woman's question landed with a scold.

"Not all of us have a wonderful mother like you, Luzita." The answer came from her friend with a loving, if envious, eye roll as the women sat arm to arm at the oak bar.

Luz dropped her empty oyster shell and sighed. She gazed at the pearly inside in the dim lights of the restaurant bar. Reflected within: the unlined, deep brown skin of Luz Tucker Lee's high cheekbones. Behind the two women, who were perched above the fray, the bustle of the busy seafood spot filled in the quiet between them.

"I know," Luz said. "But it's not like mine doesn't have her own problems, m-kay?"

"You got that right." Luz's dinner companion was her dear friend Catalina Rosa Rivera. "Cat" was a thirty-something former national television host, now a big face in Web video. She was happier now that she was her own boss, though not as financially secure. Raised by a Chicana single mother who she referred to as "Dragon Lady" ("Tiger Mom" would have been too placid), Cat wondered if and when she'd speak again to the woman who gave birth to her.

"Can I ask, Luz . . . I mean . . . Do you ever get angry at

her? For, you know . . . not telling you?" Cat stammered as she avoided too much eye contact. Luz's mother was wildly better than hers as a parent, but as they all had found out lately, she was far from perfect. Some very dirty family laundry had come to air. It was shocking to have a parent on a pedestal for decades only to see her tumble down from gold to bronze. Cat was sincerely curious and concerned about her friend, as well as looking for a wee break in the veneer of happiness and love that Luz had with her mother. Cat wanted to feel normal at being so pained by her own mother-daughter relationship. She wanted to feel less alone.

"Yeah, I mean, sure. I was mad. I was disappointed." Eighteen months prior—Luz had been keeping count, the day and date burned into her mind like char in a musty fireplace—she discovered that though she was raised by an upwardly mobile immigrant mother and a blue-blooded, wealthy, black professional father and had grown up between a historic townhouse in Harlem and a rambling colonial on Martha's Vineyard, her biological father was something else altogether. He was a now-incarcerated Dominican gangster. It was too close to a stereotype for Luz. But all stereotypes are built on some form of reality. Her privileged black-Latino family was its own cliché in some circles. But now, her circle had been redefined.

This man, her biological father, had been a brief love of her mother during a break from her relationship with Luz's father— her father, the one who raised her, the successful, educated one. *Not the one in prison. Nope. He's not my father. Not really.*

And to add to the news of that day, that scorched-brick day, the impetus for the truth bubbling to the surface: Luz was gifted with the discovery of a sister, the young teen daughter of this man. The girl's mother was dead, her father behind bars, and Luz was now raising her along with her own brood. She was her biological sister, but still just another child to care for.

"You know, I was mad for a minute, Cat. But, thinking about what she went through at that age, what her choices were . . . I think she made the right choice."

Cat raised a brow.

"Look, the lying sucks. It sucks. That just really was the worst part. And funny enough, I'm not really sure why. I mean, I turned out okay, but what would have happened had I known? What if I had had a relationship with this guy? I could have thought that I was no better than him and ended up in some bad places, *sabes?*"

Cat shrugged. "Yeah. That's true."

"Look. I know you need some time with your mother, but remember that our *mamis* come from very different places than we do. They had very different lives."

Cat nodded, processing. She munched on toasted sourdough.

Luz changed her tone a bit, moving from a lecture to an open heart. "They're not like us, hon. Our mothers are made of different stuff. They grew up in a different time. What helped me a lot was doing the whole putting-myself-in-her-shoes thing. What did the world look like to her back then? What choices did she have? Compared to us, they didn't have many."

"I know. You're right. But when she's in my life, it's like I can't move through everything—she's tied to me like an anchor, dragging me down. Like cement shoes, girl!"

Luz chuckled at her friend's dramatic visual.

A cloud of sadness moved across Cat's angular face, a foggy veil Luz didn't want to see slide so heavily over her friend's eyes. Cat continued, "Luz, I wish your mother had raised me. But what I have right now is myself, and I can't move forward with her yanking at me."

Luz had spent the past year encouraging Cat to feel strong and proud of walking away from a life she wasn't happy with.

The life that Cat felt her mother—Dolores, a name that meant sorrow—had shaped and molded for her. Straight As in school, Ivy League undergrad, ambitious local producer, even hosting her own daily TV show covering business and finance. It was a world where a brown girl with a Latin name and Mexican heritage could stand out, plow through with the force of a freight train, taking names the whole way. Cat was proud of all she'd done, even sometimes stunned at her own drive, but once her success was in place, many times she'd looked back at her bio and wondered, *Who was that, who did all that? And why?*

Luz nodded. "I get it, sister, I get it." She did understand. Not as if she'd like the idea of her new "father" in prison blowin' up her cell, always asking or pressuring for something like Cat's mom tended to do. That would be horrifying. "Okay, but here's the real question, you zzzexy thang . . ." They were both a bit buzzed now.

"Okay, now, stop that, because I am still workin' on droppin' that baby weight, mama!" Cat rubbed her barely there paunch.

"When are you and my brother getting married?!" Luz pressed.

"So this is why you insisted on a night out just us gals, huh?!" Cat teased.

"Maybe," Luz mumbled, and smiled.

Cat responded, "Hon, I just want to make sure, okay?"

"Make sure of what?!"

"I dunno. Make sure I know what I'm doing, I guess."

"*Ay,* hon." Luz redistributed the plates on their table, choreographing the clearing of the oyster platter and bread for the luxe bar bites of grilled octopus and fried manchego.

Cat dug in. "Luz, I love him to pieces. You know that. *Dios,* he's the best. Just beyond." Luz blushed at Cat's description of her younger brother. She had to agree that he was a pretty damn fine catch. Not to say that she wasn't absolutely shocked at the revelation that one of her oldest friends in the city, Cat, had been sneaking around with her brother. Well, it wasn't sneaking per se, but they did keep their relationship on the down low mostly because of Cat's mother. Dolores was an old-school racist. She was devastated to learn that her daughter was having a baby with a black man. Cat had decided not to spring Dolores on her partner, as she was already on bad terms with her after losing her television show, the biggest trophy her mother carried in her social case. She had tried to do it over the phone when she learned she was pregnant, to keep Dolores involved somewhat but enough out of arm's reach to maintain her own bravery in the face of potential discord. If Dolores threw something, it wouldn't be able to hit her over the airwaves. And, rather than having to run out the door, she could just hang up. After thirty seconds of Dolores wailing and screaming in Spanish, blasting through her cell at not only the news of an unmarried pregnancy, but the father's blackness, Cat did what she thought would save her sanity, her mind, and her heart. She did just that. She hung up on her mother. Maybe for good.

"Luz, honestly, I'm scared," Cat said.

"Scared?"

"Yeah."

Luz took a long sip of her second glass of wine while Cat sipped on her first, still getting the hang of drinking again even a year after giving birth. Cat wished she could swig it, hard. Shake off the tiny little fingers of guilt pressing into her neck, squeezing her into standing too still, sometimes, too scared.

"What are you scared of, Catalina?"

"Luz. My father left us. And look, I know that Tomas would never do that. I know that, really." She held up her hand to ward off the words she knew were about to come at her.

"Tomas would never leave you guys," Luz assured her as a big sister could.

"But, girl, my head knows one thing but my heart is yelling too loud. It's too scared of being left alone—a single mom, like my mother was—"

Luz interrupted. "But, no! No, Cat. You know he won't do that. He won't. And being married or not doesn't change if he's going to go or not. If anything, isn't he more likely to go because you're *not* married? Not that he would leave. I'm just saying."

Cat shrank on her bar stool a few inches. She felt terrible about her baggage. She felt it was unfair. Or was it? She was uncertain. "Luz, I know," Cat whispered, as low as possible while still being heard over the din. "But, I need to get there, okay? I need to know that marriage to Tomas, marriage in general, will work. And I don't know why I equate a further commitment with him going away—I don't know why, but I need to get there myself, okay? Maybe it's because he was married before. I dunno."

Luz took it in. She adored her very successful younger brother. The one who knew the family secret before she did. The one who her "father" in prison contacted to ask for help— to ask for Luz to take care of her sister. *Their* sister. The brother who kept his relationship with Cat to himself for a while, thinking it bad form to gush about his new love while his family took on the opening of a very riled-up chapter in their lives. Though Luz knew it was more likely he kept quiet because he'd come out of a failed starter marriage and didn't want anyone to think that he was going to hurt one of his sister's dearest friends, and he had to make sure, himself, that it was going to last.

But the addition of a teenage girl? A new sister from the hood who had to be loved so deeply and hard that she wouldn't slip into the cracks of thinking she was no better than the man she was born to. That man in prison. *Father.*

And now, Cat had become another member of her family. Not just a friend anymore, the mother of her baby niece, a delicious Mexican-Dominican-African-American almost-toddler, Alma Thelma Tucker. Luz's own children were half-Asian and she felt blessed that her Chinese-American husband, Chris Lee, the founder of a sold-for-millions Web business, the made-good son of immigrants who settled in Queens, was inured to the stares and questions his very blended family could get once they all ventured outside of New York City or Los Angeles. Shoot, Luz remembered all the times they still got eyeballed even on the Upper East Side. Some people.

Some people don't realize that family is family. No matter where they come from or what color they are. I should listen to myself.

"Cat. We're family now. Whether you marry Tomas or not, we're not going away. I mean, I can't guarantee what my brother will do, but I can tell you that you're stuck with us—the whole *familia!*—no matter what that *pendejo* does! Knowwhattamean?!" Luz's arms stretched as wide as she could Her smile was as broad as the long, crowded bar.

"I know, mama, I know." Cat grinned back, letting herself fall into Luz's embrace as her friend kissed the top of her head.

"But, there's my mom . . ."

"Oh yes, there's that. . . ." Luz responded but deflected, rather than getting back onto that somber track. She looked at the bright side and raised her glass to make a toast.

"Here's to our crazy little brown, black, yellow, white babies who will soon take over the world!"

Cat couldn't resist that, the image of their mini tribe of tots and now a teen, their wild hair and wide eyes filled with the promises that their own mothers wished upon them, now fulfilled. The image forced a wide grin onto Cat's once-worried face.

"*Niñas y familia!*" Cat returned the toast as they clinked their glasses and took a drink.

"And, to our crazy mamas," Luz said.

"Yup, to our crazy mamas . . . May the 'crazy' end with their generation." They toasted and drank again. Cat added silently in her head, *And may my darling baby Alma be spared my mother's poison. Then, maybe everything will turn out okay. . . .*

Chapter 2

There were no sounds of children giggling or arguing, no rustling of cereal boxes being shaken empty, no yelled requests to turn on the TV on a weekend morning. Magda felt a slight pang, missing the chaos of her children, Ilsa and Nico. Her oldest girl, bossy as all heck, just like her ma, would usually be home, trying to watch her tween shows while her younger brother begged for his cartoons and superheroes. The tug of missing them dissipated as Magdalena Reveron de Soto realized what this stillness—courtesy of her children's mother taking them for the weekend—meant. Magda smiled to herself as she lay in bed with her wife of just over a year. Cherokee's back was to her and she murmured an *mmmm,* still groggy.

Magda caressed her wife's arm. "Mornin', sexy." But as Cherokee rolled over with a smile, the landline rang.

"Who is calling this house right now?!" Magda checked her cell phone first to see if she'd missed any calls or texts from her ex about the kids, while the old-school ring blared on.

"Mags, puh-lease, pick that up," Cherokee muttered under the pillow she held over her head.

As Magda reached over to see the caller ID, she said, "Oh man, it's my dad."

"Your dad—" Cherokee was cut off by Magda's quick picking up of the call.

"*Papi,* hi. . . . *Qué pasa?*" Magda got out of bed, her phone to her ear, her long, heather gray, designer tee hanging to her mid-thigh and off one shoulder. She used her left hand to smooth down her short, wheat-hued hair.

Magda had had a zero relationship with her father for more than ten years. As his oldest, she had spent her childhood groomed by both her parents to follow the traditions of a well-off, doctor-led, Venezuelan immigrant family living in Miami. Statuesque, golden-haired, and whip smart, Magda was entered in beauty pageants and cast in commercials for local television from the age of eight. She nearly won Miss Miami her senior year of high school. If only she hadn't flubbed—possible self-sabotage—the talent portion, which in her case was playing the flamenco guitar. She loved what the guitar did to her fingers. She took pride in her callused digits, an outward sign of what she felt inside, rough. Her fingers itched when she thought back to her now-lost hobby. But back then, she was hard-worked, pent-up, pretty, but not so perfect as everyone thought.

Her father had had so many hopes and dreams for her, not to mention local Ivy League suitors to marry her off to. "Think of my grandchildren!" he'd say. *Never,* Magda would tell herself. *I'm never having children. Well, not with a man, anyway.* She had thought that her father's love for her, and the love of her mother and extended family, would mean that they would accept her for who she was and as a person. Her sisters not as much, as she was only close with one out of the three, the others resentful of the attention given to her, the firstborn, the "golden child," they called her. A sister, a daughter, who was very much female but who didn't want to wear heels and lipstick anymore, or have relationships with men.

When Magda came home during a college break scrubbed clean of the usual feminine accoutrements, flaunting her new, buzzed short hair, looking much more like a teenage boy-band idol than a former beauty queen, her father refused to speak to her again. Ever. She was iced out and financially disowned. Her mother, traditional in her own ways and subservient to her husband, seemed to follow suit. But Mama Carolina had other plans. She may not have understood her daughter's choices, but she understood that this was still her daughter, her flesh and blood, always. That trumped every decision her daughter made, every bad turn, every venture into what Carolina was raised to think immoral. Within a month, like a corporate whistle-blower, Carolina had purchased a cell phone specifically to call her daughter without her husband's knowledge.

For years, Magda's mother, Carolina, continued the secret arrangement with her eldest child, taking advantage of her husband's frequent travel schedule to sneak away on her own flights to spend long weekends visiting her daughter's homes in Manhattan and California, reveling in her grandchildren. And she liked very much their mother, Albita, a stunning woman, as girly as they came. Carolina mourned when Magda split with Albita, but supported her daughter and her decision with late night phone calls, sometimes lasting for hours.

In all that time—children born, her fortune built—there was nothing but silence from Magda's father. Cold, stern, judgmental silence.

But when Carolina was diagnosed with cancer and given just months to live, her husband, Magda's father, Dr. Raoul Reveron, finally contacted his daughter. His call was out of obligation and family leadership, initially. Their reunion in the hospital during her mother's final days was an ugly one. They argued loudly in the hallway, hurling at each other insults and barbs aimed to maim and cause pain, each wanting to inflict as much trauma onto the other as they'd suffered for years, alone.

But the funeral was full of the usual Latin drama, including a *tía* attempting to throw herself into the burial plot and onto the coffin. This scene was framed by dramatic wailing, a frayed mix of cultures present, the clash of personalities, and then oddly jolted out of his anger, Raoul found himself opening up to his daughter. Though now, nearly two years later, he still wasn't a fan of Magda's sexual orientation. He didn't have to say much. He'd just continuously and inappropriately mix up his qualifiers or stutter over her reality: "When's your, your . . . lady coming home?"

"You mean my wife, Cherokee," Magda would reply.

"*Ya, ya* . . . how you say."

There was one element of Magda's life that he could not deny and was very proud of: her professional success. A venture capitalist and philanthropist—without her father's help, except for the fodder of spite—Magda used her brain, charisma, connections, and Ivy League MBA to build a solid portfolio of investments, and through her network and reputation, become a top advisor to others in her space. She could afford a home on each coast with ease and traveled with her brood, even now, returning a few times back to her childhood home in Miami. One of her sisters, Veronica, had moved in with their father. "Nica" was a newly divorced mother of two ensconced in her place of birth with her kids and their *abuelo*. Settling into accepting his status as widower, Raoul worked to enjoy retirement from his practice, golfing most mornings, distracting himself from deep heartache with the swoosh of clubs through the salty sea air, missing his wife of forty years in a way he'd imagine missing an appendage. It felt like he'd lost his right leg or arm.

"*Papi?*"

Cherokee listened to Magda's voice as she peered out between the pillows to watch her wife walk barefoot down the long hall into the kitchen. Magda's tone—and Cherokee's lack of Spanish vocabulary to understand—made her frown with worry.

"Wait, wait, slow down," Magda said to her father in Spanish.

"I was just wondering if you could come down here," he pleaded.

"To Miami? When?"

"You know, soon."

"*Papi* . . ."

"This weekend?" Raoul never asked for favors and never had Magda heard this strain in his voice. It was new and foreign. After all they'd been through, it unsettled her. She knew something was wrong.

"*Papi,*" Magda responded, "I've got a big fundraising dinner tonight. I can't miss it. What's so big that you can't tell me over the phone?"

Silence.

"Okay, now you're scaring me. Is Nica all right? The kids? Everybody?"

"Yes, yes, everybody's okay." Raoul's voice was flat. Now that she knew everyone was safe, that no one was sick or in the hospital, Magda became mildly exasperated.

"*Papi.*"

"I just, I just really think it's better we talk face-to-face."

Magda rolled her eyes. *What in God's name is this about? It must be serious.*

"Okay. *Papi.* Listen. Let me see what I can do, okay? I'll have to move a few things around, but I'll try to swing down on Sunday morning. I have to make it back for work and when the kids come home first thing Monday, okay?"

Magda could nearly see her father, many miles away, straighten his back at the good news that she had agreed. She sighed.

"*Claro,* good, good. That sounds good." Relief was folded into Raoul's tone.

"Okay, *Papi.* I'll text you my flight info later today, okay?"

"Okay, *m'ija,* but can you e-mail it to me instead? I never can get the hang of the texting."

Magda smiled. "Sure. E-mail it is." She hung up the phone, the click lingering in her ears. She stared out the floor-to-ceiling window overlooking the whole of downtown Manhattan, the rivers on both sides hugging a nearly 360-degree view of

Brooklyn, New Jersey, Ellis Island, and the Statue of Liberty. Magda fixated on Madame Liberty's raised torch.

What's goin' on with Pops, pretty lady? What are we gonna have to do?

"Sweetie?" Cherokee called out to her from the bed. "Everything okay?"

Magda snapped out of her rumination, shaking her head as if she could shake off the worry and see straight again.

"Yeah, yeah, hon. Nope, it's fine. All fine." Magda took one last look at her green idol, her goddess, standing solo and strong in the water. She walked back to the bedroom. "Something very strange is going on with my dad—I'm going to have to make a quick trip down there in the morning." Magda leaned onto the bed and stroked her wife's arched brows as she spoke. "Sorry."

Cherokee smiled at Magda's touch, closing her eyes to enjoy it. "No 'sorry.' If you have to go, you have to go." She opened her eyes, and Magda dropped her hand. "But just tell me, is everything okay?"

"I think so. I don't know. He says everyone's fine and healthy, so it must be some other family news. Maybe he has a girlfriend or something!" Magda's eyes lit up for a moment in shock. "Wait." She raised a finger. "I mean a real girlfriend that he actually wants to introduce us to. Not one of his little side pieces . . ." She smirked.

Cherokee mirrored Magda's smile. "I'll be your side piece," she teased. "And your front piece and back piece. . . ."

Magda relaxed into Cherokee's arms and allowed herself to be distracted, if only for a few, quiet moments, before her life changed again.

Chapter 3

It was a husky and no-nonsense voice. "Hon, come here. I've got someone you need to meet."

"Oy! Okay, coming." Gabi allowed her hand to be pulled by the raven-haired executive who had arranged the screening. "When Luna says so, I gotta go! Nice to meet you." Dr. Gabriella Gomez, formerly Gomez Gold, waved and smiled at her new acquaintances as she was led away. The receiving room of a former, stately hospital in Harlem had been transformed into a lush cocktail lounge for the night. Velvet chairs, palm trees, dim lights, and strong drinks balanced on trays carried by beautiful young things. It all created a dreamy effect that Gabi more than welcomed. She was a single mother now and in the past year— her most professionally successful with the launch of her second book, *Super (Single) Mom*—she had felt overwhelmed by the demands of a relentless speaking and media schedule, as well as her most important to-do on the list, her cherubic son, Maximo. He was six years old now but continuing to act out at school, clinging to his mother in fear that she would go away, too, like his father. It was all so much. Add to that the primal need for human, physical contact and sensual love, which she hadn't had in years, and Gabi had the urge to drink a bit too much that night.

"Here." Luna pulled Gabi in close toward another guest.

"Maxwell, this is Gabi—Dr. Gabi Gomez." The executive, her designer black suit jacket shimmering, her freckles and painted red Cupid lips taking the edge off her throaty voice and formidable posture, playfully yanked Gabi to stand directly in front of the star of the premiere, the lead actor in the series launched that night. Only with Luna's pull was Gabi able to cut through the phalanx of women standing around him. Maxwell Dane was a regal-looking, brown-skinned brother with an edgy beard and the slight build of a man who needed to hit the red carpet in slim, sample-size suits on the regular. Gabi got caught up in his eyelashes. *So long.*

"Oh, hi! Hi, I'm Gabi." She shook his hand.

"Hi, Gabi, Maxwell." The actor took her hand and embraced it between both of his, squeezing gently.

Gabi's insides fluttered.

"Maxwell! My son's name is Max, too—actually Maximo." Gabi grinned.

"Oh, really? Love that! And how old is he?"

"He's six—first grade. But you know, thinks he's ten." Gabi rolled her eyes at herself, then took in what was around them. The people, the party noise, and the women giving her the side-eye, as loud and pressing in as they all were, faded into the background. Maxwell had pulled her into a quiet, velvet vortex. She vacillated back out for a second, slightly self-conscious, as she noted the other women staring at them both, waiting for their turn. But Maxwell still hadn't let her hand go.

Gabi withdrew her own hand. "Well, I don't want to take up too much of your time, but congratulations on the series and wishing you all the best with it! What we saw tonight was really fantastic." She was sincere. It was a great show and a sure success with a fantastic Hollywood director and a fresh, daring cast.

"Thank you, thank you so much." Gabi noted that he was genuine as well. As a therapist whose job it was not only to listen but to tease out the truth to better help her clients, one of

Gabi's "powers," as she'd call it in jest, was registering falsehood. A Wonder Woman fan from grade school, she'd imagine herself—particularly with difficult clients who couldn't face even their own true selves—throwing a golden lasso on them before they even sat down. She'd imagine that lasso, glowing, to remind her to always test what was coming out of someone's mouth versus what their bodies were telling her—bodies being much worse at lying than lips. Too bad she didn't use her powers in her own marriage. She'd dropped that golden lasso as soon as she walked through the door of her home. Her now ex-husband had found a way to disarm her from day one. She'd never let that happen again.

Luna watched Gabi and Maxwell from the side out of one eye as she simultaneously managed the rest of the crowd.

Maxwell wasn't done with Gabi. "So, Gabi, Luna's told me so much about you." He guided Gabi's elbow to bring her closer, right up to his side so he didn't have to yell above the din. "She told me you were a psychiatrist." Gabi nodded yes. He continued: "I'm helping care for someone in my family with some issues. I was wondering if I could get your information so maybe we could have a coffee?"

"Oh!" Gabi snapped quickly into helper mode. "Absolutely. Happy to help. Here, let me type my info into your phone, yes?" She held her hand out while he unlocked his cell. Gabi moved her fingers as quickly as she could, feeling everyone's eyes on her, particularly the other women's, whose gazes burned. Gabi wasn't sure why she felt herself flushing, blood running fast into her face. She was helping him out, nothing more. She didn't dare hope that he'd think she was more attractive than the line of young beauties waiting next to her for a moment of his time, a glimpse, a fraction of the attention he'd paid her. She was a single mom, too. This was about work. Yes?

"There. Good—please, shoot me a note or text . . . anytime."

"Yes. Thank you. I will." Maxwell looked into her eyes and

held her gaze for a beat before he brought her into a quick, fairly vanilla embrace. Gabi breathed him in for a moment. He smelled like the color aubergine to her. Musky, colorful, and deep. As soon as she made a step away from him, she was replaced by several women waiting like the rush of a river that'd been dammed for too long. The noise of the party pressed back into Gabi's head. She looked down at her hands. She wasn't sure what she was processing, but she was processing something about what just happened.

"Sooooo? Soooo?" It was Luna, her voice an eager purr in Gabi's ear.

"Huh? Oh! Luna."

"Yeeeeess?" A Cheshire grin spread across Luna's high cheekbones.

"He asked for my information!"

"And?!"

"I dunno, 'and'? He's got someone in his family who he needs help with." Gabi shrugged. She still wouldn't dare entertain that a gorgeous, working actor, who must be at least five years younger than she, would want to have anything to do with her romantically. *Right?*

"Oh yeah, his aunt. 'Das right!" Luna fell back, nearly laughing out loud. She caught Gabi's confused look and adjusted herself. "Hon, go out with him for coffee. . . . See what happens!"

"Okay, gurl, you crazy. I have no idea. I'm older than him, I'm a mom, I'm . . ."

"*Ja, ja.*" Luna, the New York–born Dominican head of global marketing for the network, waved away Gabi's protests. "And you're on TV too, and you're gorgeous and a doctor, Mama. Please . . . just enjoy!" She waved and walked away, her job done. Now Gabi knew how Luna had plowed through the ranks. Her confidence was admirable and rare.

"Whew. Okay. I found you." It was Luz's turn to saddle up to Gabi and get an update. Luz was her friend, along with Cat and Magda, for years and Gabi's "date" that night. Luz didn't have to dress up too much. Her blue eyes, walnut skin, and newly shorn natural faux hawk, dyed a heady blond, only needed the simplest accompaniment. A V-neck black top, tailored, white, wide-leg pants, and Gucci heels rounded her out. She was tall, too, placing the drink she held in her hands nearly to Gabi's shoulder. Luz stuck out a long, matte-polished nail. "Wait a hot second! Did I just see you hangin' with Maxwell Dane?!"

Gabi was pulled out of her processing. "Um, yeah! He asked for my info!"

"Whaaaa?! Gurl."

"Right?!"

The friends became twelve years old all over again.

"Oh my God, what did he say? Tell! Tell!"

Gabi led Luz farther away from the zone of Maxwell so he wouldn't catch her sort of gossiping and, even worse, giggling like a tween. Plus, Luz had a bad habit. When she was told *Pssst, so-and-so is sitting over there—don't look,* she'd do just that: look.

"Okay, so, he was super nice—" Gabi began, faking nonchalance.

"Yeah, yeah." Luz swirled her hand in a gimme-gimme gesture.

"And, well, he asked me to help with someone in his family—Luna said it was his aunt?"

Luz's eyes lit up. She took a long draw out of her cocktail straw. "Guuurl! Gurl, that's huge. That's tight."

"Um, it is?"

"Um, yeah! He wants to hang, and please, he's talkin' family to you."

"I guess," Gabi replied.

Luz narrowed her eyes at her friend.

"Luz, I mean, I just don't see it. There are like supermodels hanging all over him."

"Well, maybe the fool has some sense in his head and he wants someone who can match him in success and brains and beauty and shit."

"Ha! Well, I'll take the brains part."

Luz rolled her eyes at her friend tossing away her compliments. Gabriella wasn't a successful television shrink just because she was smart and Ivy Leagued up. It was also because she had a full, lovely face set with a strong, Mediterranean nose, dark eyes so big they looked nearly manga-comic, and Sophia Loren lips to match.

Gabi felt that she could lose ten pounds—after her son was born, she just couldn't be bothered, not as if anyone was seeing her naked anyway—and her style could use an uptick, but she knew she was a warm, sassy thing to look at. Definitely feminine, that's for sure. Puerto Rican curves and all.

"You are a pocket rocket of hotness. Don't get it twisted."

"Thanks, Luzita. We'll see!" Gabi smiled, thinking about possibly seeing the most popular man in the room again, alone. She looked his way. He was smiling, shaking hands, moving from person to person, and for a moment, he peered up and found Gabi's eyes. She smiled, he smiled back while Luz's jaw dropped.

"Luz?"

"Ya?"

"I think it's time to go home now. It can't get any better than that."

"Hey, Mama, it that you?" a man's voice called from the room just beyond the foyer. The source of light in the loft-like space came only from a yellow glow above the stove in the kitchen and the blue haze from a computer screen.

Luz tried to be as quiet as possible as she tiptoed into her home. Silence was rare in the Tucker Lee household, a hovel of rowdy children.

"Hi sweetie," Luz whispered. It was nearly eleven p.m. on a

Tuesday. Not too late if you're a twenty-something, but late when you're the thirty-something mother of three (or was it now technically four?) who also ran her own branding consultancy. After losing her last corporate client to a nemesis at her former big firm—a Latina who waved around her white skin and Anglo looks, bristling at Luz's dark skin and *"gringa"* accent—Luz forced her own hand into a large departing package to go off on her own. (*Thirteen years of my life, fifteen including my college internship, all to be pushed out by that elitist piece of work—coño.*) She took several months off to help Emelie, her newly discovered half-sister, transition into the family. At first it was "rainbows and jellybeans" as her girl Nina would say, but soon enough, Emelie's teen hormones kicked in and the sometimes surly girl worked hard to carve out her own space. It was frustrating. Luz had sought out Gabi's professional advice many times; utilized Cat as much as possible, as she shared a tough upbringing with Emelie; and even coaxed Magda into helping her get her new sister into the best private high school in town. It truly took a village.

Once Emelie's first year in her new home, new school, and new social stratum had smoothed out, Luz refocused more on her business. She pulled out her well-culled contacts, calculatingly run through with her husband's own coterie of megamillionaire buddies, and filled her initial year's coffers with enough money to load up an office on 25th, off Park Avenue South. She filled it with people she respected and paid them well, along with a gaggle of badass young associates. And at least two nights a week, she frequented the events and gatherings that either helped her business or her friends.

As Luz got home from Luna's premiere and locked the immense, antique door imported from Mexico behind her, she dropped her jacket onto a hook and shook off the bit of guilt she felt at having to go out again in a matter of days. She thought happily of her husband just around the corner of the foyer, and her face warmed up as she approached him from behind. Luz bent down and munched playfully on his neck. Chris reached one arm behind him and held the back of her head, enjoying her nibbles while his other hand found its way to her behind, his place of worship.

"Mmmm. Hey baby. How was the party?" Chris let his hands do the loving while his eyes stuck to the screen. Luz didn't mind.

"It was good." She lingered for a moment, scanning the screen, then let her other hunger lead her to the kitchen. "But damn, I barely ate anything."

"There's some Oak in the fridge. I ordered extra." Oak was a start-up food delivery service in downtown Manhattan founded and run by a team of Chris's friends. There were few Asians of their generation in the city with access to reams of capital, creative capital, too. Sure, the Southeast Asians and Chinese up-and-comers near City Hall certainly had a faucet of Wall Street money flowing. But in tech, restaurants, and brands? Slim pickings. Luz figured that through her husband she'd met nearly every single one. It was just the way of the world. For now.

"Damn. I was really rooting for Ecuador, man," Chris said to Luz as he stretched his arms behind his head.

"*Fútbol,* baby. *Fútbol,*" Luz muttered, distracted, as she wolfed down some spicy sesame tofu.

Chris shut his screen, his international soccer scores disappearing for the night.

"Please tell me you did not put a lot of money down on that game," his wife said.

Chris blushed, hand in the proverbial cookie jar. "Nah, *Mami.* It's all good."

"Jail, mister!" Luz was teasing. She knew her husband would never get caught gambling illegally. After all, that's how his father lost everything. However, she knew that he dabbled. As long as Luz controlled the household purse strings, their major assets, and her own accounts, she gave him a long leash with his own money. He was grown, after all.

"A joke about incarceration would not be a good idea right now, would it?" he asked.

"Nope."

"But you started it!"

Luz shook her head. As she turned to throw away the delivery containers in the recycling bin—*Which one? Oh yeah, the green recycling one, not the blue with these*—she said, "Oh, bro! Let me tell you the awesomeness of tonight, m-kay?"

"Hit me, sistah." They mutually enjoyed their social groups and never stopped being surprised at who they could and would meet. Chris was often happily dazzled.

"So, the star of the freakin' show, Maxwell Dane, asked for Gabi's digits!"

"Shut up!"

"Fo' reals." Luz paused to lick the dark chunk of chocolate she ended her day with each and every night from her fingers.

"That's hot," Chris deadpanned.

"Well, you know Gabi though, she's all, 'I'm not cute enough and there's all these models and it's just because he wants to pick my brain,' yadda."

"Aw, Gabs . . . Well, it can't have been easy, what she's been through."

"I know."

"If you and Maxwell Dane snuck away, I'd be sitting in a corner in a fetal position with our kids spoon-feeding me."

"*Ay,* honey!" Luz scrunched up her face, taking her husband's full cheeks in her hands and planting a chocolate kiss on his full mouth. "You're sexier than ten Maxwells."

"You're lying, woman! But, I'll take it."

They made their way down the hallway, tiptoeing. Luz peeked into the girls' rooms first, each tastefully decorated. Nina, the oldest, was in her bigger bed on one side, the books in her bookshelf thicker and with no pictures, while 'Fina slept on the other side of the room, six feet between them. She was buried in stuffed animals, her miniature library still a mix of picture and chapter books, mostly her older sister's cast-offs. While Chris waited in the doorway, he watched his wife plant loving kisses on each of their daughters' heads. Benny's room was next. Luz spent a few extra seconds kissing her small son, her only son, caressing his cheek with her hand. The boy smiled in his sleep and kissed her back, rolling over with satisfaction.

Chris waited in their large, low, king-sized bed while Luz finished her nightly ritual of face washing, creams, and treatments, wrapping her hair in a silk scarf to keep its style. Luz noticed that Chris was still sitting up, when usually by this time he was on his side, fast asleep. There was no phone in his hand.

"Hon, is Emelie fine?" Luz asked. A big believer in boundaries, she didn't want to snoop into her sister/daughter's—she sincerely couldn't tell which sometimes—bedroom. She even gave Emelie a lock for her door when she moved in to help make her feel safe. Luz loved her own lock on her door growing up. Not that she really needed it much, but it gave her some sense of autonomy and privacy.

Chris answered, "Well. Ya know . . . she complained that she hasn't been feeling well and didn't eat much for dinner."

"Yeah, I noticed she hasn't been eating much. Especially in the morning. And her color's off." Luz waved her hand in front of her face.

"Should we take her to the doctor? Have her check her out?"

Luz thought for a moment. She tried to calculate just how many days Emelie had not been quite right. Then she felt guilty for not adding it all up, seeing that maybe something was going on with her, even if it was purely emotional.

Maybe it's bullies at school. Stress? Am I putting on too much pressure?

"Yeah. I don't know but we definitely should talk to her in the morning."

Chris fluffed his pillow. "You talk to her, hon. What if it's like girl stuff?"

"Girl stuff?! What girl stuff?"

"I don't know." Chris shrugged as he lay down. "Hormones."

"Maybe it's stress from looking at colleges? Maybe she's freaking out at all this pressure—all this change." Luz had to question the expectations that she may have been putting on Emelie and her going from a tiny, riotous apartment uptown to a large, cushy home, riddled with a new family and social stratum, downtown. She was ready to pay for whatever Emelie needed— therapy, college—and wanted only the best for her. But had she been pushing too much?

"Hormones," Luz whispered as she spooned her husband.

Oh no. Could she be . . . ? Nah . . .

Chapter 4

"Cat! We've got three!" the floor director yelled out from behind the camera.

It wasn't common to have many staff on hand for online video, but Cat's show was fully funded by a multibillion-dollar network. With that backing, she got a floor director Cat brought from one of her previous networks, plus her executive producer, and a few associates. They all made Cat feel right at home. *Who doesn't want to work with friends?*

They knew her quirks and dealt with her sharp tongue and intermittent pushiness without grudge. It was clear that this was a women-run show, and *bossy* was a good word. Cat and her EP, Audrey, were never nasty but they gave everyone—and each other—a run for their money on the regular.

"Jesus! So where is the guy?! I thought they said he was in the elevator?!" Cat demanded of the floor director and anyone else within earshot, including the guest she was referring to.

At the network—and once a people-pleaser—Cat had to look the good-girl newscaster type, but now, doing her own thing, she was much more herself. That day she was decked out in trendy, dark, waxed jeans, a silk origami blouse, and stacked four-inch heels, looking like the successful, young business leader she was. To those who held onto their old-school, dying ways, moving to online from a main TV network seemed like a step down. They never got the memo Cat did that a screen is a screen is a screen. And because Cat kept the rights to her show concept, acting as a fellow executive producer and intellectual property owner with Audrey, it only took one year to nearly double her income she made from her network show. The number of eyeballs was great, uniques kept growing, and sponsors loved Cat's fresh, unfiltered focus on women's issues that leaned positive, not shrill. She was even silly at times, all too happy to never have to don network helmet hair again.

"He's there in three, two . . ." Audrey calmly gave her a countdown in her ear. Time was money on the set, and both Cat and Audrey were big on saving money when it made sense.

Walking onto the set, dropping quickly into the comfy, deep chair at an angle to Cat, was a rare type of guest of the show, a man. The show's floor director, Jim, athletic, freckled, and actor-handsome, had followed the guest, his hands down the back of the guest's shirt, working to attach his mic just before he sat down. Jim wiped his lined brow with a smirk and a pantomimed *whew*. Mission accomplished. Cat threw Jim a smile of thanks, which quickly turned into a frown at her tardy guest.

"Glad you could make it," she said icily to him out of the side of her mouth.

"Yeah! Thanks." August Tilly was a newly cemented tech billionaire. An original shareholder in early aught startups that still existed and made money, August had cashed out and invested millions in various new apps. He was here today, on Cat's set, to announce the launch of a venture capital fund for women-run businesses. August got his sincere Anglo name and tall stature from his father, a British near-royal, all title, no money. He got his looks—and his wealth—from his Indian mother's family. Floppy, thick black hair like licorice, regal nose, strong brows, and tight beard. His skin looked like sweet burnt butter, and Cat had to catch herself from looking too long at his forearms and manicured hands. *Shit, he's gorgeous. Shit. Shit.*

Cat's friends didn't even know just how many men she'd slept with in college. Working through the memories in therapy, she knew that she'd always been on a hunt for male attention because she didn't have her father's growing up. He wasn't there at all. So she danced the dangerous dance of notching her bedpost with the most attractive men on campus, one after another, canceling out any possibility of true love with her destructive, codependent behavior. It was a psychological push-pull that took years to manage. Then, once she started working in television and moving up, she turned off those needs and instead focused on being the best at everything she did—outworking, outrunning everyone she could. If her father couldn't love her, then she'd show him just what he was missing. She had to shut down the needs of the bottom half of her body, neglecting the desires once so hungry, but somehow, it worked as one drive was transformed into another. She climbed quickly on the job with her relentless focus, nearly as far as she could go. But once she was free from her daily television show and, seemingly, her television career, she became open to a real love and connection with Tomas. But she still was wary. Scared of becoming dependent and losing herself. Her hunger for success and power would nudge back against the attention she focused on her love and her child. With her new show, though, the access to rich and influential people awakened again the urge to plow ahead, whatever the means. To succeed. To show them all. To show *him,* a man whose face she could barely remember.

"*Hola,* folks! Cat here." The camera turned to hone in on her expression. Cat started the show, which she liked to be as unscripted and unplanned as possible. She ran through the pleasantries with August—Who are you; Why are you here;

smart crack; smile; say something funny; make sure he laughs; etc.—and then threw him a new, challenging one: "So, a man leading a fund to invest in women. Tell me, why should we trust you, we of the X chromosome?"

August took a breath in, not at the question itself, which he'd gotten many times before, but at Cat's tone. It was more cynical and surly than anyone else who'd asked him close to the same. "Well, Cat, it's economics, really." Cat raised an eyebrow. "All the studies show that women are a value buy—they're undervalued as business leaders and in the markets. Female-led businesses fail less than ones launched by men. Women are more cautious, take fewer risks, and tend to be more devoted to making things work."

"More committed?"

"Oh yes . . ."

"Well, we know that's right!" Cat threw to the camera.

August blushed a bit before he continued. "And you know, Ralph Nader did this decades ago—his whole office was women he employed because they cost him less—"

"Excuse me?!"

"I mean, in those days, they got paid a lot less and were less likely to move out of the company, so economically speaking, he got more for less."

August's press tour had been limited to nodding, smiling faces. Until he met Cat. She wasn't smiling.

"I'm familiar with Nader's history. You make women sound like a cheap buy off the sales rack," she said.

"No, no, that's not what I'm implying. . . ."

"Oh, then, please do tell me what you're implying by saying that women essentially are cheaper? I mean, that's what you're saying."

"No, I'm saying that they are value. That's different—"

"Back to the Nader reference . . . because that sounds like exploiting a pay gap while doing little to change that gap because it's good money-making business to have that gap exist. Even though it's based on an unfair, biased labor practice."

"Yes, there was a big pay gap. But I raised that historical point to demonstrate women actually being undervalued, whereas I see the value in investing in women-led businesses. Women get the job done."

"No kidding. And, on sale." Cat bit down.

After another five minutes of Q and A, Cat reeled it back. She didn't want to come off as too much of a stereotypical feisty Latina, and she also didn't want to stop this guy from leading a new charge, no matter his motives. She was pissed at his talking points. And possibly his motives. She didn't trust him. After years of going to school with rich kids who mocked her for her thrift store clothes, calling her "beaner" and "spic," she didn't see a fellow brown guy across from her. She saw blue blood. A know-it-all with a silver spoon. Cat worked hard to try to get her persecution chip off her shoulder, but it was difficult to shake because it was nestled so darn deep in her tendons. It would take years of careful, well-thought-out psychological surgery to remove. She was trying.

I have to. It closes my mind and that's not good. It's the same thing they do to me: stereotype. It's the same . . . right?

"And that's a wrap." Jim said from behind the camera. He walked over the cables to get to August and remove his microphone. There was a crackling silence coming from Cat.

"Well. You certainly gave it to me there," August noted.

"Just have to ask the questions that seem obvious to me." Cat turned her attention to her cell for a moment, noting her nanny's text in Spanish saying that her daughter had a great late lunch and was on her second nap of the day. Cat softened a bit.

"August, thank you. Thanks for coming and I really hope that what you're doing helps move things along, so we're not so much 'on sale.'" She put out her hand for a shake.

He looked wary for a moment but took in her eyes and realized it was okay. "You don't bite for real, right?"

Cat responded with a flat tone. "Ha. Ha."

As she gathered her notes and unhooked herself, without Jim's help, from her mic, August hesitated. He turned to leave, then turned back. "Hey."

Cat was startled at his casual tone. She looked up at him.

"You know, I was wondering, since, well, since you have a particular take on what I'm doing and you know so many women who could possibly join in, well . . . Would you be free for a coffee sometime? Or, just a meeting—you can come by our offices." Cat stood still and quiet, her eyes unblinking. August gestured toward Jim. "I mean, you could even tape part of it, for a piece, I mean."

"Uh-huh," was all Cat managed to say. It was like being invited back to lunch after biting the hand that fed you the first time.

Just then Audrey appeared from behind the floor camera. She seemed to have rushed out of the control room, rather than her usual laid-back mosey. "That sounds great, August. I'm Audrey, Cat's executive producer. We spoke on the phone." She took his hand and shook hard. "We'll set that up with your folks later today."

"Great! That'd be great." August's face seemed to light up at the approval.

Cat thought the exchange was strange. She watched Audrey usher him to the elevator, eagerly taking him by the elbow, talking, gesturing.

"Jim. What was that about?" Cat asked.

Jim was wrapping up cords, shutting things down for the day. "Gurl, I dunno." He shrugged, his muscular arms wrapping up the cameras' thick, black cables. "Doesn't seem like it's a bad thing, though."

"Yeah. Not a bad thing," Cat muttered, walking back to her desk.

His eyes.

Chapter 5

"What do you mean you can't come, Gabs?" Magda said into her phone. She was trying not to lose her cool with Gabriela, but this was too last-minute of a cancellation for her.

The event was starting in an hour and a half, and Dr. Gabi Gomez was her celeb guest, as she had been the past several years. The older folks especially liked her, as they still passionately followed the morning TV shows where Gabi was a regular contributor.

"Mags, Max is having a meltdown and I'm on my way to him. I'm sorry. I just can't make it." Gabi choked back a sob. She was great at putting on airs of stability and put-togetherness, but like anyone whose family falls apart, she was holding in a lot of pain just to get through the day. She did well, having been the breadwinner for so long, now even better than ever. She had solid checks coming in, but her son, her light and her reason for working so hard, had been suffering for them both. He was only six and had already been suspended from school three times for acting out. Gabi was at her wit's end. She knew he was in so much psychological pain. She had to stay home with him that night, for both their sakes. Gabi was in no state to put on a face and dig into small talk.

"Goddamn it, Gabi."

"I'm sorry, Mags. I have to go."

When Gabi hung up with barely a goodbye, Magda realized that she was being hard on her. But she stopped herself from looking too hard into the reason why. Magda and Gabi had been lovers back in the day. Magda was the only woman Gabi had ever been with, and probably ever would be with. They'd remained close friends but also the kind of friends who could get angry at one another and make up a day later. But Gabi's split with Bert, her ex-husband, was affecting her in ways that Magda didn't know how to deal with even though she'd survived her own split with her kids' mother. This was different. She'd never seen Gabi so torn up. She thought for a moment that surely it was because of her son, Max.

That's got to be it. Poor Gabi. Poor Max.

Magda's anger transformed into guilt. How dare she question years of friendship and love because Gabi couldn't make it to an event when her child was in crisis? She hung her head and clenched her jaw. After all, she was a parent, too. She hated the side of her that reacted without thinking, the entitlement. Ever since she'd gotten off the sauce, so to speak, she'd done remarkably better with her temper issues. No more broken glasses. No more drama with younger women she'd pick up here and there. Considering her past, she'd been amazingly faithful to her wife, and much more focused with her businesses.

Magda was never a joiner. Initially aloof in life as she masked her sexuality, she was a mix of the popular pageant-jock and the brainy, jokey yet private girl no one would ever dare cross. Magda carried herself as someone who knew better. At least she had a nugget of knowledge that no one else knew: who she really was. It was a secret that separated her from the people around her; her friends and family, she kept her at arm's length so she wouldn't show too much emotion or cry in front of anyone. Her tears were private; they happened alone in her room with the door locked, or in the bathtub when no one was home. Strangely, Magda's self-isolation had an inverse effect on her social life. The more she held people at arm's length, the more everyone wanted to be close to smart, beautiful, cool Magda. A Miami Grace Kelly ice queen.

So, opening up and asking for help? Admitting to anyone she had a problem? Talking to a support group about her alcohol issue? Never. Over her dead body. But when her mother died, Magda's frozen exterior cracked wide and deep. The truth oozed out, viscous and unassailable. She may have seemed to have her life together, her millions, her homes, her children, her ex-wife, her lovers, her freedom, but she had so little truth. Alcohol kept her icy shell together. It also was tearing her apart.

A week after she returned home from her mother's funeral, she heard her voice break at her dermatologist appointment for her quarterly acid peel; wrinkles kept the young hot ladies away. She had quietly asked her doctor, after five years of his sitting in his chair babbling small-talk bullshit, "Rafi, do you have someone who is . . . uh . . . working with some new alcohol treatments?"

The doctor, a young, gay, Ivy League Indian-American housed in fashionable Chelsea, stopped applying the peel for a beat, taking in Magda's face and, looking for a confirmation of how he interpreted her question, responded as he resumed brushing, "Yes. I went to med school with Dr. Iyer. He's fantastic." They both let out a breath. "And very discreet."

Magda nodded as he kept working on her face. "Thank you."

"I'll leave his information at the desk. Anyway, how are the kids holding up?"

She swallowed hard, so grateful for her doctor's understanding in that moment, his fine touch, his deft handling of her delicate state. She'd never been delicate, but with her veneer sloughing off like the lines on her face as she sat in the chair, she felt more naked than she'd ever been in her life. Oddly, it felt good.

Dr. Iyer agreed to see her immediately, no paperwork,

Magda's derm Rafi doing the honors of releasing her from any friction that could enable her to walk away. The new doctor was a round-faced, olive-skinned man in his mid-thirties, but his youth belied his gravitas. Magda was relieved. She needed someone she respected—it took a wall of top-school diplomas or a bucket full of street-smarts to get her to listen to someone's advice. He seemed to have both. Dr. Iyer put her on a hardcore list of supplements. He also handed her a behavioral regimen to constrict her ability to be bored for a moment or to turn to booze when triggered. It was filled with checklists and to-dos. He wanted reports, and he made her sign up for an app he'd developed—she registered right then and there so they were on the same page. The app not only tracked her behavior, gave her mantras and meditation breaks, but also buzzed her at random times of the day to come into his office so he could take blood tests to monitor her for alcohol or any other substance she might turn to.

Instead of feeling trapped by all this structure, Magda was comforted. Her life growing up had been filled with regimen. Sports, competitions, social events, studying. This was familiar. This felt right. She didn't want to talk about feelings with a therapist or AA. She wanted the warm blanket of to-do lists and pop-quizzes. It was going to work, but she also knew that she would have to be on a variation of this system for the rest of her life.

One thing Magda always prided herself on was her intense discipline. She could be out all night with a new conquest, drink five fingers of tequila in two hours, and still make a multimillion-dollar presentation in the morning, landing the deal. But this was the first time she had applied that discipline to her personal life, both sexually and with her drinking. Being called in to pee in a cup in the middle of the day kept her away from alcohol. She was an A-plus student now. The winning teenage beauty queen and competitive athlete. She was her mother's daughter again.

Too late for her mother to enjoy. But Magda always liked to think she was watching.

"Magdelena Sofia! We gotta go!" Cherokee called out from the foyer. Her silhouette was slender and shimmering in a long gown, her plaits piled on her head like a crown. She fiddled with her tiny handbag, trying to fit her cell phone and lipstick into a space smaller than her hand. Magda was handsome in a fitted suit, custom-made, of course, by a female tailor in the Meatpacking District who specialized in traditional suits for women's bodies.

"If I had known that I was going to have to have this fancy wardrobe requirement to be your wife, I dunno . . ." Cherokee trailed off as she pulled gently at Magda's jacket lapels and kissed her softly, teasingly.

"I know, *nena,* what is this, our fifth fundraiser in ten days?"

"'Tis the season."

The women smiled at each other and made their way to the event downtown. Magda's life seemed to be made of three things: her family, her business, and her philanthropy. Fundraisers had been a normal part of her schedule and life for nearly ten years. She had her main fall and winter events, and usually spring as well. At least one dinner or cocktail party a week, more often two, and sometimes, in November and April, it was three events a week. And though Magda enjoyed supporting causes and giving her money away, she also loved her friends dearly and worked hard to incorporate them into these evenings as much as possible. Anything was better than some of the people she'd see over and over again, the corporate types especially, who faked their way with smiles and "Let's get together!" event after event. Magda was beginning to wonder if she needed to shake up who she was supporting. Fresh blood. New people, new causes. New conversations. *New faces.*

As Magda's full-time driver pulled her Mercedes Gelände-wagen, luxurious, black, and boxy, into the event space, Magda ran her fingers through her top-heavy locks. "How do I look?" she asked her wife.

"Gorgeous." Cherokee kissed her sweetly and quickly and turned to the door. The driver moved fluidly, putting the vehicle in park to open the door for Cherokee. Magda exited from her side, on her own, taking her time. She felt a bit heavy for some reason. Maybe because Gabi's absence meant she had much more work ahead of her that evening. More hands to shake, explanations to make. Combine that with her father's call earlier that day and her flight out to him first thing tomorrow morning, and Magda was ready to go back to bed and call it a week. *At least the kids are coming home soon.* She brightened a bit.

"Oh sweetie! So good to see you!" Magda heard her wife call out to another couple at the door. Cherokee got pulled away quickly then, the chair of the board of the nonprofit that Magda founded and his wife, who had already taken Cherokee's arm, leading her into the hall.

"Right behind you," Magda called out. The three looked her way, assured she would be joining them, then continued on.

"Well. Hello."

Magda's skin bristled at the voice. Her back straightened. *How do I know that voice?*

She turned slowly, only with her shoulders at first, afraid of who she was about to see. It was a beautiful face. Stunning really. A long-haired Snow White, a Kat Von D without the tattoos. All pale, unlined skin, red lips, fake lashes, and a fitted midnight blue dress that ran from her neck all the way to the floor, covering nearly every inch of her body but so snug it gave the illusion of nakedness. *Déjà vu.*

"Magda. Good to see you. This is my friend, Mark." The woman gestured toward the nondescript Wall Street bro next to her, possibly a few years younger than his date, who put out his hand.

"Hi. Nice to meet you."

Magda shook his hand, her face blank.

"Oh, Mags! C'mon!" Saved by the chairman's wife's call, Magda turned from the couple, still stunned. She didn't expect a guest at her fundraiser to bring along a date like this. Especially not one that she knew.

What are the odds? Gotta keep her away from Cherokee. From as many people as possible.

Magda turned away, still not having uttered a word to the woman in blue, or her date.

Once she was out of earshot, Mark asked the woman at his side, "So, how do you know her?" He was surprised that his escort knew the ringleader of the very exclusive evening.

"Oh, we had some friends in common," she answered.

"Funny you didn't tell me before we got here."

"I didn't? Sorry. Thought I had," she replied. Her smile was slightly sour.

Mark straightened up, ready to take back control, not wishing to be had on a night he was paying for, expensive seats on his company's dime.

"You'd better not fuck up anything tonight. Whatever beef or past you have with Reveron, you keep it to yourself. I need her business. Got it?"

"Got it." Again, that smile.

"That's not a fucking question." Mark's face went dark. He squeezed the woman's arm, threatening.

"Got it." Her smile disappeared. The woman allowed herself to go limp and her voice meek. *Acting.*

"*Ay querida,* I am so happy with last night." Magda was packing her James Perse tees that her wife had left out so nicely folded. Magda's sober life may not have been as dramatic as her old one, but there definitely was something to be said for being taken care of by, and caring for, someone. She was proud to provide for Cherokee's graduate school tuition and housing.

They had met while Cherokee was coding for a Web site that occupied an office just above Magda's therapist. But once they married, the younger wife had the joy of being able to focus on getting her PhD in business analytics, aka "big data" science. There surely weren't many women of color in that space, and Magda liked to keep business all in the family. Or, at least, in her new family. Cherokee felt technically like her third wife, as she'd lived with a woman in her early twenties and then had children with another. But, marriage wasn't legal then and wasn't necessarily something Magda was hot to do. However, now, after remarrying, legally this time, and reconciling with her father, Magda wanted to make sure her wife knew as much as possible so that she could potentially take over the business someday, or at least lead it somehow, if and when she passed. Legacy and all that. She was proud of Cherokee and proud of herself.

I mean, she puts up with me when I'm sober. I'm boring when I'm sober.

"Mama, you nailed it! Half a million over your goal—amazing!" Cherokee kissed her. She was an exuberant one; genuinely happy. It was infectious and Magda was grateful.

"Thanks, baby. I couldn't do it without you," Magda yelled to her as Cherokee buzzed in and out of rooms around the apartment, making sure Magda had everything and that all was in order for the kids when they got home later that night.

"*Señora, necesita agua?*" José, Magda's middle-aged driver from Jalisco, Mexico, held out a bottled water to Magda.

"No, Jose. *Estoy bien, gracias.*" Magda apologized to him for taking him away from his family on a Sunday morning. "I could always take an Uber, you know!"

"No, señora, you never know with those guys—they can rip off your credit card. And I heard some guy just got arrested for raping a woman!" José raised his eyebrows, one eye on Magda while he spoke, the other on the road to the airport.

"Well, José, I don't think I run the risk of that." She gave him a teasing look in return. She was too often mistaken for a man or considered not feminine enough to bother. He blushed. It was rare for a middle-aged Latino man to tolerate, let alone work day in and day out for, a very out gay woman. At first, José was confused when he interviewed with Magda. But Magda liked that he was confused, rather than affronted, by her sexuality and manner. She preferred confused because to her that meant their relationship was much more a matter of education and exposure rather than of trying to turn the bow of a twenty-ton ship of machismo and prejudice. After several years of exclusively driving Magda and her family, José was indebted to her and very protective. He saw the way people looked at her sometimes. He'd even had to manage a few of his own family and friends challenging him on who he took orders from. ("So she's like a man, no? Can you imagine?! Do you get to watch? What kind of ladies does she like?") But he didn't care. She'd just sent his daughter on a full scholarship to Princeton. And he'd sent enough money back to Jalisco to his brother that he had opened a profitable restaurant. He'd move mountains for this woman, no matter who she married or how she dressed. *Buena gente.*

José watched discreetly as his boss looked out the window. She seemed pensive—this was an unplanned trip to see her father, after all. He could tell when she didn't want to talk. And Magda so appreciated that about him. She valued boundaries, space, and discretion.

As the G-Class bumped over potholes on the Brooklyn-Queens Expressway, José muttering an "*Ay, perdón*" at an especially big one, he saw Magda's face go pale. She was looking at her cell phone.

"Are you okay, *señora?*"

Magda took a beat too long to answer but managed to say, "*Sí, sí, Jose, todo bien.*" All good. Her eyes moved from the phone to stare at the back of the seat in front of her. She drew up her hand to bite her thumbnail, a bad habit of hers.

Not believing what she'd just read, she had to read it again:

Good to see you last night. You look well.

Remember that night? At The Rabbit? Those photos?

Call me. 24 hours.

Chapter 6

"*Eh, chica,* you okay?"

Luz was moving like an eight-armed deity, rapidly running breakfast prep for her three grade school children. Each ball of energy that she'd birthed worked to climb up on the stools at the kitchen island, the usual morning food spot during the week. 'Fina helped her little brother, Benny, shorter and less wily, up onto the seat. Nina was already digging into her oatmeal, scolding her younger sister for touching her.

"Stop hitting me!"

They went back and forth, normal background noise for Luz. Chris was already up and out, headed to the airport for a potential deal in Los Angeles. The couple was used to their ins and outs. Travel and days apart kept them saucy, missing each other in between. Of course, video calls helped. Though with Luz traveling less and her business gearing up steadily, she was concerned that the scales that so far had been gender-equal as to who's-at-home time were shifting a bit too much in her direction. Thank goodness for Angela, her assistant slash nanny slash lifesaving addition to the family.

Emelie was floating a bit in the background of the activity at the breakfast counter and kitchen. She was quiet—more than usual—and not interacting with her nieces and nephew as much. At first she had so loved merging into a new family with young children. Emelie seemed to be a natural with them. She told Luz that she had to babysit a lot starting at a very young age for extra money. And Luz also assumed that having little munchkins laughing, yelling, crying, all around had to crowd out many of the bad, lonely feelings Emelie may have had—or still had—with her mother having passed so young and her father in prison for a very long time.

Today, Emelie barely mumbled an "I'm good" In response to Luz's questions. She didn't make eye contact, either.

And she's looking pale. As pale as a brown-skinned girl can be. Greenish.

"Good morning!" a young, female voice called out at the front door. Angela Mack was a petite graduate student in criminology, a slight girl of Polish descent from Michigan who helped fund her studies and extracurriculars with funds from taking care of the Lee children, bringing them to school in the mornings and picking them up after school.

"Ang-EE-LAAA!" the twins called out in singsong. Benny, his mouth full, managed to mumble and wave happily.

"Oh, Ang, can you take over here?" Luz was between buttering another piece of toast for 'Fina and wiping Benny's oatmeal-encrusted face.

"Sure. No prob." Angela moved right into captain mode, her ponytail sleek and bouncy. *Pocket rocket,* Luz thought as she seamlessly moved out from the kitchen area, confident that the kids were well cared for, and walked quickly into her bedroom for one more look at her face and hair, lip gloss applied, before grabbing her bag and sliding on her biker boots. These were her commuting shoes. Once at the office, if meetings had to happen with clients, she'd switch to some bitch-ass stilettos. Why torture yourself the full day if you only needed to for an hour?

Luz listened to the sounds from the kitchen: "Okay, Benny, let's button up," and "'Fina, do you have your water bottle?"

Luz checked off the weekday-morning boxes in her head, her own and her kids'.

"Hey, Em," Luz called as she rounded the corner to Emelie's room. Junior year in high school was rough, and Emelie, though she liked Angela well enough, still seemed to be a bit cold and confused around this paid nonfamily member always in the house, almost as she was. And a white girl at that.

Emelie wasn't in her room. *Where is she?* She should have been doing what Luz was doing, final prep, pulling together what she needed before heading out the door. And she didn't like eating anything in the mornings anyway. The kids teased her about it at first, and Luz tried to pressure her into it as a new habit if nothing else, but Emelie resisted. Luz had dropped that battle. She knew which battles to fight, and as long as Emelie was eating at school—an all organic buffet, the menu changing daily, of course; that's what $45,000 a year will get you—and eating heartily at dinner, which she was, Luz was okay with her aversion to breakfast.

Standing still in the hallway for a moment, listening for signs of her sister's whereabouts, Luz heard the toilet flush from the bathroom to her right.

"Em?" Luz knocked gently. "You okay?"

The door opened quickly and Luz instinctively pulled her body back to let the girl out. Emelie slid by, avoiding eye contact, school bag with her, ready to go. "Yup," was all she said. As she headed down the hall toward the kitchen, Luz missed seeing her face—where all truths lie—and stared a beat at the back of her head as she walked away.

"Okay, Luz! We're heading out, okay?" Angela raised her voice from the foyer, the children now quiet, their bellies full, maybe even a tad geared up for their four-block walk to school. Angela was very careful with the three of them but she made sure, too, that they felt some responsibility for themselves, teaching them to look where they were going, watch out for cars, etc. Vigilant, just like Luz.

"Okay! Let me give everyone smooches!" Luz ran out to give each curly head some love, just missing Emelie squeeze out the door, offering out a weak, "Bye!" Luz tried not to look too concerned.

'Fina will feel it and be anxious all day about me. My sensitive one.

Luz usually headed to the subway right after them but this time something told her to hold back. She told Angela to go ahead without her. "I forgot something."

As Luz closed the wooden door behind her, she walked back down the hall, wondering just how far she'd take it. She was worried about the usual teenage things for Emelie, particularly considering her previous upbringing and her father's line of work. But Luz had only snooped once before on Emelie, when she first moved in. She just wanted to make sure that Emelie wasn't bringing anything into the house that the kids could get their hands on. They were snoopers, those twins. But, outside of that, Luz wanted to give Emelie a wide berth. She wanted her new sister to trust her and to trust that she'd be respected in the house. However, there were standards and expectations; Luz made it clear that if her grades were not up to speed and if she didn't help out with the kids once in a while, those privileges of privacy and electronics would disappear. "Like the rainforests!" her husband had added.

She hesitated at Emelie's door. *You've been lucky, mama. She hasn't been much trouble at all. Crying here and there the first year, yes. But she's a good girl. Right?*

Before she went in, Luz had a feeling she was going into the wrong room. She turned around and headed into the bathroom that Emelie and the kids used instead. The girl had sprayed air freshener, so that was all Luz smelled as she sniffed the air; she sniffed for the telltale signs of the acrid odor of vomit. *Eating disorder? Bulimia?* She pulled open the toilet seat, inspecting the surfaces for splatter. None. *What is it? What's going on?*

Luz looked in the shower, shaking her head, feeling guilty about some kind of breech of boundaries. She was about to leave the room when she got the idea to check the cabinets.

Under the bathroom sink was a deep cabinet filled two-thirds with old bath toys, shower caps, washcloths of various colors and states of fray. Each child had her or his favorite color since toddlerhood. The rest of it was filled with Emelie's hairstyling implements, old hairsprays, soaps, lotions, and cotton pads for cleaning her face. But just to the farthest left corner, fairly out of sight of the little ones, was an open box of tampons. They were the tiny kind; so far Emelie was not suffering from the gutted-pig periods that were common for Luz at the same age. She sat back on her heels, staring at the box. It was opened, several missing. But something still bothered her. Luz reached out and gently—she didn't want to leave a trace of her looking around—pushed the box aside just enough to see what was behind it. It was another box of tampons. Unopened.

Oh no.

The first month Emelie arrived in the home, she'd blushingly asked Luz if she had a tampon for her to "borrow" when she ran out. Somehow, the teen had thought that pads and tampons were her own responsibility and not a household necessity. Of course, living with only her father, it must have been normal for Emelie to have to go it on her own when it came to her periods. Luz felt guilty for not having thought of it before the poor girl had to ask.

"Of course! But, hon, what would you do back home when you ran out of them, or ran out of money?"

"I dunno. I just went down the hall and asked the woman who lived there. She was like in her twenties."

"Did that happen often?"

"Yeah, I guess. Money, you know."

"I do know." Luz nodded and took her hand. "Look, I bet it wasn't easy to ask your dad for money to buy tampons. I mean, yuck, right?!" Emelie smiled, relieved that Luz understood. "Listen, I'm going to put that stuff on automatic for you, okay?"

"Wha . . . what do you mean?"

"I mean that I get automatic deliveries of stuff like toilet paper, garbage bags, and, shoot, even tampons!"

Emelie's face brightened. "Oh! Okay. Thank you."

Since then, Luz noted that every box had been used like clockwork. Once one box was almost gone, another would replace it. But never were there two boxes of tampons in the cabinet. Especially one unopened and one nearly full.

Tears welled in Luz's eyes.

Her sister was pregnant.

Chapter 7

"*Jesucristo.* Are you sure?" Cat whispered into her phone.

Luz had called without texting first, which wasn't her normal MO. And though they'd always been close as friends, Cat was more like her sister-in-law. Well, at least as the mother of her brother's child, she was now officially family forever. That meant picking up the phone no matter what.

"Yeah, hi, Catalina Rivera to see August Tilly." Cat spoke to the security guard as she reached over the tall partition and handed over her ID. She was in the lobby of an immense new building, designed to a T. August's investment firm had built a Frank Gehry–esque, all-glass, undulating structure to sit on top of the historic architecture of the original seven floors of the building. As Cat worked to hold up her phone to her ear with her right shoulder, the guard asked her to look into the digital camera.

"What—no—sorry, Luz, just going through security before a meeting . . . Smile? Here?" She looked into the eye-like orb and faked a grin. "Yeah, no, this is too much, Mama. . . ." She took her identification back from the guard, proceeded to swipe the bar on her pass through the gates, all smiles and thank yous as she continued to register what Luz was saying. *Pregnant? At sixteen?*

Growing up the only child of a *Mexicana* single mother in Chicago, Cat knew just how difficult having a child could be. Her mother made sure that no matter what happened, her daughter, her only hope, would never, ever get pregnant and ruin her chances at the American dream. Most likely as she felt that had happened to her. Of course, Dolores would have loved for Cat to have children at some point, get married, *y más,* but not until she was completely stable and, in Dolores's eyes, as wealthy as possible. After Cat lost her daily, national news show on a major cable network, her mother was far from wanting to accept the news of her "special" daughter not only having a child while she was making less money on an online *"JuTube"* show, as Dolores would say in her heavy accent, but with a black man no less. Forget that he was half Dominican, educated, and successful. In her Old World mind, what mattered was that he was dark and they were unmarried. *Sinvergüenza.* Shameless.

Because, unlike Luz, Cat knew what it was like to grow up urban and to have a difficult home life, she became her friend's confidante and ally when it came to all issues with the teenage Emelie. Cat had grown to love Emelie, too. She was a smart, sweet girl, if sometimes a bit moody and unsure of herself. Unlike her outgoing father—at least that was the assessment Luz gave to Cat, that he was a "typical Dominican guy, talks too much, thinks he's the shit." Emelie must have taken after her mother. Word from Luz was that the girl's mother was a fellow neighborhood *chica,* going part time to graduate school at City University of New York for social work. She was beautiful, but bookish and quiet. She liked comic books and graphic novels, and Emelie did, too.

Luz continued to unload on Cat over the phone. Luckily the elevator had full cell service, though, and thankfully, only two other passengers. "Lu, I'm so sorry but I'm about to get to my floor and I've got folks in the elevator with me—Hi, hi." She nodded at them. "But yes, we *must* talk when I'm out of here, and I want to see you but we have to figure out what to tell Tomas—matter of fact, text me what you want me to say and do, and I'll get back to you in an hour, okay? Bye. Bye. Love you."

As the doors opened into a glass vestibule, Cat hung up and scanned for a buzzer or some way to get in. She spotted a desk beyond the glass and a spiral staircase to the right but not a body in sight. Then she heard a smooth, young male voice:

"Hello, Ms. Rivera. Please have a seat just inside and we'll be with you in a moment." The glass in front of her slid open. Cat looked up to where the voice seemed to come from. There was the telltale round bump of a camera just to her left in the corner where the wall met the ceiling. She narrowed her eyes. *Hmmm. Someone's always watching.*

As Cat was led into August's office, she noted that it was as big as her apartment. Windows floor to ceiling, open to the skies, thirty-three flights up. She gave him some points on the minimalist decor. Not too macho, slightly affected with too much chrome, but she couldn't help lusting after the large, ceramic, ornate elephant that stood near his standing-only desk. Gorgeous and specifically Indian in contrast to the cream, clean shades of the rest of the room, Cat felt a kinship with the elephant's purples, greens, and golds. The colors reminded her of the boats of Xochimilco, Mexico, candy-colored and luminous in her mind.

Cat entered to see August just behind his desk, standing, as his computer sat on a mounted platform. *He literally doesn't sit down.* August looked up quickly, seemed to blush somewhat through his coffee skin, his eyes brightening at seeing his guest. He gestured to his lounge area for Cat to take a seat after he said to her, "Oh. Hello!"

Cat responded in kind and they stayed quiet, the background buzz of an urban high rise filling the air, until both sat down on two deep, pale chairs at forty-five-degree angles to each other, separated by a Lucite cylinder coffee table.

"Sam, can you bring me another drink? Cat, what can we get you?" said August.

Ah. The royal "we."

"Just a seltzer please, if you have it, or water."

Sam was oddly smooth-faced and younger than either of them. A lean, ivory man in a vest, Sam didn't speak but nodded. His cheeks bore the sheen of possible acid peels. Cat noticed these things. Too many years on television made her overly observant of people's appearances, from the scuffs on their shoes to the pores on their noses. If she weren't so blind without her contacts, she'd welcome a day when she couldn't see so well. Noting every detail made her feel judgmental, critical. It was her mother's voice she heard when she noticed flaws. *What did ju do to jor eyebrows, eh? Dos pants look tight, m'ija. See da stretch here?*

"So, August. Why did you want to see me?" Cat had no time for bullshit, especially with a family now and her own production company. Her question was pointed, but she couldn't look him in the eyes for some reason, instead focusing on a particularly ornate building in her view. She locked onto its oxidized green parapets.

August continued with small talk, trying to get Cat to see his side in the investing-in-women matter. She noticed that he'd finished his second drink. *Was that water with lime, or something else?* His eyes were getting glassy.

". . . but here's the real reason I had to see you."

He had been droning on, though loosening up along the way, and Cat had drifted off a bit. August punctuated his statement by leaning toward Cat and putting his hand on her arm, squeezing a bit as he spoke. Cat looked at his hand on her arm. She suddenly was prickly with confusion. Her eyes went from his hand, a pleasant brown shade, to his face. *What the . . .*

"So I've now watched everything you've ever done and read everything you've ever written. You're amazing." Cat was stunned and confused. She felt something else coming, another shoe dropping, but she was completely lost as to where this was really going. Her skin prickled at what her gut was saying while her mind said, *no way.* August then made it all too clear. "I'm in love with you."

"WHAT?" Cat glared at him. He smiled back, his cocoa eyes wide and happy and, yes, under the glaze of what Cat now realized was alcohol. That wasn't water in his glass. "You don't even know me!" She pulled her arm away.

"Oh, but I do!" August continued. "I've watched dozens of hours of you and have read every blog you've written—I mean, that interview you did where you talk about your mother and your upbringing—amazing!" He paused, and Cat noted how he seemed to be winding himself up. He was. "Cat, I have spent nearly all the time since we met fully immersing myself in your world. Now, that's the equivalent of months of dating, right?"

Cat didn't know how to respond. She couldn't nod in agreement, as she didn't know if she agreed—she had no frame of reference. She couldn't disagree either. So she just stared. Her stunned silence gave August permission to continue.

"I love how you are a fortress. That's what comes across—you take no shit from anyone! There are so few women who do that . . . and to see yourself as a brown woman—because of course, we're both brown, sort of, and that I know makes a difference in this world—you see yourself as equal to everyone else, regardless of your background or gender or ethnicity. That's scrappy! That's grit! And grit, as we know now, is one of the biggest—if not the biggest—predictors of success."

Cat continued to stare as August paced around his desk, gesticulating as if he were giving a presentation to investors. It was the oddest thing. Wildly businesslike and unromantic. Or, was it?

"Now admittedly, coming from my family—my silver-spoon, so to speak—I haven't had to lean on grit like you have, and that's the missing piece for me. I need that in my life! I admire that." To all this, Cat was able to nod slightly. Yes, silver-spoon.

August took her nod as permission to address the other elephant in the room. "Now, I realize that you have a child with someone and I respect that, but I have to take a hint from the fact that you're not married yet—I mean, someone as accomplished as you having a child out of wedlock, it's positively rebellious."

"What?" Cat asked.

August said, "Well, if you really loved him and were committed to the father of your child, you would have married him, and you haven't, so listen"—Cat interrupted him by leaning forward in her seat, seemingly ready to walk out on all this nonsense, but August continued—"listen. My parents are gone, so there's no one to tell me who I can and cannot marry, and there are no old ideas of marrying 'well' or my own kind because I'm the one with the money, and that, Cat, is what's important at the end of the day, especially with a child, right?"

"What? Money?" she asked.

"Security," he answered. The word landed in Cat's chest with a thump. It was her weakness. All the hard work, all the pleasing her mother, all the freight-train madness of nonstop productivity for her was, in the end, all about security. Being raised by a single mother, wearing the same four pairs of uniform socks to school for five, six years—she'd lost count—darning them over and over, feeling deep shame at their financial state, in the end, that was Cat's drive, was her mother's drive, her mother's push. Everything toward financial security. And in the end, her show got cancelled. The business changed. She had to take a risk and adapt. And August was right. It was always grit that got her through. But goddamn it if security didn't speak to her like a long-lost companion she's shoved into a dark corner, telling it to keep quiet. *Hush!* Her life with Tomas was one where even though they both earned in the low six figures, in Manhattan, they struggled to save any money. Cat tried her best to cook more to spend less, but she wanted a cushier life. She was frustrated by limits. Tired of pushing so hard. Tired of worrying. Could August see that? How did August see that?

He leaned in to her, sitting on the arm of the chair just across from her. "Cat, you will never have to worry about money again. I'll take care of your mother too. We are meant to be, you and I! We're a global world now! We would be like the joining of hemispheres and the crossing of all lines and boundaries between my family, yours, the baby—just imagine what we would represent."

Jesus.

As he spoke, Cat processed two things at the same time. What he was saying, much of which offended her greatly, some of which intrigued her. Her other thought was: *This is ridiculous. He doesn't know me. He's projecting—this is projection. It's my public self he's seen. Not the real me. Not the me who isn't that confident or isn't that put together, the me without makeup and good lighting. Grumpy me, tired me—well, he's seen grumpy me. How do I get out of here without pissing him off completely? Why am I so afraid of pissing him off? Why do I care? I think Audrey would be pissed. She really wants to land a big piece on him and sell it to the major networks. Ugh. I have to behave here.*

"How do you think I ended up on your Web show?" he asked, Cat stunned silent as her neurons misfired.

She finally sputtered, "Why me, though? When you can have anyone in the world—supermodels, perfect people." Cat gestured out the window.

"You are different. Interesting. Plus, you're the only woman to ever challenge me—maybe the only person ever." August leaned back in his chair for the first time in an hour. "You're a woman who is strong enough to be with me."

Like Cinderella just before the stroke of midnight, Cat jumped up out of her seat. She had to get to her phone and to Luz. She was sure her friend was coming out of her skin with her newest big problem, and then the image of Cat's beloved Tomas came into her mind. What was she going to say to him about Emelie? What would Luz want to happen? What if she's wrong?

"I'm sorry, August, but if this is what this is about, I have to go." Cat put out her hand. The many-times-over millionaire still sat, a bit stunned. She stood for another beat, her hand still held out for a shake. She tilted her head and pursed her lips into a firm line. August finally moved to stand. He took her hand and enveloped it in his.

"Cat. Just think about it, okay. Promise me that at least."

Goddamn thick black eyelashes. And on a man. That's so unfair. Fuck his gorgeousness and his amazing taste and those freakin' shoes and pants and elephant and his money and success and Faustian bargain. He doesn't know me. The arrogance. Damn it.

"Okay," Cat murmured, looking off to the side of his face. It was like he was a Medusa. She feared if she looked at him she'd turn into someone else. Someone who'd give up everything for money and power.

Sam led her silently back to the elevator. As she stood tall, leaning her back against the elevator wall, she looked up instinctively at the cameras in the corners. *Can't let him see me upset and so thrown.* She put her head back down, stopped leaning, and looked straight at the doors, as confidently as she could muster. Cat wasn't particularly religious and didn't go to church, but she was a former Catholic school girl and felt always that God put people and things into her life for a reason. Like Tomas. Like Gabi, who first nudged her to get in front of the camera. Like Luz, who needed her to help with Emelie. Like the speech she gave completely off the cuff that launched her new show and career; her network head just happened to be in the audience.

So *what was that? What was that for? What is he for?*

Faust came to her mind again. The story of the man who sold his soul to the devil for success and worldly wealth. *Everything carries a price. The devil comes in many forms.* But Cat didn't really believe in the devil. So what was she afraid of?

Cat remembered abruptly that she urgently needed to check her phone for messages from Luz, and her show team, of course. She fumbled in her bag in search of her cell as she walked out the front door of the building, her skin feeling too warm. One image came into her mind like an echo: the elephant in the room. Literally.

Five text messages and two phone calls. First, though, a text of my own:

Gabs—can we talk later? Weird thing just happened—can use advice.

Gabi quickly responded: *Of course! Later good—call after kid in bed xoxo.*

Gabi had been on television before Cat, but always as a guest. She met Cat when she was a young local producer. Gabi was the first to egg her on to move in front of the camera. She believed in that girl. Gabi wondered what had just happened to her. It was the middle of the day, so she doubted it was Tomas or baby-related. Work for sure. Somehow, that made Gabi worry much less. Cat could handle anything on the work front. Though Gabi did worry about her self-sabotaging her relationship with Tomas. As someone with no role model for a healthy relationship, growing up with no father in her life, Cat had to be very independent very young. Gabi knew that as much as her friend wanted to have a normal life with a nuclear family and that it bothered her a bit to feel sometimes like a statistic of an unmarried mother, what bothered Cat even more was the possibility of marrying Tomas only for him to run away with someone else and break her heart. Just like her father did to her mother. *Oh, Cat, married or not, you can never be sure.*

Gabi's own marriage felt like a sham to her now that she knew that her ex had been cheating on her for years. And he wasn't around much with little Max, who was now getting tall and very man-of-the-house. *Please stay a baby, Maxi. Enjoy it while you can.*

She did her best. And here she was more than a year after being on her own, waiting in the West Village at a funky coffee shop for a fairly famous actor who lived nearby and needed help with his aunt. Gabi thought that it was very sweet of him to want to talk to her. How nice of him to support his aunt and seek out help that Gabi was happy to provide. It didn't hurt that Gabi had loved the episodes of the show they'd shown at the premiere and found him to be nice to look at and intelligent to talk to. Soft-spoken, actually.

Looking up from her phone to take a sip of coffee, Gabi caught his eye as Maxwell Dane made his way through the door. "Oh, I'm so sorry I'm late!" he said.

"No, no, I'm good, just working and enjoying the joe."

Maxwell embraced Gabi and grinned widely. "Let me grab myself one and I'll be right back. Can I get you anything else? A cookie?" he teased.

"Uh, no, no cookies," Gabi teased back.

Once Maxwell sat down, Gabi took in how normal he seemed. She'd always met fabulously famous people in the green rooms of the morning shows and found them all to be very human—some grumpy and cold, some insecure and wanting to be recognized and fawned over, some alone and just happy to sit and say "Hi!" to new people. But having coffee with Maxwell felt different. She wondered at the demands of his job and how it affected his family, and if they were all successful or if he was the only one.

"Okay, so, thank you sooo much for hangin' with me," he said.

Gabi pshawed, embarrassed by his graciousness. "No, no problem at all."

Their conversation flowed effortlessly. He was a first-gen like Gabi. First in his family to leave his town in the Carolinas. First to be a college grad. And, of course, expected to take care of his family as much as possible. He had already moved up some cousins to help renovate his townhouse in Crown Heights and live on the top floor. He talked openly with Gabi about his aunt, who was suffering from chronic, clinical depression. He wanted to help her out, but for years she'd said she was ready to get help and move closer to him or his cousins, but in the end, year after year, she just wouldn't commit. And he could never send her enough money. She was always asking for more, guilting him for any trips he'd take or purchases that her kids would show her on his social media. It was never enough for her. And Maxwell had had enough. He wanted to help, and he knew that throwing money her way was not the best way, really, to do so. Gabi talked to him about boundaries—the importance of building and maintaining them, especially when you're the one in the family who does well, who makes it out, so to speak. She knew the survivors' guilt, the pressure that family could exert, sometimes to the point of bringing you down and sucking you dry, both financially and mentally. She cracked a joke about MC Hammer's fate: "He put every single cousin on payroll!" And look what happened to him. And of course there was the need to understand that you couldn't help people who didn't help themselves.

Gabi's mother used to argue with her about how her daughter's studies were taking her away from faith and God, the

Catholic faith that Dolores had so lived in fear of and took as dogma. Gabi's response was always a form of: *God gave us a brain so it's a sin not to use it.* Essentially, God helps those who help themselves. Why give us all the tools if not for a reason?

Gabi gave Maxwell a one-two-three list of advice to wrap up the topic—something her media career had trained her to do. And one of these tidbits was to make sure his aunt's kids, his cousins, contributed to her care how they could. It may not be money, but it was worth a lot. Maxwell liked that idea. He had some cousins already helping him out in the best way they knew how: working on fixing up his new Brooklyn town house.

"Plus, I have to go on location so much for work that with them there, working and living there, I don't have to worry about security."

"What about house parties? They throwin' those?"

"Oh no. Too old and workin' too hard." Maxwell winked. "Hey, um, do you have something after this?"

Gabi thought for a moment.

"Uh, no, actually," she fibbed. She had a writing deadline for delivery of her monthly advice column but she promised herself that she'd just have to stay up late to finish it. Plus, her little Max would be hanging with his sitter until at least six p.m. It was only three.

"Want to head across the street to have a bite and maybe a glass of vino? I'm starving and would love to if you're not too busy?"

Gabi's brain said, *Uuuuhhh—what is happening right now?*

"Oh, sure, sure! I mean, this is why I work for myself, ya know."

Max seemed pleased. They bused their ceramic cups and Maxwell ate the last bit of his cookie. *And he's still such a thin guy.*

As they weaved their way through the line of young Village types waiting to order their own pick-me-ups, Gabi's chest felt light. *But no, this is not a date. I mean, why would he date you? He could have anybody. He's an actor, for Pete's sake. And gorgeous and probably younger than me, and JESUS, I have a kid,* carajo. *Why would he want that? And those extra ten pounds I need to lose. Shit. Nope. He's just being friendly.*

Right?

Chapter 8

"Hey, *Papi*." Magda hugged her father in greeting as she entered the doorway of the family home. There was an awkwardness about their hug. There was warmth, but it was tempered and stilted by years of frigid, unsaid history, the more than ten years that father did not speak to daughter. There was much lost between them, and the embrace, even with their arms around each other, chests touching, couldn't erase the dark matter of so much passed time with their wounded hearts. Magda hoped that one day their reunions would be absent of this psychological gap. But right now, it remained.

"*Hola,*" her father responded. Magda noted his voice was strained, like the sound of a string pulled too taut.

They both ambled down the foyer, Magda staring at the backs of her father's feet as he shuffled over the jade green tiles. He seemed weighed down and frail since her mother's death. But there was another piece of baggage that Magda could sense sitting on his shoulders. *Or is it a monkey on his back?*

"How are you, *Papi?*" she asked in Spanish as she pulled her carry-on behind her. She noticed that it was the first time that her father did not help her with her luggage. It was also the first time she was back at home since she came out to the family before college graduation. The first time she came through the door fully herself, no pretense, no makeup, and with nothing to hide. Her life now built upon truth and all the healthier for it. Raoul knew that this was still his daughter, though she wasn't the made-up beauty queen he preferred. He had said so very clearly as he reconciled with her at her mother's funeral. Magda's sister had pleaded with him before the service to make peace with his firstborn child, saying, "Just think of her as your son." Inez meant well. She was trying to make it easier for him to understand, in some way. But instead, his heart opened up, after more than a decade, to accept her truth. He said clearly to Magda, the first words of love he'd given her in ten years: "You are not my son. You are my daughter."

What he'd said that day as they laid her mother to rest, his wife, echoed in her mind as she set her carry-on near the bottom of the stairs to the second floor. The Miami sun was within hours of setting, light coming into the hallway and filling the breakfast nook with warmth. *I may not be his son, but he's not going to be helping me with my luggage anymore, as he wouldn't if I were a boy—to him, I look like one.* She had to chuckle a bit. It didn't come from a bad place in him, she knew. It came from settling the confusion as to what or who she was. She was masculine-seeming, so her father surely figured she'd want no chivalry or caretaking from him. An interesting assumption, she thought.

As Magda entered the open kitchen, Raoul was already seated at the breakfast table.

"Is Miranda here?" Magda asked about their lifelong housekeeper.

Raoul answered, "Oh, no. I only have her come here about an hour or two every other day. She's getting too old and she's going to retire soon."

"Oh! So who's been coming here for you? The place looks nice."

"Some younger Brazilian lady—she's the niece of the office assistant. Studying part time."

"Uh-oh, younger!" Magda had to tease. Her father was a Casanova extraordinaire. So much so in his day that as much as she teased, Magda always held it against him. She didn't like finding her mother crying in the bathroom a couple of times a year, every year, like clockwork. Carolina never told her daughter what she was crying about when she asked, instead saying it was nothing and changing to subject to "Let's make some cookies, no?" But Magda had figured it out. And later, when her father wasn't talking to her but her mother would secretly visit her and her own children and family both in New York and California, she would tell Magda about every single time. Every woman. Young, old, a friend's wife, a call girl here or there. Carolina would tell Magda: "This is how men are. This is how it is. And one day you understand that there's nothing you can do about it but keep yourself together."

And for once, finally, Magda understood why she was the way she was. Why she was her father's daughter. She, too, was once a hunter and devourer of women. Married. Straight. Feminine. Not. Business contacts and online conquests. Her mother's revelations were the first step for Magda's own reconciliation with who she was and how much she wanted to stop hurting herself— drinking—and hurting other people. Monogamy gave her a solace and foundation that surprised her. Strength. Once she understood what had led her to such dark places.

And she forgave her father for his sins, too.

"Oh no, *m'ija*. No. I miss your mother too much. Too, too much." His eyes welled.

They sat in silence for a moment. The distant sound of traffic and the motors of garden equipment wafted through the windows. Magda could almost see the sounds dancing in the moist Miami air.

She frowned a bit as she noted this change in his behavior. *It took her dying for you to be faithful?* "So, Papa, what did you want to talk to me about?" she asked in a firm but gentle tone. She came a long way for a conversation, and having a dicey past with Raoul, she wanted to be clear that her heart still had gates in place.

Raoul breathed in deeply. He ran his right hand through his thick shock of white hair. He used to dye it. A successful doctor with a desire for more business and a new lady here and there, he had barely let gray a millimeter out of his head. Magda's mother said he dyed his hair weekly. Even on vacation. *Funny. He never let us see that.* He stopped dying his hair the day after his wife's funeral. Interestingly enough, Magda thought he looked even more handsome now—his hair was thick, if white, but the contrast with his tan skin and blue eyes was striking. But taking him in now, Magda realized that his *guayabera,* boxy and white, was hanging a bit too much on his shrinking frame.

"I dunno. Have you been reading or hearing about the doctor here who got into trouble trying to, to . . . get too close with the senator?" Magda's eyes narrowed as he spoke. "I mean, not close that way, but close with money and trips?" Raoul clarified.

"Oh. Yes. The Castro guy, the Cuban surgeon?"

"Yes . . ."

"Wait . . . *Papi?*" Magda's skin bristled. Her father was involved in this somehow. This was big. This was not good. "Didn't he end up going to jail?" Her voice cracked with the last word.

"Not yet."

"Not yet," she repeated and took a breath. "*Papi.* What happened?" She was gentle now. Whatever this was, it was big enough that she wasn't interested in seeing her father punished, no matter how many years he didn't speak to her because of who she was, or how many times he made her mother cry. Before her was a broken man. Broken. Lonely. Business was Magda's language. Now this, this she could understand and, hopefully, help fix. She also noted that this was a powerful moment. Maybe one she'd been waiting for her whole life. When her father disowned her and canceled her bank accounts with him and with the family, she knew he felt like that was going to give her the biggest sting of all. The pain of losing his money, his financial support. He wielded the power he'd had over her mother: financial dependence. To him, a female weakness. Little did he know that for Magda, it was never about the money, as she felt herself just as capable and powerful as any man. It was the withdrawal of his love and being included in the family that pained her the most. As for money, Magda went ahead and built her own powerful business, well beyond the net worth her father had ever had. And there it was. Maybe that really was it. She'd showed him, hadn't she? And now here they were. Her father may need his daughter to dig him out.

"Well. We were close, you know, because of the golfing and his wife being friends with your mother, so." He paused. "I invested some money with him. On a big project."

"How much money," Magda stated, rather than asked. Raoul's money flow to her ended abruptly after her junior year of school. She spent her senior year taking on loans, doing work-study and waiting tables and still ended up graduating in debt. But that didn't stop her from networking and busting her smart ass into nearly nine figures of assets. Money. Magda knew money.

Raoul seemed to breathe harder. He still couldn't look his daughter in the face. "All of it."

"What do you mean, all of it?!" She raised her voice.

Her father waved his hands across the table as if he were sweeping it clean. "All."

"Get specific, *Papi*." Magda folded her arms and sat back on the bench. It was still covered with her mother's vinyl, a crack in it snagging Magda's pants, pinching her thighs. She lifted her leg and smoothed out the fissure. Then, she waited.

"Interest rates were low so I borrowed some money. Against the house."

"Okay. Fine. The house." Magda calculated the damage. At today's valuation, she figured $1.1 million. Awful. "What about the business?"

Raoul's practice had grown to three in-house doctors, and Magda figured there had to be at least $5 million-plus there for a buyout. Though, he may have given the other doctors more equity than she would have.

"The business took a big hit with the recession."

"*Papi*. Is that gone too?"

"Yes. The partners have my remaining equity."

"What about other cash savings? Retirement money? Anything?" Her voice was starting to get shrill. She was angry at him. She had thought better of her father. Yet at the same time, she wasn't too surprised. He was an old-fashioned man with some old-fashioned ideas. Including the one where he was smart enough to outthink any market and how he knew with absolute certainty what was the right thing to do with his money. Except when he didn't.

"I have a little bit. But I'm going to have to declare bankruptcy."

"Not personal bankruptcy, just business, right?"

Raoul went silent. What had happened since her mother's passing? What had he done?

"*Papi*. Who's been advising you?"

"*Psssffft*. I don't need advice."

"You don't . . . need . . . advice." Magda dropped her head on the table. She breathed in deeply and thought twice about losing it on him. *The arrogance. I should hurt him like he hurt Ma. Like he hurt me. And where were my sisters, huh? He gave them so much money over the years,* Mami *told me about it. Paying their bills. Paying their schools. Their kids' schools. And where are they now? Why am I the one here? The only one who didn't get any help from him? The one who made it on her own. Isn't that life, though. That's life.*

Magda's face bristled as she held in a torrent of irritation and distress. It all pushed against the inside of her skin as if it were going to ooze out of her pores if she didn't stop it. It prickled.

Magda brought her head back up, her arms still hung under the table. "So. What do you need, *Papi?*"

"I don't know. I don't know what to do now." He was ashamed and couldn't look her in the eye. His hands together, he played with his thumbs. They'd both turned into little kids trying to have a stressful conversation. All jumbled up inside, the mess leaking out of them with body language.

"What about Inez and the other girls?" Magda asked about her grown sisters. Where were they in all this? Helpless?

"You know, *m'ija,* the girls have their own kids, and Nica, well, I've been helping her for a while but I told her I can't anymore . . ."

"Doesn't she have room for you in their house?" Veronica, Nica, lived ten miles away. But with three children and a husband with little drive, they were struggling and much too proud to ever ask Magda for help.

"No. The mother-in-law moved in last month. Her diabetes got too bad to move around."

"And Diana?" She was the youngest.

Raoul chuckled a bit at mention of his youngest. "Magdalena. She lives in a tiny studio with *cucarachas.*" That's right, Magda remembered. She was "finding herself."

"Inez?" She was the daughter after Magda. The yin to her yang. The carefree hippie to Magda's razor-like approach to business. *Wait . . . Why am I passing him off to them when I know that I'm the only one in any position to help?* She put her head in her hands, ready for another story of rejection.

"*M'ija!* She lives up north! I can't live in the snow! I'm too old for that. Not good for my stress."

Magda had to chuckle at her father's dramatic reaction. "Or your golf." She rolled her eyes. Dios, *he hates the cold so much. I don't think he's visited her once.* Besides, Inez, too, was in no financial position to help. It would be up to Magda.

"*Papi.* What do you want to do? You want me to float you a loan so you can keep the house? And maybe your practice, too?" She paused to let him answer. He didn't. He remained still. His mouth closed, his eyes looking into space ahead of him.

Magda adjusted herself. She couldn't bring herself to touch him, to put her hand on his arm or his hand. She thought of it for a brief moment but was quickly cold to the idea. The wounded side of her took the reins. Wanting to forgive one day, but never forget.

As she sat, looking at the right side of his face, his hands so still on the table, she saw a solitary tear build up in the corner of his eye. She'd never seen him cry before the day of her mother's funeral. Now, here it was again. Never in decades of her whole lifetime. Now, twice in two years. The tear grew until his lower lid could not contain it. He blinked and it fell. Magda swore that her mind made the sound of a *splat* when the drop hit the table. It was so big, that drop of salty water filled with so much.

"I don't want to be here anymore."

"*Papi?*"

"I don't want to live here. It's too much."

"Okay. I understand." Magda had been back home for less than an hour and she'd already felt the need to pack it all up and leave. Too many memories, and now the ghost of her mother and even her beloved housekeeper hanging above them, weighing the air down. She wouldn't want to live there either now that her mother was gone.

"Maybe I can live in New York for a while," Raoul said.

Magda's eyes went wide. "But, Pa, it's cold up there!"

"That's okay. I won't have to go out much."

And with that, Magda saw her father as he was for the first time. A separate person—just a man. A sad, older man who made some bad and some good decisions in his life. An immigrant who built up his own American dream only to see his wife die before he did, even before their children, who all took on the qualities normal to American children of their generation. They moved away, both in distance and in day-to-day life. He had pushed Magda away, though. That was his doing. And Magda suspected that her sisters were pushed away, too, as their American qualities conflicted too much with their macho father's. Where he was from, Caracas, a man's children and wife, especially a doctor's, wouldn't go far at all. They had little choice to do so, even if they married someone wealthier. The culture frowned on it, and social pressures created and maintained formidable barriers to leaving.

But here, here in Miami, US of A, Magda saw her father now hit with the reality of what he'd created. Not only his financial mistakes and his pride, too big to take counsel, but his pigheadedness toward his late wife's needs and his children's. Magda wanted to punish him to no end. Wanted him to feel the pain of his mistakes and his choices. But he was just a man, as she now realized, and in him, she saw regret. She saw that he had been punishing himself a lot already. She knew what she had to do.

"Okay. I'll get a place for you, *Papi,* near me and Cherokee and the kids. Okay? But it may take some time so you're going to need to stay with us for a while."

Magda got her answer via a surprising hug as Raoul fell into her arms. *So broken.*

"*Gracias, m'ija.* I'm so sorry. So sorry." He sniffled as he spoke, his voice cracking into a near bark.

She was alarmed. Magda knew that in the morning she'd have to call her psychiatrist friend to get a referral so he could get on some medications. She knew now that he'd likely spent most of the last year or more clinically depressed. She was so used to not talking to him that she didn't think much of the fact that she didn't hear from him often, instead getting updates from her sisters. But his weight loss especially was a sign that he needed help.

How did the girls not see this? No. It had to be me. He probably only felt safe with me because he knows they depend on him too much. If he fails, he's let them down. Magda felt a bit of pride as now another advantage of making it without his help became even more clear. However, the thought was more a sorrowful pride than sweet.

"Okay, okay, listen, *m'ija.*" Wiping his face, Raoul rose from the banquette. "I'm just going to go into my office and make some calls, okay?" Magda nodded. "Miranda left your favorites in the fridge, so help yourself. Just give me an hour or two." For someone in his sixties, Raoul moved quickly. Magda's concerned eyes followed him up the railing of the staircase until he disappeared.

Once Raoul closed the master bedroom door, Magda peeled herself off the vinyl breakfast nook bench, picked up her bag, and sat herself down on her childhood bed. Instead of feeling the years that had gone by, she felt detached. A spectator in her memories. *So this is what being a grown-up really feels like.*

Stroking the decades-old bedspread, with green tropical vines zigzagging up and down the mattress, she remembered trying to kiss her best friend when she was twelve in the same spot. That went badly. Melissa Moran nudged Magda away with her shoulder as they both were lying stomach-down, leaning on their elbows, talking about a female star in a movie they'd both just seen. How beautiful she was and how they wished to be her. Her friend, a neighbor from two doors down, looked shocked after Magda touched her lips with her own, then pretended nothing happened for the next half hour. But as she left to go home for dinner, Magda knew that she wouldn't see her again for a while. Though she still spoke to her in school, Melissa never came into Magda's house again.

I have to find out how bad his finances are. Cherokee is going to not be too happy about this—Hola! I'm home—with Papi! *Then again, my wife is amazing. Ma, I did good with this one. You would have loved her.*

Magda pulled her cell phone out of her jacket, laid down neatly next to her. She started a group text to Gabi, Luz, and Cat, grateful not to see another threatening note from Miss Rabbit.

Ladies—my father's broke. He wants to move in w/me + C in NYC. In FL now—dunno how this is gonna go—miss u all—

And as it's sometimes easier to tell your friends things than to tell the one you love, Magda waited a moment before texting her wife:

Mami—u home? Will call xoxo

As she watched the telltale bubbles on her phone indicating Cherokee typing a response, she let her mind drift. She wrestled with the strange feeling of calm that was seeping into her body. She knew it was not really tranquility or satisfaction but the state she shifted into in times of stress. Being thrown into self-sufficiency at barely twenty years old after a young life with a monthly family expense account forced Magda into a survival mode wound so tight it was nearly zen. Unfortunately, she only slid into this high-pitched serenity a few times in her life. When her mother died, for one. But normally, stress had led Magda to alcohol. And women. She realized years later, once she became sober, that for years she'd become a version of her father, a womanizing, functioning alcoholic. The tequila warded off the searing pain of being rejected by her father and her siblings, for the most part. Also, the years of suppressing who she was. The mask and costume of years of beauty pageants, gowns, and makeup, so anathema to her inner idea of who she was. It was all to please her mother and father and to fit into the society in which she was born. But the masquerade took its toll. It was an expensive toll. And now, someone was going to try to make her life even harder. For a moment, she'd forgotten. Taking care of her father, doable. But, this?

Rabbit. Of course I remember. How many hours do I have? . . . She said twenty-four—that text was six hours ago. Caramba.

After she filled in her wife, who, as she suspected, was understanding and kind-hearted about her father-in-law moving in for a while, and answered texts from the girls back home, Magda lay on her bed, her eyes closed but her mind very much awake. So many logistics. So many questions for her father. The other issue would just have to wait. Even another hour or two. Family first.

I have to ask him to show me all the paperwork on this deal. Gonna sue the shit out of this guy who is screwing my father over. Note to self: Set up appointment with Ira once we're back. He's a wolf. And need to look into how to keep Papi *busy. Can't have him driving Cherokee crazy. And the kids will be back. They'll be happy to have* Abuelo *around, but . . .*

Suddenly she heard a thump. Magda quickly realized that maybe an hour had passed. She shot up from the bed. She waited to hear another noise, more movement.

"*Papi?*" she called out. No answer. Her door was open but his was closed.

Magda's skin began to prickle in premonition. She ran to her father's office door.

Opening it quickly, she didn't see him at first. Just his wide, masculine, Brazilian wood desk. There was a glass decanter, the top off, sitting on the desk. Clear liquid was inside, only a quarter left. *Tequila.* Then she saw his foot, then his leg, on the floor.

"*Papi!*" Magda yelled as she ran to him. He was lying facedown on the carpet. "Carpet, in Florida!" Magda would tease her mother. "It's stylish!" she'd call back, every time.

Magda didn't see any blood and could feel him breathing with her hand on his back. *He's alive.*

She looked around, doing a sweep of the periphery in a quick second. She looked for a gun or weapon or where he could have hit his head or hurt himself. Nothing. Though she knew that this could be a stroke or a heart attack, she was strangely relieved it wasn't a mob hit or some other kind of violence. Quickly, she focused again on her father and rolled him over onto his back. Raoul's right hand and arm had been trapped under his body. As Magda turned him over, she saw the most likely culprit, a bottle of pills that fell out of his hand. A few were left and fell onto the carpet.

Ay, Papi, no.

Magda looked at the label as fast as she could, preparing herself to call 911 and report clearly what had happened to up his odds of surviving. It was OxyContin. Mixed with tequila, which Magda could smell wafting up from Raoul's face, it was possibly lethal. With one hand she made sure his breathing stayed regular and with the other, she dialed her cell.

As she relayed to the responder the situation, catching her breath and holding back sobs, Magda thought to herself, Papi, *don't leave now. We were just getting started.*

Chapter 9

The sun was warm on Luz's shoulders. She stood outside her Range Rover across the street from Emelie's school. Her children went to a more progressive grade school on the West Side, but by pulling a few strings, and thanks to Emelie having killer test scores, Luz was able to get her into a top-three private high school. Her backstory helped for sure.

Damn, this school needs more brown. She watched a flow of students with light-hued faces and multishaded hair trail out of the door. She had to cancel a few appointments that day but she knew her crew could manage. This was not the time for thinking about business. This was bigger than business. It was family.

Luz finally spotted Emelie, with her thick, textured hair pulled into a side braid, her brown beauty a standout in the crowd. She had to get her attention before the teen headed to the subway for dance class. Luz never picked up the kids, unless they were headed to the airport or there was a doctor's appointment, and she certainly hadn't picked up Emelie in months.

"Emelie! Em!" Luz waved broadly. She saw her teenage sister's head turn in her direction. She felt bad that she had expected a wide smile at seeing her big sister-slash-quasi parent there to give her a ride, but instead she watched whatever color was in Emelie's face drain rapidly. The girl said goodbye to her friends, and after they all looked over Luz's way curiously, they moved on.

"Hi." Emelie made it to the car. She was apprehensive. "What . . . um . . ."

"What am I doing here?" Luz asked. Her sister nodded. "Well," she started as she gestured Emelie to get into the car. As they both sat down and closed their doors, she continued. "I just thought I could drive you to dance—I was in the neighborhood."

"Oh."

"Hope that's not a disappointment?" Luz felt herself taking on a hard tone. *Nice, sistah, nice.*

"No. That's fine." Emelie stared straight ahead. "I just get a little carsick."

"Shit. I forgot. I'll go slow. Want some gum?"

Emelie shook her head.

Luz's mission was to have one-on-one time with her outside the home. The loft was a manic place filled with kids and noise and mess. And, thin walls. Luz needed time alone with Emelie for this. If she got queasier than usual, Luz had the guilty thought that it would be a way to get her to admit what was going on. Or, it could work against her, be an excuse. *I'm getting to be as nervous as she is.*

Luz noted that Emelie was fiddling with a tiny piece of paper in her fingertips. She had a strange habit of rolling little pieces of paper into one-inch tiny rods. Not a joint roll, more like a nervous tick. It was curly origami, except no creatures or figures were made, just little rolls of paper the family would find scattered around the apartment, and in Emelie's clothes in the laundry, and in between the back seats of the Rover, where she'd sit with the little ones during their weekends away so she could sleep.

Luz made it through the pleasantries of *how was your day/what's your favorite subject/everyone treating you cool?* Emelie responded in monosyllables. *Teens.*

As they pulled up to the dance school, Luz pulled the emergency brake and left the doors locked. They were on the side street across from the building and just enough down the block that they were not on full display to the other students. Some might walk by, but they'd be heading in the same direction, not head on. Luz tried to think of everything.

"Okay, so, I'll see you later." Emelie reached for the door handle.

"Wait, E," Luz said. Her tone made Emelie widen her eyes and swallow.

"Hon." She placed her hand gently on Emelie's upper arm. Such a position to be a big sister, not so much a mother. "E, are you okay?"

"Yeah. Yeah, I'm fine." Emelie huffed, feigning indignation and irritation.

"No, Emelie, you're not fine." Somehow, this statement made the girl relax. Luz popped her bubble of play-acting quickly. It was a weird form of relief, but also an acceptance at being trapped, discovered. Emelie sighed but still didn't look at her older sibling. She looked at her hands. She started again rolling her paper between her middle finger and her thumb. She rolled as she wrote with her right hand. She rolled while she typed texts. Her rolling was slower than usual now.

"I'll be okay," she managed to let out.

"Em. Is there something you want to tell me?"

The girl looked out the window, giving Luz a view only of the back of her head. Luz heard her sniff. "Nope."

"Em, please." Luz waited for the girl to turn around, or at least show her face. Finally, she did both. "I saw the boxes," Luz said. "The tampon boxes."

Emelie scrunched up her face, confused. She didn't understand.

"I know you're not having your period."

That made it clear to Emelie, and she put her right hand up to her head. Holding herself up, or maybe preventing herself from turning again toward the window, looking to escape. A tear escaped down her young, high cheekbones. She stayed silent. Luz's heart hurt for her. She couldn't for a moment think that she understood this girl, half her flesh and blood. Sharing a father's genetics only, but as Luz's mother reminded her, "That's half of something big."

The past year, Emelie had spent all her time adjusting to a new school, a new culture, a new home, an environment so completely different from how she'd grown up, yet still on the same island of Manhattan. How does just a couple of miles and some money mean navigating the distance between Jupiter and Venus? Might as well have been that far. And Luz thought they did a pretty good job, she and Chris. The kids adored and admired Emelie, and she seemed to lose herself in them when she felt lonely. More like, she prevented herself from entering the state of loneliness by making herself available to Luz, helping out as much as she could. It probably assuaged any guilt she had over feeling like a freeloader in all that affluence.

School was another matter. Luz didn't know how Emelie managed to test so well coming from a public school uptown, where the graduation rate was dismal. *Genes?* She wasn't the nerdiest kid, for sure. She was stylish, urban, more a design student Pharrell than gangsta. Which meant, of course, that when she landed at Dean Prep as one of the few students of color, especially a pretty female, she was instantly crowned the coolest kid in school. She was real, urban, all that was hot in youth culture. And thankfully, Emelie seemed to know how to use who she was to open people's minds as much as possible. She also took her studies seriously. Though, every week, Luz had to make a check-in call on Fridays and have once-a-month check-in meetings with Emelie's homeroom teacher, school therapist, and head of the high school division. It was exhausting to fit in with everything else and everyone else she was responsible for, but it was worth it.

Or was it? I mean, here I am now, right? A pregnant teenager? What was the point?

"Emelie. How could this happen? I took you out of that world—you're out. You've been doing so good. Why did you let this happen?" Luz tried to be more curious than accusatory but Emelie didn't take it that way. What Luz said was judgmental. Emelie sniffed again, crying more. Luz handed her a tissue.

As the girl blew her nose and wiped her eyes, she let the words flow.

"You know, I'm still me, okay? And you didn't take me out of anywhere—I was dumped here. I didn't have a choice!"

"I know you didn't have a choice, honey."

"I didn't! I didn't have a choice . . ." Emelie trailed off.

"But you do now."

"What do you mean?" the girl asked.

"Well, I mean, you have a choice now. Whether to keep going with school and your new life, and all its opportunities, or . . . not."

For the first time, Emelie looked Luz directly in the eyes. "Are you telling me to have an abortion?!" She was horrified.

"I'm just saying. Let's just talk it through."

The teen turned again toward the window. She spoke to it. "I've thought about it."

"Okay, but hon, you're still not eighteen so we have to handle this together, okay? As your legal guardian—"

"I know! Okay! I know." She huffed, flapping her hands in frustration. Luz noticed that her rolled paper popped off Emelie's lap and onto the floor. *Gotta get that.*

"I know, I know you know. Let's just . . ." Luz moved her mind around to try to find the best spot to get to Emelie—to get to a place where she didn't shut down and shut her out. This was a huge development, a huge change and challenge. So big that Luz couldn't even begin to think about what could or would need to happen after this conversation. She just wanted to get through it. Then, they'd deal.

"Em. Who's the father?"

At this question, the redness in Emelie's face blanched out. She looked pale green again. She stopped crying and stared straight ahead.

"Em. Is he a guy from back home? Or . . ."

"No." She shook her head. "No. Not back home."

Luz berated herself for sighing with relief. *Thank God, Lord Baby Jesus, thank you.* "Then . . ." She waited. Luz didn't want to push too much, push her sister away. She definitely didn't expect to be having these kinds of conversations so quickly. Her oldest was only seven.

"It was Peter."

"Peter?"

"Peter Quinton," Emelie said.

Jesus Christ.

"Emelie. Peter Quinton."

"Yeah." Emelie reached for another tissue out of the packet Luz left out.

"Are you sure?"

"Yeah."

Luz sat back in her driver's seat. She placed her hands on the steering wheel at ten and two and gripped. And breathed heavily. "Isn't that . . ."

"Ben Quinton's son, yeah."

Ben Quinton was the biggest actor, producer and writer in comedy box office. He was ten years plus into a career of international franchises, starring in them as well as co-writing and leading them with his production company. Huge star was an understatement. But this was Manhattan. And private school. Nearly all the private schools in the top twenty had kids of famous parents. But this guy? This guy was the one percent of the one percent. And her sister, Luz's just discovered, younger sister, whose mother was dead and father was in jail and who was only sixteen years old was pregnant by his son.

"How old is he?"

"Seventeen. He's a senior."

Seventeen. Emelie's only sixteen.

"Em, I don't want you to get into particulars but please, tell me, how did this happen? What were you both thinking?!"

Emelie shrugged. She fiddled with the end of her braid and looked at the floor. "We just weren't thinking."

"Of course you weren't." For a moment, as Luz felt herself venture into mean-mommy territory, she noted that unlike what she'd think the stereotype to be, Emelie didn't lash out. Yet. She didn't scream or yell or lose it, despite all the stress she'd been under. Luz thought, was this just her personality? Or, was this the way she was, repressing and sublimating her resentment at being taken from all she knew, and instead of theatrics and throwing things, she acted out by sleeping with the son of a movie star? And then got pregnant by him? Or, maybe she was happy about this turn of events. Stressed. But happy.

"Wait, Emelie. Did you do this on purpose?"

The girl turned quizzically to Luz. "What?!"

"Did you get pregnant by Peter on purpose?" Luz enunciated every word, the frisson in her welling toward the surface.

"No!" Emelie nearly shouted for the first time. "Are you accusing me of gold-digging or something?! Like a baller girl?!"

"Shit, Emelie, no!" Luz lied. "No, no." She pulled back, as if bitten. "You don't have to worry about money stuff now, it's just that maybe this is normal to you."

"Normal?!"

"Yeah, I mean, normal. For home."

Emelie narrowed her eyes at her. "Oh, like how it'd be 'normal' for you to be old enough to be my mother back home?" she threw back, with a bite. Luz had to admit it stung.

"I dunno. I didn't mean . . ."

"Yeah, you didn't mean."

They both glared out the windshield, each hurt by the other. Hurt by their circumstances. Hurt by all the changes required of them in such a short time. Changes choreographed by their parents—like puppet masters of their lives. *Here, you, here's who you really are, and you, here's where you really belong. Well, we're certainly arguing like sisters.*

"Okay," Luz breathed out. "Does he know? Peter."

"No," Emelie responded a bit too quickly.

"Are you guys still together? I mean, I didn't even know you were dating anyone. . . ."

"Luz, we don't, like, date."

No, you just fuck around. . . . Ugh. Luz. Just stop.

"Okay, Em. What's your situation with him? This is important—it's an important part of this," Luz asked as calmly as her most adult self could manage.

"I dunno. I mean, I see him in school and stuff. It was more like a one-time thing, though."

"I should have put you on birth control, I mean, when we went for the vaccine I just really . . . just should have . . ." Luz welled over and she started to cry, which alarmed Emelie a bit. Em was used to women of Luz's age and experience yelling and screaming their emotions. Scolding and shaming. Emelie knew that her late mother meant well and did her best to protect her, but her methods were old school. She'd seen her cry only a few times and each time was in a fit of rage. Not sadness or despair, or anxiety. Just anger. The girl was confused. Was this anger? But it seemed so much like sadness and disappointment.

"No, look, Luz . . . It's not your fault. I just wasn't thinking," Emelie mumbled.

"Oh yeah, well! He wasn't thinking either, was he?!" Luz reached for one of the last tissues, blowing her nose with an elegant honk. "What was *he* thinking?! And you, to take advantage of you like that! I mean, he should have known better—you're new to all this!" Luz caught Emelie's confused and concerned look and knew she had to pull it together. But one more thing: "I mean, is this because he's white and he thinks that that's what you're for, or that . . . that . . ." She stumbled. "That he's like rebelling or something?!" Luz sobbed. "He's awful! Just awful!" She took one final blow into a very wet tissue, pulled in a deep breath, and with it, all her stamina and strength.

Emelie was holding onto her tissues tightly, in a ball. Her hands hadn't moved out of fists since her big sister started losing it. It frightened her.

Pull it together, Luz. She needs you. This is not about you, it's about her.

"Okay. Hon." Her composure back, Luz started problem-solving. The sun had gone down a bit and the tree the Rover sat under spread its polka-dot shadows all over their legs. "Okay. We're gonna get through this, right?" Luz took Emelie's left hand in hers.

Emelie gulped and turned the sides of her mouth up just enough in response. She nodded.

"We're gonna get through this," Luz told her again.

"Yeah," the girl said, with less heart.

My Lord, how are we gonna get through this?

Chapter 10

"So, did you get Dr. Raj for him? Has he seen her?" Gabi pushed through Magda's apartment door and started grilling her without an *hola* or a peck hello. Raoul had been at the loft for just a day. One day after Magda packed two suitcases for him while he was in the hospital and jetted him home after he recuperated from an overdose of pain killers and alcohol. There was a flurry of psychiatrists who hadn't wanted to release him to Magda until she'd confirmed solid psychiatric supervision outside their hands. Magda simultaneously juggled the handful of her sisters and their husbands dithering about, wanting him to stay at the house in Miami.

Why do you have to leave, Papi? Why don't you stay with us? I'll come visit you every morning.

Magda shut it all down, quickly and firmly. And then once Raoul, the patriarch, decided to speak twenty-four hours later, he made it clear that he was going with Magda, and his oldest was now in charge of what happened to him. Nica and Diana were understandably resentful. They had had all their father's attention for more than ten years, his sight temporarily cut off from the original apple of his eye, and then here she came. He let her step right back in and take over.

And take over she would. She had to. The doctors, many

who knew of him socially, talked in hushed tones with Magda about needing to report what happened to the board, which could mean the loss of his license to practice. He was already quasi-retired, but now broke, too, which was precisely why Magda had to do all she could to ensure that her father could work again. Once he was lucid, she persuaded the director of the hospital to visit Raoul and ensure that the full reason for his admission would remain off the record. Was this special treatment fair? Or right? No. Did Magda think twice about it? Not one bit. And she got her dear friend and former girlfriend, nationally known psychiatrist Dr. Gabi Gomez, to refer him to the best treatment in NYC. Of course, Gabi would have preferred to have Raoul admitted to a rehabilitation center immediately, but the *viejo* wasn't willing to go.

Bustling down the hallway with her ever-present load of bags, Gabi had two missions for her visit. First, get this man to agree to be taken care of at a facility. Second, make sure her dear Magda was going to be okay. Seeing a parent like that, finding him unconscious, well, Gabi didn't want to imagine. Her parents were still fairly healthy and happy. Not happy about her divorce in the slightest—Ay, m'ija, *for better or worse!*—but, at least healthy and still working.

"Geez, hi there, how are you," Magda deadpanned. "How was the show?"

Gabi came barreling in after her regular appearance on the top national morning show. Her makeup still caked on, her hair unmoving.

"Fine. Fine." Gabi put her bags down all at once. "*Whoof,*" she exhaled. "Got here as fast as I could. So much traffic. . . . How is he? Where is he?"

Magda had to smile at her devoted friend. The Problem Solver. The Fixer. "He's in the guest room. Quiet. I think Cherokee's bringing him some coffee."

"Oh! Good, good." She wrung her hands. "So, you okay?" She put on her doctor eyes, squinting a bit, using her truth lasso, looking for nonverbal clues.

"Yeah, yeah, I'm good." Magda walked into the kitchen. The apartment great room was a wide-open loft space full of warm grays and chrome. The kitchen overlooked the thousand square feet of open space, the epicenter of all that happened so many floors up. "I mean, I haven't slept in two days, so there's that." She walked over to make another coffee. *Just one more.*

"Mags, you look like shit. Can't you work from here today?"

"Nah, nah. Big client coming in. And I missed an event. I'm operating on fumes but I just gotta make it through the next couple of days." She took a long sip from a souvenir mug bought by Gabi years ago on a trip to Paris. It was from the Louvre, red and slim with the Mona Lisa's sultry smile on one side. Commemorative mugs were the only non-modernist, non-conforming pieces that Magda allowed to live in her space. She couldn't resist the sentimentality of them. But they were hidden away in a high cupboard when not in use. Yet every morning, without fail, it was the first place Magda reached into to start brewing her only fix these days.

I have to talk to Gabi about being blackmailed. She's the only one. Cherokee can't know. But, Papi *first.*

Cherokee entered the room, her shoulders drawn down in defeat. "Okay, Mags, I just cannot with him. I'm sorry." Her hair was piled high on her head, tamed with a band. She was in a tee and cargo pants, her usual casual self, but despite her darker skin, even Gabi could see that her color was off, and the skin under her eyes held the shadows of no sleep. "Oh, hey Gabi," she said as she pecked the doctor on her cheek. Gabi appreciated Cherokee so much. Not only for loving Magda in a healthy way, but for keeping watch over her, helping her stay sober. *So far, so good.*

"Hi, hon, what happened?" Gabi asked Cherokee as Magda took a large gulp of her coffee, her eyes shut to the world as she swilled.

As Cherokee answered, her eyes welled. "He just doesn't like me. I'm trying."

"I know you are, *querida*." Magda kissed her on one side of her head as she passed by, fiddling with her father's empty cups and the refuse she'd removed from his room. "He likes you—he just doesn't know you well enough yet, that's all. I mean, he just started talking to me again, so *imagina!*"

Cherokee smiled a bit. "I know, I know. I just want to be helpful."

"Gurl, you are so helpful, you don't know." Gabi weighed in. "Keeping this big one over here"—she gestured to the tallest person in the room, Magda—"is more than half the battle. Plus, I have to assume that he's still figuring out you two."

"Figuring out?"

"Well. He's an old-fashioned guy, just understanding his daughter's, uh, way of life. It's a lot of changes."

Cherokee and Magda both shook their heads in agreement. "But"—Cherokee felt compelled to address another elephant in the room—"what if it's just because I'm black?"

Magda's face blanched a bit and she looked away for a half second. Just enough to contradict slightly what she was about to say. "Oh, no, no. That's not it." She waved her hands for emphasis, dismissing the idea, though it looked more like she was trying to sweep the elephant out of the room. "No, *mi vida,* he's much more weirded out by us being a gay couple than you being black. Trust me."

Gabi watched for a beat. She bit her tongue. She knew that this wasn't likely to be true. A man like Raoul was very likely to be racist. Even Gabi's own parents, one much darker than the other and definitely of African descent at some point in their Puerto Rican history, tended toward discrimination due to shade. *That generation.* But Gabi also knew that at such a time of high stress, the last thing they needed to do was go there.

"Look, hon, it's normal for him to be apprehensive. He's never even been in this apartment! And look at why he's here. . . . Most likely, it has little to do with you." Gabi trailed off as she gently squeezed Cherokee's arm in reassurance. "Speaking of family, where are the kids?"

"Oh, Ilsa and Nico are gonna hang with Albita another day. I didn't want to overwhelm *Papi.* So much noise and they'd be too curious, *sabes?*"

"Absolutely. Smart." Gabi nodded. "Though, I'm sure they're going to be excited to have him around. . . ."

"Not for too long, I hope!" Magda said.

"You really want him in rehab, huh?"

"Well, don't you think—in your professional opinion— that's where he belongs?!" Magda raised her voice. "I mean, you should have seen him. What he did to himself." She breathed in deeply as the women looked on, concerned. Magda rubbed her temples. "I'm sorry. I'm just, just spent right now . . . and I gotta run. Shit!" She dropped her mug in the sink, quickly kissed Cherokee goodbye, cheek-pecked Gabi, and started running out the door. "Gabs! Please text me in a bit and let me know whazzup, and C, love you!"

The women waved at the *whoosh* that went past.

"I'm going to go ahead and see how he's doing, okay?" Gabi made it her turn to deal with Raoul. She wanted to assess his state and convince him to try rehab for a bit. She knew he most likely needed it but that it would be a battle. It was hard enough to get him to agree to a script for antidepressants a few days ago, let alone to not be with family at such a hard point in his life, to accept being taken care of by strangers.

There is no worse patient than a doctor.

"*Hola? Señor Reveron?*" Gabi knocked at the slightly open door of the guest bedroom. She heard a mumble of permission.

"Hi," she said, smiling, then switched to Spanish. "Do you remember me, *señor?* I'm Dr. Gabi Gomez—"

"*Sí, sí.* Come." Raoul was sitting on the side of his tightly made king-sized bed, fiddling with the long, slim remote control in his hands. "How does this thing work?!" Gabi followed his eyes to the fifty-plus-inch screen attached to the wall opposite the bed. There was a grid of boxes, apps, and movies and shows. He was scrolling and pressing buttons in frustration. "You're a doctor—how does this work?!" He handed the remote to Gabi. But as he did, he took his first look at her as she accepted the device.

"Ah, yes. I remember you, from the funeral, yes? The psychiatrist."

"Yes, that was me. I'm a longtime friend of your daughter's."

Raoul pulled his brows together. He looked on her hand for a wedding ring. "Friend-friend, or . . ." he asked.

"Ah, yes. Well, there was a time when Magda and I were a couple, but I got married—to a man—and had a child. I'm divorced now." *Well, that was a lot of explanation.*

"I see." He scowled first, but then, as he admired her makeup, her expertly done hair, and her very fitted dress, all for television—Gabi blushed in a mix of discomfort and pride—he smiled. "Where are you from?"

"Uptown, actually," Gabi replied with no warmth. His smile faded.

"So, my daughter sent you here to check up on me."

"Well, not as a doctor. You're seeing my dear friend since med school, Dr. Raj, this afternoon. I'm here as a friend."

"*Bueno.* Are you taking me or is that . . . other one?" Gabi knew what word he would have preferred to say but, wisely, didn't.

"Magda's wife? Cherokee?" she asked. Raoul nodded. Gabi figured that if he was going to be pissy about Magda's choice in spouse simply because of her race, she could afford to take off a few layers of respect for him. "*Señor,* she is the best thing to happen to your daughter in years. Magda needed her desperately and we're all so happy that they're together."

The older gentleman took all this in, his chin raised and jaw tight. "*Bueno,*" was all he said in response.

"So, let me see what I can do here with the TV, and hopefully we can talk about how you're doing, yes?" It was more a direction than a question that Gabi delivered as she expertly handled the remote. "News?"

"Yes," Raoul responded. Gabi turned on the most neutral news she could find and then showed him how to toggle between live television, the channel guide, and the on-demand services, apps, and games. Not that she suspected he'd use them. Though, Gabi had seen many times older patients completely change nearly all their regular behaviors once a spouse passed or left them.

"Okay, Magda will be back at three to bring you over to Dr. Raj. You're going to love her. She's Ivy and knows what she's doing. She'll take care of you really well." Gabi placed her hand on his in a doctor-like way. "And maybe you can talk about being somewhere where you can get more help."

"I don't know about that but . . . thank you." He seemed both humbled and quickly tired. As Gabi started walking out the door, he asked after her: "Why are you and my daughter not together anymore?"

Gabi stopped abruptly and turned around slowly.

"I mean, look at you. You're beautiful, you're a doctor, Latina. I mean, what happened?"

"I think that's a conversation for another day." Gabi sensed that his was both a genuinely curious question, maybe even mildly flirtatious, and a bit of a plea from a lonely man for some conversation and company.

She smiled slyly and winked. "Let's just say, like father, like daughter."

Chapter 11

"Nina, 'Fina and Bennyyyyy! You listen to Angela, okay?!" Luz yelled out to her children to respect their sitter above the sounds of their happy screaming, mischievous giggles, and the clanging of pots as she worked to nab the one pan she needed to finish dinner. It was all the way in the back of the cabinet, of course.

"Mama, whenever you say their names all in a row, I feel like I'm in a bad sitcom," Cat teased as she sipped a red wine and stood on the other side of the kitchen island. Tomas, strapping, dark, and rocking a downtown-hip beard in contrast to his shaved head, chuckled as he dove into the refrigerator for beer for himself and his brother-in-law, Chris, who was checking his phone.

"Shoot, wait 'til Almita Thelma's old enough to start rollin' with them," Tomas said as he snuck a peck on Cat's cheek as he passed her by.

"Speaking of babieeees," Cat started in a whisper just to Luz. She was about to finish her sentence when Emelie walked in from her after-school coding class.

"Hey," she mumbled, barely looking at anyone. Since she'd moved in, Emelie had been taken by surprise at how loving and supportive her sister's friends were and how much the genders mingled. The men would eventually go off but they'd all talk, and there was little belittling of either sex. That was new to her. And the lack of jealousy between the women was refreshing. She warmed up to them fairly quickly, especially Cat. Cat understood her more. She came from a similar background.

"Hey girl," Cat threw out as she took in every nook and cranny of Emelie's appearance. She was looking for clues and hints to something no one was supposed to know.

"Hey," Emelie tossed out.

"Wait—where you goin'?" Luz called out as the girl fled down the hall, past the kitchen and the two women. She usually at least swept up a snack from the kitchen when she got home.

"Oh, I got a big test tomorrow. Later." She closed her bedroom door quickly.

The friends sighed. The men pretended to look out the window and talk, though they had taken it all in.

"Lu, where are you at with her?" Cat asked.

Luz was putting together place settings while simultaneously cooking. It was Friday, the one day she allowed herself to come home at a decent hour and make something easy for the family. It was possibly one of her favorite blocks of time in the week.

"Babe, Tomas and I will head into the office and leave you gals, cool?" Chris snuck up behind the women and spoke in a hushed tone. Luz shook her head. She seemed to be fighting something back.

"Sure. Thanks, hon." She gave him a slight smile of gratitude.

"You want me to help, though?" Cat asked.

"Oh no, hon. I love doing all this. Please. Relax." She waved for her friend, mother of her baby niece, to sit down on the stool at the counter. Little Alma gave a snuffle from her stroller. The women stood stock still, like statues, until they were assured that she was going to stay asleep. The noise was all now coming from the other side of the brownstone, Luz's cooking limited to stirring and slicing. Latin jazz came softly from the speakers.

"I think sometimes she loves the noise so much—the quiet means she's up. City kid." Cat winked.

"Mmm-hmm. 'Fina was like that. Even in my belly! Needed noise and movin'. Second it got quiet and still, girl was rollin' around."

"Okay. You brought up belly—talk to me, Luz." Cat leaned in so Luz didn't have to raise her voice. Before she answered Cat, however, she had to get a clear view of the hallway, which she checked one more time from her perch. She felt so bad but needed some support.

"Girl. The father is Ben Quinton's son, Peter Quinton."

"What the fuck . . . The actor?!"

"Yup. And he doesn't know yet. And, get this. They're barely a couple." She threw the salad together, tossing in her homemade dressing. Shallots were key. Sherry vinegar and finely chopped shallots.

"Oh no." Cat took a long, hard sip of her wine. She nearly drained the glass but caught herself. She hadn't gotten back to her pre-baby tolerance so she had to be careful. Cat tried to soak this in. As a member of the media for years, she knew just how bad this could get. Tabloids. Paparazzi. Poor Emelie's name all over social media. And she was just a kid. This couldn't get out.

"Luz. What are you going to do? Well, wait." She raised her hand. "Forgive me. First, how is Emelie doing and feeling?"

"She's got morning sickness and she's less than eight weeks. I took her to the doctor this morning. She'll be fine. It's just . . . just . . ." Luz stuttered to a stop. She steadied herself on the counter.

"Do your parents know?"

"Not yet."

"Don't tell them, Luz. Not yet. The fewer who know the better." Cat got up from her stool to help herself to a bottled water from the fridge. She got one out for Luz, too, cracked open the seal, and set it beside her before she went back to her seat.

"I know. It's too much."

"And is she keeping it? I mean . . ."

"I know. It's a hard question. It's hard for me to even think about it. All the trouble our friends have had with fertility and there you go, a teenager, it just happens. And it's not an easy thing to think about."

"No. It's not."

"It's been a day so we haven't gotten there yet, I mean, definitively. She's still too scared about dealing with his family and them finding out. Shoot, she's so upset that I found out!" Luz pointed to herself.

"Are you kidding? What would have happened had you *not* found out?" Cat asked.

"What do you mean?"

"I mean, she could have gone to get it taken care of by herself or let it go so long that it would be too late to make any other decision, and I know that that would just break your heart if she wanted to give it away. . . ."

"Oh no! No! No! No!" Luz's face got hot. "No. I can't let that happen." She wiped her eye.

"But Lu, you have to be ready for these things. She's not your daughter."

"I know, Catalina. I know." Luz sniffed. "But she's still only sixteen, and I just can't imagine my own flesh and blood, I mean, it's not like we don't have the ability to care for the baby—"

"But what if she doesn't want it?"

"*Ay*, Cat." Luz shook her head, shook the thought of giving away her niece out of her mind. "If she goes to term, that child is not leaving this family. Shit. Another baby? I can take it." She started to pull herself together as the sounds coming from the hallway grew louder, like a clock ticking closer to its alarm.

"Is she going to go to term? I mean, what's your take on this?"

Luz sighed. "Honestly, I just want this all to go away."

"I know." Cat knew not to press. She knew her friend was bighearted and patient, but with all she'd been through, all the changes, the family secrets revealed and her own identity up for grabs, she knew Luz was exhausted. "I know. The famous father—or should I say, grandfather—doesn't help."

"Nope. Nope, it doesn't."

"Okay, listen, be kind to her, okay?"

Luz stood up straight, a bit taken aback. "I'm kind!"

"I'm not saying you're not," Cat soothed. "I'm just saying that right now, the most important thing is to make sure that she doesn't end up a teen runaway."

"Runaway!" Luz said a bit too loud. She repeated herself more softly, though it came out in a hiss. "Runaway—from all this? From us?!"

"Hon, remember where she comes from. It's not too crazy to think that. If she feels too much pressure, who knows what she'd do?"

"Oh my God, you're right."

"Just give her lots of love right now and understanding, okay?"

Luz nodded as she took out the silverware for dinner.

Cat continued, "So, what's next?"

"Visiting her father."

Cat raised an eyebrow.

"Yeah, yeah, that guy, person . . . upstate. This weekend. We have to tell him. She's too young and I could get into big trouble."

"Totally. Understood." Cat poured them both another glass of wine. "What do you think he'll say?"

"I dunno. Probably to have it. Lock this guy down or something. I'm going to assume that all he'll see is more opportunity."

"Most likely . . ." Cat agreed. "I'm here for you, okay? Want me to come? Maybe just drive?"

Luz smiled and relaxed her brow. "Oh no, babe, no, but thank you so much for offering. I may call you screaming after, though. We'll be done by three. You've been warned!"

"You got it, girl." Cat let the heavy air stay still for a minute. She let it breathe. So much to hold up in the air, like juggling weights. She felt much love for this family. They were blessed in so many ways—supportive, successful husband, beautiful children, great parents—but then, family secrets and new family members come around, and there you go. That's life.

"Okay, so before everyone shows up here, I have to tell you something to distract you." Cat leaned in conspiratorially. Luz's face lit up just a bit. She could use the distraction.

"What?! What?"

"You know that tech guy, August Tilly, who was on my show?"

"Oh yeah! That hottie majillionaire—dang, girl, you came down on him hard. I saw like a thirty-second clip someone tweeted of you. Poor guy!"

"Yeah, well, he can cry into his money," Cat sassed. "He's after me."

Luz stopped her multitasking and stood still. "What you mean, he's *after* you?"

"After me, after me." Cat shrugged.

"Okay, gurl, that ain't gonna fly. Fill a sista' in now. And fast. You've got one minute before the whole crew comes barreling down that hallway, hungry!" Luz waved a spoon in their direction.

"Okay. But listen, I'm telling you this as a friend first, not as your brother's woman and your niece's mother."

"Well. That's a hard one, now."

"I know. But nothing's gonna happen. I just have to tell you. I went to his office for a meeting, thought it was going to be more about the show, and Audrey pushed me along because girlfriend was thinkin' potential sponsorship."

"Mmmm-hmm. I'm listening," Luz said as she took a swig from her glass, one hand on her hip.

"He told me he loves me."

Luz's wine dribbled out of her mouth as she tried to pull it all back in, nearly spitting it all over the countertop. She grabbed a dishcloth and wiped her face. "What the fuck?! Loves you? He just met you!"

"I know." Cat was nonchalant. She wanted to make sure that Luz got the message that she was not interested in the slightest. She was tempted a little. Curious even. But she couldn't show that. Not one bit. "He crazy. *Un loco, de veras.* Not happening." Cat twirled her finger at her head.

"He doesn't even know you!"

"I know. Says he's watched everything I've ever done, read everything I've ever written, all this stuff. But that's not me— not all of me, anyway."

"I'll say." Luz's face grew concerned. "But, you're not going there, are you?"

"*Ay,* no, sweetie! No." Cat waved the idea away. "Hon, I love your Tomasito so much and our little Almita." She looked over at the stroller and saw the little girl wiggling away. "This guy is projecting completely. He could have anybody, anyway. What the hell would he want with me?"

"Well, Cat. I think the real question is, what would you want with him?"

Chapter 12

"Oh, hey munchkins!" Magda hugged and kissed each child in succession as they came through her apartment door. Nina, 'Fina, and Benny, all in a row, with Benny attached to Emelie, who was letting his little hand guide her like a seeing eye dog. Her round, large eyes rarely seemed to look up anymore. She offered the smallest smile to Magda as they cheek-kissed. Magda let the teen be. She was glad to see her there at all, considering the antisocial tendencies of her age, but also possibly knowing—or not—that people might know about her state. Though when Luz briefly called Magda the night before, she made sure to ask her to please, please give no indication that she knew or that anyone knew. *It's only supposed to be me.*

"And you, *Mamacita,* lookin' grand as usual," Magda offered Luz as she passed through.

"*Ay,* can you and I just compare the bags under our eyes for a minute?" Luz teased.

"Come. You guys head in there and the kids can join Cherokee, Ilsa, and Nico."

"Is Albita here?" Luz asked, wondering if Magda's ex, their children's mother, was going to add to the fortifying mix of family.

"Nah. Thought I'd give her this one off."

"Got it."

It had been one week since Magda had returned from Florida with her father, and this was going to be her way of indoctrinating him into just what her life looked like. Luz, her husband, Chris, their gaggle of little ones, and even Luz's parents were coming. Magda wanted Raoul to meet some folks his age, and to meet parents who were also experienced with their kids marrying someone, well, unexpected. Chris was Asian, Cat was Mexican-American and not even yet married to Luz's African-American brother, and then Gabi had a special family of her own, just herself and her son, Maximo.

As Magda entered the room and took in the image of all the kids lolling about, playing on the floor, climbing on the couch, she noted her father, Raoul, looking smaller than usual in the overstuffed chair he'd decided was going to be his perch. He seemed pleased, if tired. He threw out comments to the kids once in a while, directing them like a conductor with his right hand, his left holding onto the armrest as if he were sitting on a throne. *King of the castle.*

She watched Luz greet Cherokee and reintroduce herself to Raoul. His eyes brightened a bit as Magda watched him remember Luz's big blue eyes from the funeral service for his wife. Luz presented her husband again. The men shook hands, Raoul even bringing up his left hand to embrace Chris's completely. *He always liked him. Reminds him of his Chino-Latino golfing buddy—plastic surgeon, I think—from Miami.* Luz called up little Benny, and the boy raised his tiny hand to give Raoul a high five. The older man hooted and praised him in his accented English, giving the boy's mini arm muscles a squeeze. "So strong!"

Magda caught her wife's eye as she sat on the floor, one part of her attention on the kids, the other taking in how Raoul was reacting to everyone. Cherokee smiled at Magda, letting her know that she was okay. *I wish he'd treat her better. I have to make sure she knows that it will get better.*

"Helloooooo!" came from the hallway. Gabi and her golden-haired son, Maximo, walked in. "The door was open." She handed Magda some bags.

"Bags, bags, Bag-Mama. Watch'u got here?"

"Just some munchies for later—cookies for the kids and pie for us big people." Gabi smiled. *Always taking care of us, Dr. Gabriella Gomez.*

"*Gracias, Mami. Y Maximo! Ven!*" Magda gave the little one a hug and kiss. He warmly hugged back, giving Magda a big kiss on the cheek.

"*Mmmwwwah!* Hi, *Tía.*"

"You. Are. *Delicioso*. Did you know that, monkey?" Magda asked, crouched down so she could be eye level with little Max.

"Mmm hmm," he agreed.

"Okay, *Papi,* go see your *primos, vaya!*" She patted him on the bum as he ran into the living room, and then she grasped Gabi's arm to stop her before she could follow her son.

"Hon, I have to talk to you alone later, before you go tonight, okay?"

Gabi was surprised at Magda's delivery, whispered and urgent. "Okay. Sure." She was about to ask more but got the hint that, as the woman said, later was better. Magda let go and Gabi went on her way, concerned.

Before Magda could follow her far down the hall, the front door opened again as Luz's parents, Altagracias and Roger, much more quietly than the guests with children, ambled in.

"*Hola,* Magdalena!" said the handsome, older woman, her cropped, natural hair a matching salt-and-pepper to her husband's, who followed just behind. Mama "Alta" never failed Magda in the fashion department. She and Roger spent their time in retirement going from art galleries to museums to restaurants and shops.

Not so much ostentatious as admiringly well-thought-out, the two of them reminded Magda of a portrait of what architects from Harlem would and should look like. Which, in actuality, was close to who they were.

"I cannot pass up an opportunity to spend time in this gorgeous home of yours, Magda," Roger commented in greeting.

"Well, just watch all the toys on the floor, Roger. I know they break your eyeline and give your aesthetic sensibilities a rash, but pay no mind!" Magda teased him.

She led them both to her father, who stood up in respect for people who were actually his own age and generation. Raoul seemed pleased to hear Altagracia's Spanish, and Roger handled himself just fine, walking over politely to Chris to talk business. Alta sat herself next to Raoul's chair as Cherokee came over to greet her and offer her a drink. Cherokee met Magda in the kitchen, where she was overseeing her supplies. Or, avoiding the madness for a moment. It was a bit overwhelming.

"Oy, hon, I think he's liking me a bit better!" Cherokee genuinely seemed relieved. "Of course, it may be because he's outnumbered by us brown people." She winked.

Magda snuck a squeeze of her wife's waist. "*Querida,* he knows he'd be missing out."

Cherokee kissed Magda on the cheek and whisked off with one red wine and one white for the new arrivals.

"Whazzup, whazzup!" Tomas walked in holding his daughter up in her car seat like a basket of plenty. "Check one, check one, two." He set the sleeping baby down on the kitchen island, far from the food, closer to the pile of mail. "This cool?"

"Of course," Magda said. "How's the lovely Almita?" She bent down to breathe in her soft, sleeping face. "Dang, she's looking Asian, Catalina!"

"That's my Mexican roots, yo." Cat, much smaller than her partner, emerged from behind him, laden with a diaper bag that she dropped as soon as possible. "How you doin' girl?"

Magda bent down to give Cat an embrace.

"You know, I'm good. I'm okay."

"And your *Papi?*" They were enough out of earshot and the children were so rowdy that there was little chance Raoul would hear Cat's question.

Magda sighed. "You know. He'll be okay. I worry. I mean, of course. He's here. He hasn't warmed up enough to Cherokee, his old racist ass." Tomas, the same shade as Magda's wife, raised an eyebrow. He was very familiar with the prejudice—some subtle, some not so much—in the Latino community. "But, this is helping a lot, having you all here. Thank you so much for coming, hon."

Cat gave Magda an additional, platonic, hug. "Of course. Shoot, soon enough he'll be so swallowed up in all our awesome craziness, he'll forget all the crap he used to think."

"From your mouth to—"

"Catalina Rosa Rivera! The TV star!" Magda was startled by her father shouting out to her friend. "*Ay,* I used to watch you all the time!" He kept on his fan-clubbing as Cat approached him. Magda thought, *So funny. All these years. He was watching one of my closest friends. Watching her. But not seeing me.*

Tomas smiled as he whispered to Magda that he was going to set up sleeping Alma in the adjacent room. Magda nodded.

An hour into the gathering, a few drinks set back—except Magda, who now, nearly two years sober, was happy to sample from her collection of flavored seltzer waters—the women all gravitated to the kitchen. Tomas and Chris kept Raoul company as they watched a soccer, *fútbol,* game as Roger stared out the window, taking pictures of the great expanse of city that lay before him so many flights up. Altagracia had all the children in the next room, watching the most recent Pixar release on a flat screen.

"Ladies, Cat has something to tell you about that August Tilly guy," Luz slyly let out.

"Tilly? The guy on the cover of *Fast Company* last month?" Magda asked.

Cat groaned.

"Let it out, sistah!" Luz teased.

"He's . . . uh . . . ." She blushed as much as her skin would allow.

"He's in love with her," Luz blurted.

"Love?! Like in love in love?" Cherokee asked.

"Yeah. That's what he says." Cat rolled her eyes.

"Hon. First of all, that's weird. Didn't you just interview him?" Magda looked to confirm her timeline.

"Yup. And then did a follow-up meeting at his office."

"And this is where it all went down?"

Cat nodded.

"Gurl, he didn't jump you or anything, did he?" Gabi chimed in protectively.

"No! No, it wasn't like that. He just went on and on about how he'd seen everything I've done and how no one stands up to him like I did, et cetera." Cat waved her hand dismissively.

"So. How did you leave it?" Magda asked, an edge to her voice.

"Of course I was like, 'No way!' And, 'You're nuts!' 'You don't know me!' " Cat responded, betraying slightly her confusion at the whole matter. "I mean, I love Tomas." She nodded to Luz, his sister. "And Alma is my life, outside of the show. . . . So, no. It's a no. It's ridiculous."

"But, you must have been flattered, no?" Gabi asked. "At least somebody's getting a powerful, rich guy to love her!" Magda gave Gabi a side-eye.

"Gabs, what happened with the actor dude? What's his name?" Cat asked.

"Maxwell Dane."

"Holy shit—the guy from the new series? On the bus stops all over the city?" Cherokee was surprised.

"Yup." Gabi nodded. "He ghosted me."

In unison, all four women echoed, "Ghosted?!"

Gabi nodded again, frustrated. "It was like a five-hour date and he was all, 'I'm gonna ring you when I get back from LA and then we'll hang out again, right?' And of course I was all, 'Um, yeah!'" She paused. "I fucked up."

"Dr. Gabrielle Gomez Gold, shut the fuck up." Magda pointed at her. They might not have worked out as a couple but she still cared for her deeply and wanted her to not hurt anymore, especially after her cheating ex-husband tore her heart out. "You didn't do a thing wrong. The guy probably freaked out or something came up in his family or something happened in LA—who the fuck knows! But it's not your fault, okay?!"

Gabi nodded. "I know, hon. I know. . . . It's my job to know!"

"He did you a favor by ghosting now, not after you all had slept together or something." Leave it to Luz to be practical.

"Word," Cherokee said in agreement.

But Gabi knew what happened. She could practically taste when it all went sour. It was the second she realized that Maxwell really did like her, not only the help she was giving him. This was Gabi's problem. She was a fixer. Her ex, Bert, essentially threw the well-earned title at her during the fight that began their separation. Sure, she was sick of his lackadaisical ways, his pot smoking, his entitled attitude, his yelling at their poor son for the slightest thing. And of course, in the end, the icing was discovering his multiple affairs. Not only one woman or two, but maybe a dozen at least—dating profiles on singles' apps and sites, e-mails from public relations girls missing his touch. It made Gabi retch still to think of it. Though, she was grateful that as time went by, her visceral reactions dissipated. She knew that soon, she'd feel very little if she worked to let it go. But she couldn't let go the one truth—a gift—that Bert had given her: the realization that her tendency to fix and help was a form of control. She was a trained psychiatrist so that was her job, but she spent decades functioning as if that role were her life. In the beginning, men loved it—well, Bert did. They leaned on it. Saw her capability and drive as sexy. But when that fire in her to make everything right, to smooth the edges off of everything, to make all of life's labels face front on the shelf, was directed at someone she loved, well. It was too much. She was beginning to discover that it was a way to hold people at an arm's length. To not see and accept them for who they were, but instead to only see problems that needed fixing. It saddened her to learn this about herself but she also knew that she'd never have a healthy relationship unless she changed. So she knew when things curdled with Maxwell. She kept pressing him on his family and his aunt instead of stopping, breathing, letting the two of them just . . . be. *Stop the help train, Gabi. Not everyone wants to be on it.*

There were a few seconds of silence in Magda's kitchen, filled with the friends' reminiscences of lovers past and lost, before Cat, staring into her cell phone, blurted an anxious, "*Ay, Dio'.*"

"What?" asked Magda.

"I just got a text from Mr. Presumptuous."

All the women held their breath, their eyes unblinking. "Tilly?" asked Gabi.

Cat read the loaded words in a flat, almost angry voice. "It says: *I have to ask; if you're so happy, why aren't you married yet? Let me make you happy.*"

"You have got to be kidding me." Luz joined Cat in annoyance. Her jaw set, internal battle mode instated. This was her brother's woman, her niece's mother. Family. *Fuck this interloper.*

Cat dropped her phone into the back pocket of her jeans. "You know, I just can't with him."

"What are you going to do?" asked Cherokee with a bit of awe. She was the youngest of the group and much less experienced in managing the ways—and attention—of aggressive multimillionaires.

"I dunno."

Gabi swooped in, per her usual role. "Cat. You have got to tell this man to quit it. This is more than inappropriate. He's part of your show—"

"He was just a guest." Cat defended herself.

"Yeah, *was,* and then Audrey wants him to be a sponsor."

"And can we just talk about how this is also about my brother here, and my niece?!" Luz had had enough.

Cat sighed and the air shifted. "Nope, nope, you're right. This is wrong and he really needs to back off."

"All these assumptions—inserting himself into your business and your decisions is a big red flag, *chica.*" Luz bobbed her neck. "I mean, who the fuck does he think he is, huh?"

"A famous tech titan," Magda responded to the rhetorical question.

"So the fuck what." Luz poured herself another drink.

"True. True. So the F what, though, that's the question here. Right, Cat?" Gabi probed.

Cat looked at Magda, wanting to catch her eye. She did. Magda was in nearly the same tax bracket as August Tilly. She understood how people at this level thought and she knew how people treated others like her and Tilly. Cat also assumed that she could understand how she'd be tempted, slightly, by the promise of economic security and access to more power than she even had now as a member of the media.

Cat had never had wealth in her life. She'd been supporting herself and helping out her mother financially for more than a decade. Shoot, even in high school she waited tables to help her mother pay bills. Cat looked to have it all together from the outside: successful former television host now with a popular online show, hundreds of thousands of followers. She owned most of her business, but yet—but yet—she was still paying off student loans. And, though Tomas was an amazing lover, father, partner, and made just in the six figures, Cat got the sense that as smart and solid as he was, she was going to end up ahead of him. It could just be age. She had some years on him, and those years in between meant he made less money now. He had great promise, but Cat also feared that since he was a gorgeous black man on Wall Street, it was just a matter of time before she found out that he was sleeping around. *Am I just being insecure? Is it me? Or is it just a fact? There's no way I'm going to make it with Tomas without him cheating. No way. And I can never forgive that. But wouldn't August cheat? Sure. But money and status helps assuage those wounds. Right?*

"Huh?" Cat snapped out of her thoughts.

"Cat," Gabi asked as all the women stayed quiet, waiting, wondering, "are you tempted by this guy?"

"No! No . . . I mean it. It's crazy and it pisses me off to no end."

"What pisses you off, exactly?" Gabi kept at it. Magda was leaning on the counter, Cherokee's head nestled onto her chest. Luz was looking partially away, wishing she weren't in the room having to face a potential family betrayal but glued to the moment by years of friendship and in the moment, curiosity.

"The whole thing. Just the whole fucking thing."

As Cat deflected the question more than anyone would have liked her to, and Gabi geared up to ask another while Luz pressed her temples and Magda narrowed her eyes at Cat, working hard to figure out if her hunch about her friend being conflicted and tempted by money and status was right, and how money and success could really mess relationships up, her own life included, the sound of a baby's cry filled the hallway.

"Whoop! Saved by the baby!" Luz blurted.

Cat didn't say a word beyond "Oh!" as she put down her glass and raced down the hall to comfort her crying Alma. Though, satisfying Alma's needs would be just as comforting to Cat.

The remaining women waited until Cat disappeared into the room where Luz and Tomas's mother held court with the children.

"Well," Magda threw out like a lure for her friends to fill the air.

"Well, what?" Luz asked.

"I think we all need to give our Cat a little reality check."

"Of what kind?" Gabi was curious.

"She's a good girl, that Cat. But I think she doubts that your brother will stick around—"

"What?!" Luz blurted.

"Hon. Let's be real. It may have little to do with Tomas and a lot to do with Cat's family history. Just sayin'. Girl is insecure and she needs us to remind her that she's on solid ground. And that this ground is the best ground to stand on." Magda sucked the pimento out of an olive. "Before that fool Tilly has the chance to build her a new ground to stand on."

"Oh, shoot, one second, *mi* Almita," Cat assured her baby girl, gurgling on a bottle in her arms as Cat balanced her ringing phone with one hand, holding up the bottle with her chin. She didn't recognize the number but it was a Manhattan 212. *Could be a source.*

"Cat here."

"Am I right?"

It was August. Cat came to attention, straightening her

head, managing the bottle with the tips of her fingers on her other hand, coming up just behind her baby's back.

Cat froze. Her stomach dropped. She was so angry at the intrusion. Angry. *How dare he?!* And if she was so upset, then why didn't she just hang up?

He asked the same question, again. This time a bit more pleading, plying.

Cat's jaw was set. Her baby in her arms, her man just in the other room. Her friends and family all around her. "I am at a family function. This is not the time," she hissed.

"Okay then. When?" August sounded hopeful.

"I don't know." *What am I saying?!* Cat heard the thump of someone approaching in the hall. "I gotta go. Good-bye." She hung up a bit too hurriedly, guiltily.

"Hey, baby girls!" Tomas rounded the corner, his grin warming the room, washing the initial adrenaline out of Cat with its honesty.

"Hi, sweetie."

"Were you talkin' to our little boo?" He came over to kiss Cat on the head and stroke his baby girl's face.

"Yeah, yeah," Cat lied. "She's such an angel. So good." They both gazed at her lovingly.

"She is, she is!" Tomas agreed.

And what does that make me?

"Gabs. I'm in trouble," Magda said.

The two women managed to land a spot in the hallway, Magda's bedroom being much too loaded a place, considering their history as partners. Most everyone else was now sauced on wine and tequila while Magda managed to maintain her sobriety. The smell didn't bother her so much anymore, or tempt her. Surprisingly, she found herself almost repulsed by it. It made her feel nauseous. She chalked it up to having had too many bad experiences, it being a door that opened up dangerous times. And physically, her kidneys and liver just screamed *no*. Her father was impressed. He'd been warned to lay off all forms of alcohol—joining his daughter in sobriety—and Magda stocked him up with his favorite, sugar-loaded sodas to distract him, but she thought she caught him going to the bathroom with his cup in his hand. *That's not good.* However, he looked okay. They both were functioning alcoholics for years. She'd talk to him in the morning. Right now, the men were all comfortably reclined on various seats, yelping out at the sixty-plus-inch screen before them, another soccer game on from somewhere in the world. After three hours or so, Luz had taken the children home with Chris and her mother, Alta, leaving her father, Roger, there to keep Raoul company. Tomas stuck around as Cat bonded with Cherokee, the younger woman looking for some career advice. Baby Alma slept away in her car seat, and Gabi's little Max was passed out on the couch nearby, rounding out the multigenerations of men in front of the screen.

"What kind of trouble?" Gabi asked. For once, she had no clue. "Wait—is it money?!"

"Well, sort of," Magda said. She seemed ashamed of something. Gabi picked up on her body language quickly. At first, Gabi thought her incredibly brilliant businessperson of a friend had for once made a bad investment decision. But in the seconds that Gabi waited for Magda to finish her thought, she realized what this was about.

"Mags. What did you do?" Gabi scolded.

"I didn't do anything, Gabs!" Magda leaned her back against the wall. "I did something. Once. Before."

"Ah."

"And it's come back to haunt me."

"Jesus." Gabi felt for her. She was never a fan of how hard Magda used to live, and ultimately, her infidelities drove them apart and broke her heart. But Gabi was able to forgive her with time, once she understood just how deep her pain was, a pain that only drinking and sex could help until she decided to help herself. Her mother's death and her reunion with her father had sobered her up quickly.

"Do you remember that gala last week that you weren't able to come to—"

"Yeah, yeah, it was last minute. . . ." Gabi tried to wave off any guilt.

"Okay, well, someone was there—and I don't know how she got in, well, actually I do, she was there with some banking dude. Do you remember Sharon?"

"Sweetie, I can't—I didn't keep track of all the hoochie-mamas you put your face into, mmm-kay?" The other women who had come between them still felt too close to home for Gabi to discuss. She knew it was her own insecurity but still, she didn't feel like running her mind through all the pretty faces. She'd had too much wine herself.

"Fine. Well. Sharon was the super pale one, black, black hair. BDSM chick."

"*Ay,* please, Mags. Seriously?"

"So you remember her?"

"Yeah, I remember a girl fitting that description and you bringing her to some party, but are you telling me that she was like a dominatrix or something? Like for money?" Gabi's face was getting hot at this conversation.

"Well. No. Not really."

"You know what, Mags, I don't want to know."

"Okay, listen, so maybe Sharon has video of me somewhere—somewhere I shouldn't have been, or wouldn't like to be seen . . . people in my business, the press."

At this, Gabi grew pale. Magda had more money than she really needed in this lifetime, but with how far she'd come personally, and her children, *carajo,* this was not something that could get out.

"Okay, Mags, be specific with me. How many videos?"

"One."

"Supposedly."

"Right," Magda said.

"And, you're doing something, or . . ."

"No. Nothing. Just waiting."

Gabi sighed. "Right. Okay, that's somehow better." The women stood quietly for a moment. Magda needed her confidante's problem-solving powers. "And how much does she want?"

"Doesn't matter."

"Doesn't matter?! Magdalena Sofia, I will not be able to help you if you arc not straightforward with me!" Gabi pointed at her friend. "How. Much."

"A hundred."

"Hundred thousand?"

"Yup."

"Mags, you could go in your closet right now and get out that much money."

"I know. But Gabs, it's a rabbit hole. You pay once, they want you to keep on paying." Magda took on a pleading tone.

"You're right. Hon, you're right. Tell me, today, with everything going on in the world and sex videos making the Kardashian empire, you're an out and proud gay woman with a reputation for being a lady killer anyway. . . . Would it be a big risk to just, well, go dark on this girl? Call her bluff?" Gabi asked.

Magda thought for a moment. She ran her fingers through her hair. Squinted her eyes tight. Imagined the headlines in the blogs. Imagined the apology she'd have to go public with. Imagined her children finding out—seeing that video. Her eyes started to water.

"Fuck, girl. I just don't want it out there. Cherokee doesn't know how bad it was, really. Yet. I have another life now. My kids are growing up."

"I know, *chica*. I know." Gabi put her hand on her shoulder. They heard a low-level "Goooooooaaal!" come from the other room. They'd have to wrap this up.

"Is she showing up at the apartment? How is she communicating with you?"

"She's texting. But it's escalating. I'm afraid she's going to be outside the building or at the office soon. I'm trying to hold her off."

"Okay. Hold her off for one more night. Let's talk in the morning. Have you talked to your lawyer yet?"

"No! Jesus. No."

Gabi assumed Magda was too embarrassed yet to make that move. She was flattered a bit that she was the only one who knew. So far.

"All right. *Ya*. We'll take care of this. It's not going to be easy but you've got to keep your eye on the ball, okay?" Gabi took Magda's shoulders, which she was only able to do because her nearly six-foot friend had sunk so deeply against the wall. "Don't let her get into your head. Text me when you need me—all hours, okay?"

Magda nodded her head in agreement.

"Damn. And we were all pissed that I was being ghosted by an actor!" Gabi remarked.

Magda had to laugh at that. "Yeah, well. Leave it to me to have a *cucaracha* from my past crawl back into my life."

"True. But we're gonna crush that little bitch like the bug that she is, *sabes?*"

"*Sí*." Magda cracked a smile. She loved Gabi's spunk. Whenever she stressed too much, Dr. Gomez was there with some laughter medicine. She used it on her patients, on her son, and on her friends. It worked.

They hugged and walked back into the kitchen. Cat and Cherokee had joined the men for what seemed like a great game. All at once the room jumped one last time for the night: "GOOOOOAAAAALLL!"

Gabi looked at Magda. She mouthed and winked, "Goal."

Chapter 13

"Get the door, honey, will ya?"

"I got it." Emelie opened and closed the car door again, making sure it was shut. She looked particularly put together for a teenager on a Sunday. Luz noticed a bit of extra blush, Emelie's hair out and free, not braided as usual, and she had on her best coat. *Wants to impress her daddy. Um. Our Dad.*

Meanwhile, Luz had stripped herself of status. She had taken off her best jewelry, applied only minimal makeup, and wore the blandest clothes. *Can't look too good for prison. Daddy or no Daddy.*

"You haven't told him yet, have you?" Emelie asked Luz once they left the borders of the city, gaggles of trees taking over the skyline from the billboards and buildings of home.

Luz didn't answer.

Emelie took the omission as an answer even louder than *Yes. I have.* Emelie started to cry.

"Oh, come on, hon. C'mon." Luz gave her tissues and put on a soothing tone. *Lately, I'm always handing this poor girl tissues. This car is crying on wheels.* "I didn't want to have to."

"You didn't have to!" Emelie yelled. Luz tensed up.

"Yes. I. Did. Sister." She glared at the girl, one finger pointing in the air. Emelie looked out the window, her face teared-up and angry. "You are under eighteen years old. He is your father. I may be your guardian and your sister but I would get in trouble if we did anything without telling him."

"Oh, so, *you'd* get in trouble!"

"Yes! Me! Because I'm supposed to be taking care of you, which is *all* I've done and now, under *my* watch, you're knocked up!" As soon as she finished, Luz knew that was going too far. She was still so emotional about the situation. Shoot, she was still so emotional about taking in a secret sister and leaving the company she'd been at for ten years to make it on her own. (*Thank God I'm making it there.*) And of course, finding out who her real father was and wrangling with all the feelings that had conjured up in her about her mother, her saintly mother, and her father—well, her stepfather now, but the man who raised her. So many feelings. Too little time.

"I'm sorry," Luz said.

Emelie sniffed. Her sister's apology took some of the air out of her anger. But she didn't speak for the full two-hour drive. Luz allowed the heaviness of their situation and their destination to just sit with them for a bit. There would be plenty to talk about on the way home.

Eugenio already looked pissed. His chin in the air, jaw set as he embraced his daughter Emelie. Luz wasn't up for hugging him, biological father or not. She soon found out, though, who he was going to blame.

"How you feelin', *nena?*" he asked Emelie. His hair was buzzed shorter than last time they visited, several months ago. There was more gray in his temple, Luz noted, more lines and creases on his face. But he'd beefed up. The muscles connecting his neck and shoulders were bulky. Luz imagined him working out in the prison yard. She wondered why he'd work out like that, a man his age. Vanity? Or, to stay alive?

"I'm okay," Emelie mumbled, her hands under the table, her shoulders hunched.

Eugenio sucked his teeth. "And you?" He nodded at Luz.

"I'm good," Luz answered.

"I bet." The man leaned forward. "So. You wanna tell me how 'dis happen'?"

Luz looked to Emelie. The girl looked to Luz.

Luz said, "However it happened, it did. And now we need to deal with it."

"Fine. Ju don' want to tell me. Fine." Eugenio leaned back in his chair and gave another guy in a jumpsuit a nod. He looked back at Emelie. Pointing his finger into the table, right under her nose, he asked, "Who is da father?" It was threatening. Luz could only imagine what he was thinking of doing to the male responsible. Her mind raced and her hands began to sweat. It was a clashing of worlds—people coming together, crossing classes, cultures, that Luz felt wildly unprepared for. And she was embarrassed by her lack of prep.

"Just someone from school," Emelie mumbled.

"From school, eh? And he a teacher or teenager or what?"

Emelie's eyes grew wide in offense. "Not a teacher, *Papi*, sheesh."

"Well. Das a relief because I was going to have to take care of him if dat were de case. I have people here dat do dat."

"Okay, now, no one is 'taking care' of anyone here—" Luz piped in. Eugenio crossed his arms and gave her a look.

"An' what ju have to say about dis? I expect my daughter to be taken care of by her older sister and dis happens. *Rich* older sister."

"Listen—"

"No, ju listen. Ju have money. Ju have lots of education. Ju put her in da best school. And some *pendejo* student knocks her up? Ju tell me how ju let dat happen, uh?!"

"It's Peter Quinton," Luz responded.

Emelie looked off to the side. She was trying to hold back her tears.

"Who dat? Who Peter Kwin-TON?"

Luz looked at Emelie, who said softly, "Son of the movie star. Ben Quinton."

The father was so new to this stratosphere, this class system that was suddenly a part of his life, his face went blank. The females watched him think and process.

Eugenio brightened and leaned back in. "Da guy in da big museum movie? Da funny guy?"

"Yeah."

Too loudly, Eugenio blurted, "I jus' watch dat movie like las' week with my boys! He was hilarious! *Tan* crazy . . ."

Oh God. Here we go.

"Eugenio. He doesn't know yet. We wanted to come here first, it was your right to know, and I'm talking to Emelie about speaking with his parents tomorrow, Monday."

"Oh, no, dis is how it's gonna be managed." Eugenio pointed his finger again at the table. Luz felt as if she could see the surface give under his jabs. The man turned his attention to Emelie. "Ju are gonna keep dis baby because it is the answer to the rest of jor life—"

"But, *Papi*—"

"No 'but *Papi*' me—ju listen. Ju are gonna be set, and he's gonna haf to take care of ju, and we can be all set when I get out and you won' haf to worry about anyt'ing."

"Listen!" Luz put her hand in between his jabbing finger and Emelie's face. "This is a big decision to make and because of us, because of me and my family, Em won't have to worry about anything anyway for the rest of her life, so she is *not* keeping a baby just to be rich and famous and take care of you. She'll keep it only if she wants it." Luz's eyes were fiery. This was mama lion mode, and she was used to going toe to toe with men across tables. But not so much men like this.

Eugenio's eyes simmered. He fell back in his chair, unblinking at Luz. Emelie, more familiar with this mode of her father's, shrunk visibly in her seat. Her body compressed into itself, making her appear a third of her real size. Luz stood her ground. She noted in the corner of her eye that her sister was shrinking. She absorbed the fear coming off of her like a quiet vibration. She felt her skin prickle at Eugenio's stare. But she refused to cower to this man she barely knew, her biological father.

"See, here's the thing, Eugenio," Luz emphasized the "eu" at the front of his name. "Emelie is with me now and you . . . you are here for a very, very long time." Both of them had yet to blink. It was more sibling rivalry than parent to child, which was what happened when tables were turned and casting was by biology only. Luz looked at Em to make sure the girl was okay. With Luz's assertiveness with her father, standing up for her and her rights, Emelie seemed to rise a bit straighter, her chin raised slightly. Luz took it as permission to move forward on her behalf.

But in her pause, Eugenio took his opening. "*Ja,* and she's going to be eighteen very, very soon and can do whatever she wants. Right, *m'ija?*"

Emelie didn't look at him. She didn't make a peep. Luz nabbed the ball now in her court; it was clear that the females were on the same team. "She won't be eighteen before this baby comes, and again, this is her decision to make with our guidance— particularly mine as I will stand by this girl no matter what and support her, as family and financially, no matter what she decides to do."

With that, Emelie looked up slowly at Luz, her gaze wide as she absorbed the weight of what her sister just said. Had anyone ever said such a thing to her? Such a deep, bonding, accepting thing? Her eyes welled and she was back to nearly sitting up tall and taking up her full physical space.

"No matter what, huh?" Eugenio taunted. "Lee-sin. No amount of money is da same as fame. Being famous is bigger than money. Look at her." He gestured toward his daughter. "She gorgeous, *tan belleza* . . . and she can be a es-star. Dis baby do dat for her—reality shows, that Instagram thing, social media, all dat!"

They heard a whisper coming from Emelie's direction.

"What, hon?" Luz asked.

The teen said in a flat tone, "What if I don't want that?"

Eugenio's hand slammed down and sent the whole table and their benches into vibration. Both females jumped, and Luz looked instinctively at the guard in the corner. He made a step toward them in warning, or protection.

"Ju had to go and open jor legs to da first white guy who comes jor way—I am jor father, I am jor family! Ju will listen to me!" Eugenio's voice boomed. Luz instinctively placed her hand on Emelie's leg to assure her that she'd protect her.

She didn't have to.

Emelie enlisted her strongest voice. "And *you* chose your business—your drug business—over me. So no. You made your choices, now I'll make mine. *Adiós, Papi.*"

It took a moment for both Luz and Eugenio to process what Emelie delivered. They both stared at her, mouths open. After Em was done, with little emotion for someone her age, she put her own hands down on the table, raised herself, and stood up.

"Can we go now, Luz?"

"Uh, yes. Yes, we can go now." Luz picked up her bag and made sure as she got up that their father wasn't going to lose it and grab them both by the throat. "Good-bye," she said to Eugenio. She nodded at the guard.

Luz's heart was racing as she took Emelie's arm in her hand and walked her out of the prison, through each gate. Neither of them looked back. Neither of them wanted to give their father a chance to scare them again, to bully them. To lay claim to their female bodies and all their powers, thinking that somehow his daughter's ability to create belonged to him. He had signed over all guardianship rights to Luz. It was generous of her to even bring Emelie there and to fill him in. It was going to be up to her now to make sure this girl did what she felt was right. *And I said I'd support her no matter what she chose. Shit. Another baby? A famous baby? Let's just get out of here.*

Once they got in the SUV for the ride home, both locking the doors as quickly as possible, they simultaneously sucked in a deep breath of relief. They looked at each other, surprised, and smiled.

"Luz?"

"Yeah?"

"I think I want this baby," Emelie said.

The girl looked directly at her older sister, her caretaker, and let tears run down her cheeks like a brook. Luz gently wiped her face, cradling her cheek in her palm.

"Honey. I understand. We need to talk to his parents, okay?"

"Okay." Em sniffed.

"Wanna just turn on some music from your phone and we can just chill the whole ride home?"

Emelie smiled with relief and dug up her phone, scrolling for what would make her feel better.

Staying calm on the outside for the girl's sake, inside, Luz was screaming at her declaration about keeping the pregnancy.

Dios.

Chapter 14

Cat rounded the corner of the prewar, subway-tiled hallway, the iron railing cold in her fingers. She breathed in the memories. She grew up in this building, full of railroad apartments, tiny, clanking elevators and narrow, marbled stairs. She hadn't been here in years. And though she now had a family of her own, she was alone here. This was hard, going to her mother. Visiting the apartment was loaded with not only memories but dreams, both good and bad. Reaching out and asking to see someone—her mother—who had been so difficult to live with at times, Cat felt like she couldn't breathe. Dolores's needs, demands, and expectations were suffocating. And once Cat had lost her television show and decided to take a big step back to do the show she wanted to do online, then, the sin of all sins, had a baby with a black Dominican-American, out of wedlock! Well . . . That was the last straw for Dolores.

But today was an expedition, an exploration of sorts. Cat needed to know what this fear was that she had living inside of her like some symbiotic parasite. Tomas was everything she needed and wanted. So why did the thought of committing to the father of her child have her breaking into a cold sweat? And why was she tempted by someone who was nearly the opposite of Tomas, the man she loved? Calculating, unstable, even coldly ambitious. Cat had a deep sense that her mother hadn't always been straightforward about what kind of man her father had been, and she hadn't seen him since she was four years old. She only knew for sure that her mother had a love-hate relationship with the whole male gender. She acted enamored of her Telenova stars, yet Cat never once saw her mother on a date or alone with someone of the opposite sex. She knew Dolores wasn't a lesbian, so why this intense holding-at-a-distance of men? And why did Cat seem to share some of this pathology? The knot in Cat's stomach yelled at her to turn around and go home. But her head prevailed. She needed answers.

"Hi, *Mami,*" Cat said, her voice cracked. She surprised herself with her emotion.

Dolores stood in the doorway of the apartment, waiting for Cat to come out of the elevator, just as she used to do when she'd come home from school or when her mother would yell down the hall toward the open doors at the other end, all the children on the floor hanging out with each other, the hallway an extension of everyone's home, making the floor one big, communal apartment.

Usually in this stance, Dolores's face would be stern and Cat's anxiety would come from what punishment was coming her way that day, whether it was a whop on the back of her head as she walked in or a trail of shrill admonitions following her in Spanish. Cat had trained herself to shut down that part of her brain and not hear a thing but chatter. But this time Cat saw her mother's face filled with pain and sorrow, and soft. She was holding tissues in her hand with even more—probably used—jammed into her shirt sleeve. But as Cat approached, Dolores opened her arms and smiled broadly with relief and joy. "*M'ija!*"

Cat was late to the hug and distrustful. But once she let go of those feelings, she embraced her mother and allowed herself to believe that Dolores really missed her and was genuinely feeling joy and remorse, she found herself tearing up. It was just enough to loosen her nerves. The mutual feelings, for once in sync, melted the two years lost between them. At least for a moment.

As her mother ushered her into the apartment, Cat noticed Dolores seemed thin. Smaller than usual, too. She set those thoughts aside to take in the space. It was the same; barely an item had been moved in years. Thankfully, there was less plastic on the furniture and breakfast table. Cat had convinced her mother that the fumes from the vinyl were not good for her lungs and head. Dolores rarely listened to her daughter, but this time, because Cousin Manuel said the same thing to her on the same day, she took it as a sign. The scent of chamomile tea wafted through the space. Cat to this day avoided chamomile tea. It was the smell of her mother. To her, the odor of oppression.

As they settled in and Cat refused the tea, asking for a *cafecito* instead, Dolores remained fairly quiet, most likely waiting for Cat to apologize for not talking to her own mother for so long. It was always the child's responsibility to keep in contact and tug the apron strings. Always. *But it takes two.*

Instead, Cat pulled out a picture of her beautiful Alma on her phone. "This is Alma, Ma. Alma Thelma Tucker." Dolores put on her bifocals and slowly received the cell phone her daughter handed to her. "We call her Almita."

"Ooooo. *Preciosa,*" Dolores said. She barely hinted at a smile. Cat knew full well why this was one grandmother, one *abuela,* who was not too happy at seeing a picture of her grandchild. *Wait for it. Wait for it. . . .* "So, ju are still with the same guy, the black guy?" Dolores used the slang Cat hated for Tomas, "*el negro.*" She handed back the phone to Cat and smoothed out the front of her skirt.

The women sat perpendicular in the cramped nook near the kitchen. This position always made it easier for Cat to not look her mother in the eyes. This time, Dolores was the one looking away.

Breathe, Cat. Breathe. You're a grown-up now.

"Tomas Tucker?" Cat paused. By using his full, formal name, Cat wanted to give him agency. Make him real. Not some "*negro*" to her mother. "Yes. He is Alma's father and we have a place together on the West Side."

"*Pero,* I don' see a wedding ring on your finger?" Dolores pointed at Cat's left hand. "Or, did ju just not invite me to the wedding?"

"No, Ma. We didn't get married. Haven't. Yet."

"Why not?" Dolores asked.

Cat paused and took a few beats to catch her mother's eye even if their bodies were not facing each other. "Do you want me to be married to him?"

Dolores shrugged. She was caught between a rock and a hard place. As an old-school immigrant to the States laden with her home country's racist baggage, she certainly dreaded her flesh and blood dating a black person, let alone marrying one. And having a baby, too! But even worse, they had that baby and were unmarried. Cat watched Dolores struggle with the conundrum. *Better to be married with a family even though he's black, or unmarried because he's black?* Dolores shrugged again.

"And how are you, Ma?" Cat wanted to make sure she ran through the niceties before she lay into her mother with the questions she needed answers to. Dolores complained about the new neighbors, the *Anglos* taking over the area (Cat surmised gentrification was making her mother grumpy), but all in all, Dolores didn't seem much worse off than when Cat last saw her two years ago. This knowledge gave Cat some room to feel less guilty about her upcoming line of questioning.

"So, Ma. I need to know more about *Papi*."

Dolores went cold at the word *"Papi."* Her movements slowed and her pallor grew green.

"Why?" her mother asked, staring at the table in front of them.

"Why? Well, because I have a family now and I think it's important to know more. The last time I saw him I was only four. Is he even alive?"

"I don't know," Dolores responded, staring straight ahead of her at the refrigerator door. Cat followed her mother's line of sight. It was the permanent plastic magnets of fruit and weathered photos of her youth. Not one new picture. She made note to print out a photo of Alma. *She'll put it up eventually. Or I will.*

"You don't know?" Cat asked.

"No."

"When was the last time you heard from him?"

Dolores sniffed and shifted her gaze out the tiny, barred window that looked out at a brick wall. "It's been years."

Cat paused, assessing the best way to keep her mother from getting too upset, reopening wounds between them before she had the chance to find out what she needed. "Ma. What happened with *Papi?*" she asked.

"What do ju mean, what happened?"

This is not going to be easy.

"Why did we leave? Why didn't you ever want to talk about him to me?"

Fiddling with her tissues, Dolores straightened her back and spoke with some force behind her words, as if she'd been holding them inside her in an overstuffed box in her mind now being opened. The words started to come out in a kind of unrolling or unwinding. One word after another, one revelation followed by the next.

"He didn't go away. We left. It was the gun that did it. I had it with him and his violence. And you were so scared. Your face when he pulled it out. I never wanted to see that face again. Your face." She paused to blow her nose and wipe her eyes. "So, that night, after he fell asleep—he was drunk, you know, always drunk—I packed us up and put you in the car and we left. I never looked back. I never wanted to see him again and I never wanted him to see your face again."

Cat didn't move. Her mother continued. "Nona took us in for a while—do you remember Nona? No? Well, she was so beautiful, that woman, with her hair dyed blond and her dark eyebrows. We became friends when I was working in that restaurant and your father didn't know her so I knew that we could go there without him following us, at least for a while. Because he used to beat me, Catalina. Hit me. A lot. Mostly my back, where people wouldn't see the bruises. I don't know how he knew to do that. And then he'd force himself on me when I was so tired—oh, *nena*, I was so tired sometimes—and he'd do it when you were right there, sleeping in your crib. I was so ashamed when you'd wake up and see him on me and you'd cry and cry. But you didn't know what was happening. No. No. But I knew that you could see it was wrong, even as a baby. I was so ashamed. But I thought I needed him, *m'ija*, you know?

"He came by once. You were at school. He found us. Thankfully I had my friend Miguelina over so I think that he knew he'd have to take on two of us. And Miguelina, oh, she was tough, a tough lady. But he wasn't that mad. He looked tired and sad. I didn't let him in. He said he just wanted to see you. I told him no. But I was so scared, *m'ija*, so scared that he'd take you from school, so I acted so cool and calm, but once I saw him drive away, I waved down a car and went to the school. I made sure that you were there and told them that you were never to leave school with a man you didn't know, even if he said that you were his child. I ended up having to file with some lawyers, it was maybe two hundred dollars, but that was a lot of money then, and I had to make sure that just because he was your father he couldn't take you away from me.

"But here's the thing, *m'ija*. Here's the thing. Miguelina's son watched the whole thing, his visit, from the window, watching him park his car and come into the building. And you know, Marco, well, Marco is a curious kid, so he snuck downstairs and looked through the windows of the car and then told his mother, told Miguelina, that there was a mess of baby bottles and diapers in the backseat. Smushed-up cereal, *sabes?* So your father recovered—he did just fine—with another family, I'm sure. But I didn't want to know more. He's dead to me and he should be dead to you, too. I never wanted you to know him because I never wanted you to feel like you came from such ugliness, such violence. Never wanted you to feel like you were less than anyone else because your father was such a terrible person. I never wanted you to carry that with you. Never."

Dolores finally took in a breath.

Cat's shoulders lay hunched. She was stunned, staring at her mother, nearly unblinking the whole time she spoke. This was the first she'd ever heard these things. There was so much to process. So much to understand. About herself and about her mother.

"Ma. I didn't know."

"I know, *m'ija*. I know. I didn't want you to." Dolores blew her nose. She got up from her seat to get another tissue.

Cat felt like she should hug her mother, but it was an urge out of obligation, a *should*. It wasn't what she *wanted* to do. Not yet. But it all made sense now. Why her mother was so hateful and fearful of men. Why she worked so hard to push her daughter. Her girl was not going to be like her father, she was going to be as far from her father as she could be. She was going to be the best of her mother, of Dolores. The vessel of all her hopes and dreams, and she would take advantage of all the independence that this country offered her, a woman, a working mother.

They sat in silence for a while. Dolores got up to refresh and reheat her tea. Cat had run through the questions she'd prepared in her mind and in her journals; she'd even rehearsed them before getting here. But each question had been answered. She didn't need to know more. She realized in that moment as the sun started to fade from the tiny kitchen window that any and all desire to see her biological father had started to disappear, just like the light. She saw the image of a man holding a gun at her mother's temple.

She wasn't sure if she was imagining it, putting herself into the scene of the story she was just told, or if she was remembering it. She could see the duskiness of the room. Her point of view was from the floor, sitting, like a child. He was wearing a light blue T-shirt, sweaty, tight in the arms and belly. His belt seemed like a thick, unfinished leather. Her mother was in a light color, but Cat couldn't see details on her. Couldn't even see her face, hidden by her arms trying to protect her head. She could, though, see the glint of Brylcreem on his thick black hair. The wideness of his face. A grimace. His yelling. She could almost hear it. Guttural and in Spanish. He thrust the gun harder, downward, threatening.

Cat had no idea how much time had passed once she looked up. Thirty seconds? Three minutes? Dolores had started tidying up the kitchen. Her favorite thing to do to occupy herself. Cleaning and straightening, order, was a compulsion for her. *To control what she could control.*

"Ma?"

Dolores answered as if nothing had happened, her back to her daughter as she cleaned something in the sink. As if it were a regular day and they were two women just having tea in the kitchen. "*Sí, mi amor?*"

"I'm sorry."

"Sorry?" Dolores put her sponge down, leaned on the edge of the sink, and looked at her daughter. "Sorry for what?"

"That that happened. That all this happened."

Dolores turned back around to finish scrubbing whatever kitchen implement she was intent on making immaculate. "*M'ija*. It was never your fault." She pulled a paper towel off the roll, the ripping sound loud to Cat's ears. "We're okay."

Chapter 15

As Magda dug for the keys to her home before walking through the revolving door of the lobby, she prayed that the kids would be in a great mood and not giving Cherokee a hard time. Her wife wasn't a full-time stepmother just yet, but she was adamant about wrapping work by five, if not earlier, and then picking up the kids from their after-school programs when it was Magda's turn to have them at home. But now with Magda's father, *Abuelo,* living there too, there was tension in the house that wasn't there before. Granted, before, Magda could barely manage being present and focused during the week. Now, she knew her priorities.

"Hi," a woman said from the lobby bench. Her face was scrubbed clean of makeup and her blue-black hair was up in a ponytail. She was maybe in her thirties, her clothes covering up what Magda knew was really there. It was Sharon, normal-person disguise or not.

Magda's throat clenched and time stopped. *This woman is in my lobby. Near my kids. My home.*

"Hi, Ms. Reveron." The doorman greeted Magda as she brushed by him. She didn't like his tone. Like he was in cahoots with Sharon. Like he now knew something he hadn't known before.

Magda pulled up close to the woman as she stood up from

the bench. Magda was annoyed at how she pulled her purse's shoulder strap over her right side and held onto it too tightly. "What the fuck are you doing here?"

Sharon was all smiles. "Oh, I'm just here as a reminder."

Magda stared at her and stewed. She hated surprises, ferociously.

"I saw your lovely family come in! Your new wife is so cu—" Before Sharon could finish her sentence, Magda grabbed her arm and jerked her into the elevator bank. "Hey!"

"You wanna talk? Let's talk," Magda said as she continued to not-gently guide Sharon into the maintenance hallway, past the elevators, where she hoped no other tenants would see her. She still had to get out of the building if she wanted to avoid cameras. Pushing Sharon ahead of her toward the door of the loading dock that led to the back alley of the building, Magda didn't have to say another word, even as the woman turned around to protest. Magda's eyes were not seeing. They were blank with rage and her body language warned Sharon that if she wanted a chance at what she needed, she'd better just go along with it and see what was next.

In the alley, Magda looked around to make sure there were no discernible cameras. She shoved Sharon against the brick wall.

"Listen, bitch, you stay away from this building, you stay away from my home, and my kids and my wife, you got me?" she said, her finger pointed at Sharon's neck.

The woman's face was defiant, alluring even. She was used to these power plays. After all, it was what she did for a living. Her pointed chin was raised, her bottom lip pouting. She arched an eyebrow. "What's a hundred grand to you, Magda? What's the big deal, huh?" Magda breathed in. "Just do a quick transfer on your phone and poof, it's done."

"Who the fuck do you think I am?! You think I'm stupid?! Is that it?" Magda said, noting with satisfaction the split-second break in the confidence of Sharon's expression. "You think you're the first one?! Fucking special, huh? Twat, I wipe the floor with people like you—you're a fucking cockroach and will come back again and again asking for more, like a junkie. So think again, *puta*. It's. Not. Happening." Magda was nearly spitting in Sharon's face, she was so close to the woman, looking down on her smaller frame. She pulled back, her point made.

"Well. Look at that. You figured it out. Good for you," Sharon said, then stood up a bit taller. "But like I said, what's a couple hundred Gs for you? Even over time, huh? Probably what you pay one of your executives, hmmm? Well, just as worthwhile as paying them is to you, I'd think that you'd want to make sure that one day, when your children are old enough to go online, maybe at a friend's house for a playdate, and they Google your name, they don't see *Mami*'s sex tape—I'd think that not letting that happen would be very much worth the price."

Magda's face felt like it was on fire. Her hands shook, and like a reflex, one she used to full effect when she and her first girlfriend were jumped walking along the Seine in college, the men looking to rape them out of their lesbianism, Magda raised a fist, ready to punch Sharon straight in the face. In her moment of hesitation, she heard the woman hiss, "Go ahead. Hit me. You'll make me rich."

Magda couldn't breathe. Her fist stayed clenched above Sharon's head. She heard the door they came through open.

"You have until the end of the week. Friday. Or it's done," Sharon said. She skirted past Magda's body and walked down the block, the lights from the building leaving Magda looking at a moving silhouette she never wanted to see again. Her chest hurt and she noted her shirt gripping to her torso with sweat under her suit jacket.

"Good evening!" A building porter that Magda was fond of had come through the door and walked by on his way home from his shift.

"Hi. Hi, Jerry," she responded as normally as she could. Magda could dispel the shaking in her voice but she couldn't move yet. She was stock still, standing, frozen, in her spot. She felt her phone buzz. It was Cherokee. Magda texted that she'd be home in ten minutes. After quickly hitting *send,* she called Gabi.

"Hello. You've reached Dr. Gabi Gomez. I'm sorry I'm not able to take your call at the moment, but if you will please leave a message, I'll get back to you as soon as possible. If you are in need of immediate assistance, please call 888-555-6000. If this is an emergency, please call 911. Thank you!"

Goddamn long ass message for her patients . . . Goddamn it, Gabi.

"Hi. Hi. Gabs. I need you to call me. Just . . . I can't say, just call me. Okay?!" Magda hung up. She followed up with a text. Almost immediately she got a reply:

Speaking at conference. Going into session. Will call ASAP after.

"Fuuuuuuuuuuck," Magda said out loud. She stood for another moment, wiped her eyes, rubbed her face, and shook off as much of her tension as possible. She hated her children seeing any of this, and her wife was too good at sniffing out when something was wrong. Spousal guilt tapped Magda on the shoulder. *I know I should be telling her, but I can't. Too much going on. My father. The kids. Her work. I just don't want to expose her to this. Gotta contain it. Contain the situation.*

"Ma's home!" Magda made her usual holler as she came in the door, but in her past-eight-p.m. voice. The kids were already in bed—*guilt, guilt*—but she felt the need to cheer herself up somehow. The ritual of greeting them made her heart heal just a bit, her hands shake less. It put a smile on her face, even if underneath that smile, there was something else.

Cherokee's back was to Magda as she walked in. "Hi, hon,"

Cherokee said. Something was off; even in light of her nearly smashing a blackmailer's face in, Magda could feel it.

"*Amor . . . ?*" Magda asked.

Her wife turned around, wiping tears from her face.

"*Ay, nena! Qué paso? Amor.*" Magda took the small woman into her arms. She held her as she cried for a moment then lifted her face up to hers with her hands, deeply enjoying the soft cradle she made for her face, feeling the warmth and cushion of her beautiful cheeks.

"Mags, I just can't with him," she said. "I'm trying, I'm really trying, but he hates me!"

"*Ay,* sweetie, he doesn't hate you." Magda detested the patronizing words as soon as they left her mouth.

Cherokee pulled her wife's hands off her face, hurt. "Yes. Yes, he does, Mags. And it's simply because I'm black."

"Okay. Okay." Magda rubbed her forehead again. She'd done it so many times today that she wouldn't be surprised if by midnight there was a trough running across her brow from the pressure of her fingers. "I hear you. He is a bigoted old man. I am so sorry, my love."

Cherokee seemed to appreciate being heard. "Thank you." She blew her nose.

"Magdalena? Is that you?" Raoul called from his room, the closest to the kitchen. Magda rolled her eyes at his voice, making an exaggerated face of disgust. Cherokee chuckled.

"*Ya, Pa, ya vengo!*" she yelled in answer. To her wife, she said, "*Amor,* I'm going to talk to him. I'm going to make very clear that he has to respect you, as my wife, in our house." With that, Magda focused on Cherokee's eyes, then kissed her on the lips. Taking her right hand, she said, "And what I'm finding strangely amusing is that it's not being gay that's bugging him— now, that he seems to be okay with after all these years, the *viejito.*" She was making light of it as much as she could. "I love all of you, my Cherokee—I love your blackness, your brains, your body, every bit." Magda kissed her wife's hand and felt herself desperately wanting to jump into bed with her, tearing off her clothes and taking every inch of her dark skin into her mouth.

"Magda!" Her father's impatience snapped them both out of their romance.

"*Carajo! Papi,* I'm coming!" She pecked Cherokee quickly. "Ten minutes, *amor. Diez minutos.*" She winked as she patted her wife's backside.

And she did take ten minutes. Ten minutes to make sure her father was well fed, had taken his medicines and vitamins, had a plan for the morning, no alcohol hiding in his room—they kept it all in a locked cabinet that only Cherokee had the key to, so both Magda and her father would not have easy access.

Magda badly needed time to think and to check her phone and talk to Gabi. But she promised Cherokee to be present. And as a sober spouse, she was going to keep that promise. *Ten minutes.* But as she rounded the door jamb to their bedroom, she saw her exhausted wife, in her favorite negligee, passed out cold on the bed. She looked peaceful. And very, very tired. Magda smiled at her. She walked over and kissed her on the forehead. Cherokee smiled in acknowledgment and rolled over, humming. Magda took that as permission to let her sleep and then do what she really needed to do.

Magda dropped herself into the wraparound couch, wishing it would swallow her whole, if but for a moment. She closed her eyes and pulled out her phone. There was one text from Gabi:

Taking long. Might be late—will call ASAP.

Magda sighed. She looked straight ahead. Then to her right. There was a row of cabinets. She knew that behind one of those doors was a shelf of liquor, and on it her favorite, tequila. Had Magda actually been to Alcoholics Anonymous instead of the more slight pressure of doing it on her own with one advisor, she'd be scolded. She knew that there should not be alcohol anywhere at home in any form. She should even be avoiding parties and situations where it was being served. But, she reasoned to herself, with her line of work, her business, she entertained often. She needed it there for her guests, her friends. Even though they were always aware of being respectful of her and her choices.

But right there, in front of her, there were only a piece of wood and a key separating her from her favorite taste in the world. Her tequila, *añejo*. This time, her mouth watered. She remembered the feeling of peace that would come over her, the numbness, when she drank. It lured her. All this anxiety. This stress. *Just one. Just one taste. That's all I need. I promise. Just one. I'll probably even hate it.* After all, she knew where Cherokee kept the key. She had followed her wife without her knowledge. She saw her take it out of her jean pocket and slip it into her panty drawer. *Panty drawer. Always a good one.*

Panties made her think of the video. The video with Sharon. That night. So useless, actually. The opposite of tantalizing. But there it was. And Sharon was about to go public with it, and Magda's children would see it. Magda didn't give a shit about anyone but her children seeing it, really. And Sharon was counting on that. She pushed that button.

What have I done . . .

Just one shot. That's all I need. I promise.

Chapter 16

Luz walked up the town house stairs. She found it odd that one of the biggest stars in Hollywood wouldn't have security everywhere. Then again, that was why famous people lived in New York. The illusion of being normal. *They're just like us!* A fifteen-million-dollar, four-story town house on a tiny little overpopulated island in an expensive neighborhood was not quite normal. Luz was still comforted, slightly, by the ability to walk to the front door unbowed.

She rang the buzzer. Dogs barked. But not guard dogs. To Luz's urban-hound-trained ears, they sounded under twenty pounds.

"Hey, hey, Vic, Barbara, shush it. Maria, can you please put them in their room?" Luz could hear a man behind the door, probably the grandfather of her sister's embryo, Ben Quinton, giving directions to Maria. The click-click of the dogs' nails drew away from the door. Luz tried to look to her right and not seem overeager. Or nervous. But she was. Very. This was going to be a difficult conversation no matter how she cut it. No one wanted to hear their teenager got someone pregnant. No one. And even though Luz and Chris had their own hard-earned millions, this guy had both many more millions and the power of fame. *This can't get ugly.*

"Oh, hi! Hi, I'm Ben." The door opened halfway with a

whoosh. Luz noted that it was a thick door and made a metallic echoing sound as it moved. Utilitarian, she assumed. Fireproof, probably bulletproof and crazed-fan proof. A small-built white man reached out his hand in greeting. Luz recognized him right away, as would probably a billion people on the planet, but she took in how much he just seemed like another person who put his pants on one leg at a time. Normal. Ish.

"Hi. I'm Luz." She smiled out of courtesy, not necessarily warmth. The judgmental voices in her head too loud. *And what kind of father raises his kid to have unprotected sex? And what if she's just a brown conquest to him—like an urban street trophy? The little entitled shit.*

"C'mon in." Ben gestured. As he waved Luz in, she watched him look over her shoulder, most likely to assure himself that no one else was with her, following her or taking pictures. He wore no shoes, just expensive-looking socks under his expensive-looking jeans and his thin, surely cashmere, pullover. As he walked her through the foyer into the grand living room of a double-wide town house, Luz absorbed every detail as much as she could. She was naturally curious, never nosy, more of a Sherlock Holmes type than a gawker, garnering clues on who someone really was based on their surroundings, their clothes, even the way they spoke. At times she felt disapproving, but it was more a reflexive way of sorting. Maybe a side effect of her mother's sometimes untrustworthy nature, maybe a natural aesthetic inclination to note every surface, every clue. The skill had served her well so far in her career. She might as well lean on it now, a time of high stress.

"So, Luz—Luz, is it?" Ben asked as they sat down diagonally from each other around the coffee table. Luz noted the disappointingly cookie-cutter decor of a rather basic, but over-priced, interior designer.

"Yes. Luz."

"Is it Luce, or . . . ?"

"No. L–U–Z," she said.

"Z? Got it. Got it." Ben nodded his head.

"It means *light*. In Spanish."

"Oh, yeah! Right. That makes sense." Ben took a quick sip from the coffee mug a staff member put in front of him. It happened so automatically Luz assumed such prescience was normal for his staff. He ran a tight ship, she could see already.

"So, what, what brings you to my *casa?*"

The false smile on Luz's face grew even more circumspect as he played at Spanish for her sake, and at his tendency to repeat words. It was a tic that seemed funny in his movies, a New Yorker's way of speaking, but in person it was part of his affect she had hoped was only for the cameras, only to find out now that it was the real deal.

"Your son, Peter—"

"Yeah, yeah, my Petey!"

Luz hesitated for one extra beat, seeing if Ben registered her annoyance. He didn't. The man sat with his dark, graying hair and eager blue eyes, looking at Luz as if she were about to deliver him an investment opportunity. *Possibly so.*

"Peter, yes. Well, he knows my sister, Emelie, well."

"Wait—Emelie is really your sister, not your daughter?!"

"Yes."

"Wow! I mean, wow! That's amazing. What's the story behind that?"

"Uh. Well. That's probably for another time," Luz said with a strong pause for emphasis. Then she continued: "Let's just say that's how we roll."

"Right! Right."

Good Lord, please stop.

"So you've met Emelie or heard about her, or . . . ?" Luz asked.

"Oh, yeah, Petey has mentioned her a few times. I think they were getting close at one point?"

"Yes. You could say that."

Ben leaned in, finally getting a sense that something might be wrong. Luz continued. "Ben, Emelie is pregnant."

The billion-dollar funny man's eyes went wide. Then, just as quickly, they narrowed. "Are you saying that you think that Peter's the father?"

"I'm not only saying that. I know."

Ben got up from his armchair. Another member of the staff, Luz assumed, came by, and the man of the house shooed her away with his hand. Ben turned his back to Luz and paced. He sighed. She was ready to give him all the time he needed. She'd already consulted with the best family attorney in town to run through all the permutations of how this meeting—and its results—could go. Luz was about to be very grateful for thinking ahead.

"Are you sure?" he asked, finally turning around to face Luz. "Yes."

Ben paced and sighed again. Luz addressed the elephant— one of several—in the room. "And if you need a paternity test, that can be arranged."

He waved her off again. "I need to talk to Pete about this. Get his input."

"Sure. But Emelie is not eighteen, so this is a very delicate situation."

"Well, she's not going to keep it, is she?" Ben's energy was raised. "I mean, they are way, waaaaaaay too young to be having a kid, I mean seriously . . ."

"She is thinking about it."

"Thinking about it?! I mean, what's there to think about? Petey's way too young to be a father—I mean, the press will have a field day. Remember Chet Haze?"

"No. I don't know who that is."

"Well, let's just say that the children of celebrities don't get any passes; if anything, they come down harder. I mean, the privilege . . ." Ben continued to pace. His hands would gesticulate anytime he spoke. Actually, Luz noted, only when he spoke. It was as if his hands and mouth were connected with puppet strings. *The strangest thing.*

He ran his fingers through his hair. Luz could see the wheels turning. She said, "We have to be prepared for the fact that Emelie may want to keep this baby and if so, I have no choice but to support her decision."

Ben sat back down, plopping himself into the upholstery. They sat in silence for a moment. Luz felt no need to fill it.

"She's sixteen years old."

"Correct." She knew what he was implying: that because she wasn't legally an adult yet, her legal guardian, her sister Luz, should be making the decision for her, and it was an easy one, right?

"Is it money you want?" he asked.

"Excuse me?!" *Oh, he's gonna be the fool.*

"Money. Is this about money?"

"Mr. Quinton. Ben. Does it look like this is about money? Do I look like that to you? Do you know who my husband is?" Luz delivered with ice.

Ben studied his guest a bit more. Surely all he saw initially was her blackness. Not necessarily her blue eyes or her diamond rings (one with black diamonds, one with brown diamonds, the other two her four carat engagement ring and her wide white gold and diamond band). Not her expensive clothes or bag (though her tee had cost five dollars and was from H&M). Blackness. That's it. And all the assumptions that came with it. Sneaky. Underhanded. Looking for a handout. Trying to work the system. Land a sugar daddy.

He glanced away once he'd gotten a partial answer from looking beyond the shade of Luz's skin. But he had to ask, "What do you do, Luz? I mean, I don't know anything about you or your family. . . ."

"I own a marketing firm. Twenty employees. Twenty million annual gross, four million net." She wasn't happy with having to answer to him, but she tried to put herself in his shoes for a moment. "I'm the former SVP of Idol." Ben's brows raised. "My husband is one of the founders of Tarp-dot-com—"

"The insurance agency with those ads with the beaver?"

"Yes."

"Wow. Okay," Ben said. Luz hoped that he read the business section and knew that Chris got bought out for millions. It seemed he knew enough.

"My father is fifth-generation Martha's Vineyard, second-generation Princeton." Luz couldn't let that go. Even though now, as she said it, she felt the tiny weight of the truth pull down on her words. He did raise her. He was absolutely her father in that way. Not in the way that her sperm donor incarcerated father factored into her life.

"Your father—you mean Emelie's father, too?"

Luz hesitated for half a second. "Yes," she lied. She'd deal with the truth later if she had to.

"Okay. Well. Look. Everything is spin, right?" he asked. Luz cocked her head. She wasn't sure where Ben was going yet. "Look. We have a beautiful mixed girl." Luz rolled her eyes at "mixed." "I mean, she's gorgeous, Pete showed me a photo once. And this is the time of social media, right?" Again, Luz was lost only because she couldn't believe what she was hearing. This conversation seemed to be headed down the same mucky river where Eugenio had been taking it. She was incredulous. "Look." Ben leaned in to her conspiratorially. "If Emelie can't be convinced not to have—well, not to bring this situation to term, then, we gotta deal, right?" Luz nodded. He continued, now seemingly excited about possibilities. "They don't have to get married or anything like that—"

"Definitely not," Luz said. Ben noted her sharp tone.

"But it could be like a Benetton family!"

Luz gave him a sarcastic smile. *Haven't heard that reference in a while, old man. Fuck you.*

"Okay, okay, look, all I'm saying is that this could turn out okay if we just look at the bright side here."

Luz's expression was flat. She was just too pissed at this guy. "Bright side," she said, then breathed in and started picking up her bag and raising herself up off his chair in his house with as much dignity as history gave her after overcoming hundreds of years of white men and their bright sides.

"Ben. My teenage sister, for whom I'm paying a substantial amount in tuition, is now pregnant because of your son. Your son got her pregnant. As a teenager. A black girl. Now, though she comes from a very well-off and less disadvantaged family, I see no way that her becoming a statistic is a benefit. Now." Luz raised a finger. "Would this child grow up with many benefits, benefits that we older folks didn't have, sure. But there is no way, and I have no plans of supporting the idea, that my sister's misstep is going to be a boon to you."

Ben's face blanched. His nice-guy demeanor slipped away and Luz started to see the real Ben Quinton. The one who was certainly a shrewd businessman. One who surely pounded subordinates into the wall if need be. The one who probably wasn't around much when his kids were young, but as his wife seemed to have disappeared (according to the tabloids) with a billionaire in Florida now that their kids were much more grown, here he was. He got up.

"Yeah. You're right, Luz Tucker Lee. I'm good. And my son's going to be good. I'll make sure of that."

"I bet you will."

"Expect a call from my lawyer in the morning. We'll need a paternity test."

He stared down Luz and she gave as good as she got. Her jaw clenched.

"See yourself out," Ben said, and he walked out of the room.

Luz didn't even reply. She couldn't. It was as if her jaw were wired shut with fury.

Fuck you.

As she made her way out the door, which felt heavy to her hands, the small rush of fresh air consoled her for a moment.

She looked up at the sky. She squinted, then walked down the stairs and pulled out her cell to hail a ride. Luz paused, looking at the wallpaper on her screen. It was a merry photo of her big, dazzling family, laughing and holding each other on the floor in a pile. Her mother had taken the picture during the summer. Luz zoomed in on Emelie's face. Her smile wasn't as broad as her nieces' and nephews', Luz's kids, but there was a smile. A true, peaceful smile. And the face of a girl who probably felt safe, secure, and accepted for the first time in her life.

I'm sorry, baby girl. I won't let you down.

Chapter 17

"Yup. Just give him the nuggets in the freezer and he'll be fine."

Gabi was in full makeup after wrapping up a segment for a national news show on a celebrity divorce battle. *Bad enough I had to go through my own, now look at me, loads more work as the expert on breakups. Lemons, lemonade.* "Okay, thanks, and I should be home in an hour, okay? Want to be able to tuck him in."

"This it?" the driver asked.

Gabi looked out the window and saw the restaurant sign confirming that she was at the location of her mission. "Yup. This is it. Thanks."

Magda didn't know what Gabi was about to do. Magda would tear her head off if she knew. But Gabi just couldn't have her friend taken advantage of. She couldn't just be a helpless observer when she had some power, even if might get her into trouble. What she was about to do could mean that she'd end up dragged into a scandalous quagmire, but she'd just do what she knew worked much of the time if she were confronted by it: deny, deny, deny. She wasn't jeopardizing anything. They were in public. This was on purpose, as she didn't want things to escalate into a drag-down fight. After all, Gabi Gomez was from the Bronx. Straight-up Vaseline-on-the-face, pullin'-hoops-out-of-ears BX. At least that was her childhood. She was here to bring it.

"Sharon, right?" Gabi asked the tall, buxom young woman who looked to be the cohostess, her hands holding menus, her face lit by the tablet screen where she checked reservations. It wasn't too hard to find Sharon. Magda had told Gabi her full name, which Gabi then searched on social media, finding her old Facebook account (which she seemed to have abandoned a year back), listing the restaurant where she worked. Just to make sure, Gabi then found her Instagram and noted several recent postings from the same restaurant, called them, and asked if Sharon worked there, which they confirmed. *All that med school research training has yet to fail me.*

"Yes. Do you have a reservation?" Sharon said, with a mix of snot and seduction.

"Sharon. Do you have a minute? It's urgent." Gabi acted like a friend. Or, at least, the friend of a friend. Get her away from her cohost and catch her a bit off guard.

"Um. Uh." Sharon looked as if she was vacillating between asking for more information and realizing that due to her other line of work, that might not be the best idea in front of someone else. Gabi was smart enough to catch her well before the dinner rush. There was only one couple seated in the cavernous space. It was geriatric dinner hour—before six p.m. "Sure. Follow me."

Wise choice.

Sharon's hair was piled up in a musty black bun as her low-back, spandex black dress displayed her tattoos. Gabi couldn't be bothered looking at them, some cut off in odd places by her clothing, but she registered their aggressiveness. She knew that odds were that a girl who grew up to do what Sharon did for a living might not have had the best upbringing, but not all girls in her business turned to extortion of their clients. Gabi could never be mad at a woman's hustle game, but she sure as hell could rail against the idea that you hold someone's secrets against them for money. She was a psychiatrist after all, her business was ugly secrets. And Gabi knew that Sharon's role for many of her own clients was as a quasi therapist. This made her betrayal sting that much more for Gabi.

"So, what's this about?" Sharon asked, leaning against the empty oak bar. The clink of glasses being washed by the bartender far down the row of the bar was almost a melody.

"I'm going to make sure that you don't get a dime."

"I'm sorry?" Sharon asked.

"Not. A. Dime," Gabi enunciated with threat in her voice.

"Are you recording this?"

Smarter than I thought. "No."

"Again," Sharon sniffed, her puckish nose curling upward with her upper lip, "I don't know what this is about."

"Okay, sister." Gabi knew she sounded a little square, but that was what too many years working in Anglo environments did to you. She drew herself a few inches closer to the woman, though even with her four-inch heels on, Gabi was probably four inches shorter than Sharon, her large bun not included. "See, I'm media. And I know everyone who could counter anything you put out there." Sharon didn't answer. She just raised her right eyebrow. "And, we're lawyered up. So there is no way that I'll let my girl go down that road with you—no way!"

Sharon looked over Gabi's shoulder and shifted her weight from one platform-shod foot to the other, her hips moving counter to her shoulders. "So I take it you're here for a friend."

Gabi didn't respond. *Is she doing this to so many people that she doesn't realize who I'm talking about?* This girl and her shenanigans were pissing her off. Straightforward was how Gabi liked it. *Give it to me straight, pendeja.*

"Well . . ." The pale woman reached for the upper hand. "Does this friend know that you're here talking to me, on her behalf?"

Gabi simply stared at her in answer. She was never a good liar.

Sharon sniffed. "I didn't think so."

"Cut the shit, Sharon. Magda's not gonna go down that road for you. If she did you never would stop, and she knows that— we all know that. I remind her every day." Gabi noted that Sharon had yet to ask her what her name was. She couldn't just yet put her finger on why that didn't make her feel good. Either the girl knew who she was already or she really was that arrogant and just didn't care.

"Let me guess. You're acting like this friend's muscle here because you're such a good friend." Sharon waited a beat for a reaction. Gabi didn't give her one, but she played her card anyway. "Oh, maybe a girlfriend!"

Again Gabi didn't answer.

Sharon said, "Well. I wish I had friends like you, lookin' out for me. It's cute."

Oh, I just want to smack a bitch right here.

"That's it, Sharon. That's all I had to say. You've got a bunch of us backing Magda up and we've got plenty of, as you say"— Gabi delivered with a neck roll—"muscle. So, just kick back and stick to what you do best, mm-kay?"

"Oh! You know, now I know who you are!" Sharon's voice got louder, her eyes wider. Gabi didn't care for the newly satisfied look on her face. She diagnosed the smile of a devious, most likely borderline-disordered or narcissistic person. Someone you couldn't engage with because there was no winning. Every volley you threw at them, they turned right back at you, like light into a mirror. They functioned as if on another realm with no one actually getting through to them, ever. *I should have known.*

Gabi remembered back to her first love in college. A white guy from Massachusetts, over six feet tall, black hair and pale skin like Superman. Could have been Sharon's brother. He brought his "representative" to the table for the first year of their relationship, his personality all romance and charm. He was so understanding, full of compliments, supportive. He put her on a pedestal. Gabi would tell her clients—and herself—for years afterward: *Beware of pedestals. They're not stable places to stand for longer than a hot minute.* Initially she resisted this man. She didn't trust him much and was more focused on school. It was up to her to be the first in the family to get a college degree. She wasn't going to be distracted by some drooling guy, though her mother loved that he wasn't Latino. Talk about pedestals. But once Gabi was sucked in, once she committed herself to being with him, he changed. He started complimenting less and picking on small things more. When they'd argue, Gabi's mind would be sent into a frenzy of defending herself, not aware that every ball she lobbed at him he'd just lob back. And, she'd catch it. She'd hold it and take it until she lobbed another. And it would come back. And once he'd get her into a state of near tears, he'd launch that smile. The smile of someone who knows they're playing a game. And winning.

Sharon had that smile right now.

"Aren't you Dr. Gabi Gold from TV?" she said as she wagged her finger.

"Gomez. Not Gold."

"Right, right." Sharon pretended to think for a moment. She put her finger to her mouth, her lips overlined with red. "Your ex-husband is Bert Gold, the chef."

Gabi's face started to prickle. She started to sweat. She came here to surprise someone. Not to be surprised herself.

"I know Bert." *That smile.* "Real well."

Gabi couldn't speak. She was stunned at how quickly the scene—and her mission—devolved. She felt the Catholic weight of God's hand punishing her for thinking she could fight fire with fire. Her fallback was guilt, and right now, it knocked the wind out of her lungs.

Sharon leaned in and spoke lower. "See. I know Bert. And I don't think your son or your viewers need to know what he's been up to lately, hmmm? I mean, shoot, that would hurt his business, too, and his investors. Or"—she turned her finger to point at the ceiling—"or, maybe it would be good for his business—you know, sexy chefs and stuff—but just a bad thing for yours."

Gabi stood stock still. She noted the muffled sound of people being seated at tables around them. The lame electronica playing in the background, louder now in parallel to the voices of incoming patrons.

Sharon abruptly threw her head back and laughed. "Oh! I am so kidding. That was funny. I mean, yeah, I know Bert, but feel free to ask me anything and I'll tell you. I've got nothing to hide."

Gabi found her voice. "I bet you do. We all do. But one thing that is very much out in the open is who you are. Try looking in the mirror to apply something other than makeup. Like, your conscience." Sharon's smile got smaller. "We all have families. And you once came from a family of your own. No matter what they did to you, how much they hurt you, hurting others is not going to make it better." Sharon's smile disappeared.

Gabi took that as her exit cue. Without another word she left the girl at the bar. Gabi strode out as confidently as she could, grateful that she could not see the pained look on Sharon's face before leaving. Gabi made it out the heavy glass and iron doors of the restaurant and down the stairs, holding onto the railing, as her balance was off, and not only because of her heels. At the bottom landing, Gabi was fuming with righteousness, but at the same time, sad wounds were called up. She flashed back to when she discovered all the horrible betrayals on her ex-husband's computer. She had scrolled through Craigslist requests for midday sex, dating site profiles, gushing and explicit e-mails from media girls Gabi knew personally. She had run to the bathroom and thrown up. Her gut clenched at the memory.

Ain't this a small town. Too small. Bert's still at it. Still gettin' his, while our son and I are alone. While I raise this boy. His child. Dear God. What door did I just open that I never wanted to open again? Lord, if this is punishment for going behind Magda's back, I'm sorry. I'm so, so sorry. I didn't want this. I didn't want to know.

Gabi walked in a daze to the street corner. A few cabs went by and she didn't hail them. She just kept walking.

Chapter 18

Cat sat her bags down on the narrow table in the foyer. It was quiet. Alma must be taking a nap, she thought. She sighed. She'd end up staying up late tonight because five o'clock was way too late a nap. She'd have to scold her au pair (again) for not trying harder to keep Alma on a regimen.

Instead of the au pair, Cat encountered a very odd sight as she walked into the open dining and living space and her eyes searched for her baby. There was a vase—the biggest vase she'd ever seen—filled with what must have been three or even four dozen long-stemmed roses, too many to count. At the base of the glass vessel was an unraveled blue ribbon, baby blue. The telltale baby blue of a globally recognized jewelry brand. Just behind the ribbon was a small bag, also baby blue. And as Cat's eyes adjusted to this surprising welcome-home, she saw just behind the installation of flowers the legs and hand of her love and the father of her child, Tomas. She couldn't see his face, but in his posture, slack and splayed, she realized that the miniature box in his hand, the bag and ribbon on the table, the massive flowers, did not come from or for him.

"Babe?" Cat said.

Her answer came with the sound of Tomas shifting in his chair. He moved forward, his handsome, youthful face now visible from behind the monstrous bouquet set in front of him.

"Wha—?" Was all Cat managed to say as Tomas squeezed the flesh between his eyes with his fingers, wiping what might have been tears off of the bridge of his nose.

"What do you need to tell me, Cat?" Tomas asked, the small jewelry box in his hands, his elbows now resting on his thighs. He looked up at her with red eyes.

"Where's Alma?" Cat saw the storm about to come between them and wanted to make sure the baby wasn't a part of it, or first, whether she needed attention. After seeing Gabi's divorce and what she'd told her about babies being affected strongly by arguments and tension in the house—even before they could understand what was happening—she worked to protect Alma from angry, raised voices. She didn't want to hide conflict, necessarily, which would create a bizarre bubble of politeness just as damaging to a child with its lack of truth. But Cat needed to make sure Alma was going to be all right.

Tomas sniffed and sat up straight, moving the chair into her line of sight. "I asked Freya to take her to the playground for a while."

"Oh." Cat felt the nauseating sickness of guilt, though it was tinged with rage. *How dare you do this to me, August Tilly, you motherfucker.*

"Tomas . . ." Cat pulled up a chair opposite him. Tomas's tears unnerved her. In her three-plus decades on the planet, she just hadn't found herself in a situation where a man cried. She didn't grow up with a brother or a father. She barely had relationships that lasted long enough to elicit tears in a man. Tears from her, sure.

"Cat! Do you have something to tell me?!" Tomas's pained voice snapped Cat out of her thoughts. This pain, now directed her way. She felt ashamed of herself.

"Tomas. Tomas, please trust me when I tell you that I have had nothing to do with this man—"

"Oh! So you know full well who this is from? This August?"

Tomas said as he produced a note from behind the vase. He handed it to Cat. It read: *Be my real woman, forever.—August.*

Fuck.

"And this," Tomas said as he opened the box in his hand. Inside the box was a solitary diamond ring—probably four carats— sparkling like a dwarf star. Cat would not hold it against Tomas in the slightest should he want to leave her ass right then and there.

"Tomas. He's crazy."

"Who's crazy, Cat?! Someone you're cheating on me with? Some fuckin' rich guy?!"

"No! No! I am not cheating! I am not going near this guy—I interviewed him once! Maybe twice."

"Oh. Maybe twice. Make up your mind, Cat! Maybe it was three times or four times or maybe you even slept with him and forgot!" Cat could feel his pain. She had to stop this. She had to stop acting like she was guilty of something when she wasn't. She had to remember what it was like to feel hurt like this.

"His name is August Tilly. He's a tech guy—yes, big money," she said. Tomas's right eye flinched at the mention of money. He did well, but Cat suspected that though he was hardworking and smart, he was going to be okay with making six figures for the rest of his life. Like her. It was a blessing to be at the levels they were at. But she had to admit, coming from nothing, working so hard to succeed, there was appeal in big money— bigger money. It meant security. Freedom. Things she'd never had before. There were many other places in the country where what they made together annually would put them in a brand new four bedroom with two nice car leases and money for Alma's college. But in New York City, a couple of low-six-figure salaries and a baby meant living paycheck to paycheck.

She continued. "He came on my show once and then I did a follow-up meeting at his office, because Audrey was talking to his people about sponsorship. It was all business—for me."

"For you?" Tomas asked. "And what was it for him?"

"A fantasy. He's put together some idea of me, some projection. He's in love with it."

"With 'it'?"

"*Amor,* he's not in love with me. He doesn't know me. My videos, my writing, those things were my work—it's not who I am. He doesn't get that and has made up in his mind that I'm some kind of partner solution."

"Partner solution?"

"Right," she answered.

"You're my partner, Cat."

"I know. And I told him that," she said. Both their bodies formed arches of emotion, of weight and despair. Cat reached out for Tomas's hand. She gently took the box from him, closing it and setting it on the table without turning her body away from him, her love.

"Tomas." She exaggerated the Spanish toe-MAHS when they were being affectionate. "I don't in any way, shape, or form want to be with this guy. I don't want to." She pressed on his fingers with hers in emphasis. Tomas looked up at her. He was looking for truth. His wide eyes examining. "You're all I want, hon. All I want—and our Almita. It's everything."

"So why won't you let me get you a ring?" It was a question that Cat knew had to come up, because August hadn't given her, or them, a choice, sending that tacky-ass engagement ring. "You won't even talk about marriage with me, but this guy seems to think that that's what you want. Is it?"

"No," Cat said. "I mean, no, I don't want it with him."

"And what about me?"

Cat sighed. "Tomas." She thought back to her conversation with her mother. She thought of all the roadblocks she'd put in the way of having any formal commitment with a man. Of how after Jason, her first real love, she shut herself down. He ended up blaming Cat for going back to his ex-girlfriend. "You're leaving me anyway! Your career will always mean more than any guy." She had internalized the idea that he might have been right. She accepted it. She ran with it. Living and working became one. And it worked out, right? She got her own national television show. She was invited to all the best places. Daily car service. It was glamorous. She felt like all the work, all the focus, had been worth it. But, she had a revelation after she lost her show that life had to be more than work. She took her current show initially for much less money. She settled down, or so she thought, with Tomas and finally had the family she wanted. She just couldn't make that last step. That commitment. What was that about?

"I went to see my mother this morning."

"Your mother?" Tomas was surprised. "You haven't spoken to her in . . ."

"Years. Yeah. But, I had to figure some things out. I needed to hear more of the story. Her story." She had Tomas's attention, and he knew that this was leading to some answers. "For now, I'll tell you that my distrust . . . of . . ." She was having a hard time. ". . . of commitment is hard. But, I want to work through it with you." She peered into his eyes, pleading with hers. "I want to be with you and I want to marry you—someday." His eyes brightened. "But . . ." She made the mistake of looking at the table, at the bounty of gifts, the pile, in effect, of money that another man had dropped—obnoxiously—into her home and her life.

"But, what?" Tomas's brightness shifted.

"Just, please. Be patient with me?" Cat asked.

Tomas was no fool. As much as he loved his woman, the mother of his child, he was no chump. "Understand something, Cat. I have all the patience in the world, but I'll tell you that there is no way that I'm going to lose my ability to parent our daughter—I'm her father, no matter what. And I want very much . . . I've shown you . . . I've shown you, haven't I . . . that

I love you and want to be your husband, want to make this a real family. But I'm not going to put up with you keeping someone on the side, waiting, just in case."

"Wait—Tom—" Cat protested.

He shushed her by blinking slowly and shaking his head. "I need to feel that you're bringing it, Cat—bringing it to this family, to me, not just Alma. That I'm your man. Because I tell you, whatever this guy thinks he can give you, he don't know you. He'd dump you for a new model in no time."

"Well, that's a risk everyone takes—"

"Really? Is that what you think of me? That that's what I'm gonna do?"

Cat hung her head. Her silence spoke for her.

"Look, Ma, I don't know where your insecurities come from, but I don't know what else you need from me to make you realize my commitment to you—to our family. If you're always afraid that your man is gonna leave, well then, there's nothing that you can do to stop him from doing just that."

Cat looked confused.

Tomas continued. "If you're always afraid, then you're the one not committing. It takes two."

Cat nodded. She knew this now. Knew that it might not be men who were the issue, at least her man, but her fear of him leaving. It was as if he were trying to hold her but her arm was locked, palm out, pushing him away, always. Who would blame someone from walking away from that? She was saying "no" regardless of how much someone loved her.

"And I mean it, ma. Alma is the world to me and I won't have any other man take my place. So help me." With that, Tomas let go of Cat's hands and got up from his chair. The now-closed ring box sat on the table, loaded with what felt like guilt to Cat. She had it so good with Tomas. She knew his family, loved his sister and her family dearly. She was the child of a single mother, a one-two punch of a mini family; now she found herself embraced by a large, warm, multicolored, joyous family. She stared at the roses, their smell so strong she could almost see waves of odor, like heat off a candle flame, lapping at the air.

Cat stood right up, picked up the incredibly heavy roses and their enormous vase—half the size of her—walked them out the door, and set them down in the trash room just down the hallway. The flowers nearly took up the whole space. She was sure someone would be happy to find this surprise—and they'd be able to enjoy it, no strings attached. No marriage proposal to answer to.

As she got back to the apartment, picking up a stray petal along the way, then throwing it in the kitchen garbage under the sink, her eyes couldn't leave the box on the table. Tomas hadn't gotten her a ring yet because she said she didn't want one. She had rambled something about it being a waste of money and how they should save up for a bigger apartment instead. But his proposal had stood on its own.

I went from not getting laid for years, or even a date, to having two men wanting to marry me. Two pretty amazing men. Huh. Cat allowed herself to be proud and pleased just for a moment. Then, her guilt kicked in again. But guilt, as she knew, was a sucky emotion—self-indulgent. So, what was she feeling? Or, what was the feeling behind the mess in her head?

Time to figure it out, Catalina. You love Tomas. You love Alma. So much love, right? So, how does one give back an engagement ring, anyway?

Chapter 19

"Mama! Mama! Wake up, wake up!" the little voices said.

"*Ooof!*" Magda woke up to her children, Ilsa and Nico, crawling onto her, pulling at her face, Ilsa trying to open an eyelid, Nico doing his best to tickle her. Magda was on the couch, never having made it to bed the night before.

"Ma—why are you on the couch? Did you sleep on the couch?" Nico asked.

"And you have your clothes on. Where are your PJs?" Isla added.

"Oh, hey, good morning! How about a good morning, Ma!" she said.

"Good moooorning, Maaaaa!" they said in unison.

"Thank you. That's better." Magda kissed them both and snuggled them in warm hugs from her extra-long arm span. It wouldn't be much longer, though, that she could fit them both into one embrace.

"All right, kiddos!" Cherokee said and clapped her hands twice. "Let's get breakfast goin' and get to school! *Ándale . . .*" As the siblings un-Velcroed themselves from their mother, Cherokee herded them with her hands and turned her eyes to Magda, searching for what state she was in. Magda nodded at her wife and gave her a slight *I'm okay* smile. She assumed that Cherokee might be upset with her for not coming to bed the night before, but she needed to manage that later. In the moment, as soon as her children woke her, she started processing the fact that she was amazed that she didn't feel too much like shit. Magda did an internal check and was incredulous. *I'm not hungover. Did I drink? I could have sworn I did.*

She rose from the couch, the kids a controlled chaos that punctuated every weekday morning they were there with her. Magda looked at the liquor cabinet. Cherokee kept an eye on her as she moved around wrangling the little ones, watching Magda trying to work out for herself what had happened. The tall blond, her eyes puffy but lucid, noted the volumes of each bottle in the case. She noted the door was still locked. There was no key sitting beside it. There was no glass sitting around, either, near the couch or near the cabinet. She ran her fingers along the dark walnut of the furniture. *I didn't do it. I didn't do it.* Magda went quickly into her bedroom. A flood of relief hit her physically. She could not contain it, nor could she truly understand why she suddenly found herself in her bathroom crying, loudly, in heaving waves, each washing over her with a mix of pain and relief.

The past ten hours were a blackout of some sort, but not one caused by her demon, alcohol. It must have been exhaustion, stress. She remembered the pull of drink, staring into that liquor cabinet, wanting the taste so badly she could conjure up the flavor by memory, by desire. As she cried into the sink re-membering the urge of the night before, she could nearly taste it again, but this time, it was sour. But it was a sensation of relief, sweet relief. She had done it. She'd kept herself away from what once nearly ruined her, what always sat on her shoulder ready to bring her down at any time. Relief. But, for how long? Where was the light at the end of this tunnel with Sharon? How was Magda going to keep her business going as fiercely as in the past while she juggled her kids, a newish wife, and a father who not only now accepted her for who she was after decades of disowning his oldest child for being gay, was now living under her roof? He was ruined financially and personally, and there she was, supporting him. *Trapped.* That feeling again of being trapped, stuck in a sandwich of generations and a specter of her sordid past. But the triumph of not succumbing to temptation imbued her with a bit of welcome power.

"No, no, honeys, your ma needs a minute. . . ." Cherokee said from the other side of the bathroom door. Ilsa knocked.

"Ma? You okay? We gotta go to school and I want a hug," her daughter said.

Magda sniffed deeply in an effort to erase the emotion from her voice. "Yeah, yeah, Ma's okay, I just have a stomachache. Gonna give you *besos* through the door, okay?"

"Okay," both children answered.

"Mmmmwwwaah!" Magda said and put her palm on the door, making enough of a noise, gently, that they knew she threw them a kiss.

"Mmmwwaah! Mmmwwaah!" each child said as they slapped the door back in response.

"Okay, meet me in the hallway, grab your bags, right behind you!" Cherokee called out. She tapped the door. Magda opened it slightly. "Are you all right, hon?" Cherokee asked.

"Yeah. Yeah. I'm sorry. Just exhausted. Talk when you get back, okay?" Magda said.

"Sure. I love you."

"I love you," Magda responded as she shut the door on her wife's concerned face.

Clean yourself up, sister. You're good. You're good.

Magda started washing her face with a washcloth, using the coldest water she could handle. She began to feel another state well up, strength from not going down that very slippery slope. She thanked God, unreligious as she was. She was grateful for whatever stopped her from opening that cabinet. She suspected it was sheer exhaustion. That she'd sat there, slumped in a comfy couch, staring at that cabinet for as long as she could and merely, well, fell asleep. *Relief.*

"Pa. What you need?" Magda emerged freshly showered, hair wet and slicked back, clean suit, into the kitchen. Her father had his head buried in the refrigerator.

"*Coño,* do you guys have any real milk or no?"

"No, Pa. Just one percent."

"Fine, fine." They spoke in Spanish when no one else was around. Raoul grumbled as he pulled out the low-fat milk for his coffee that he'd made in his favorite old-fashioned Cuban press—a Miami staple. His back remained facing his oldest child. Magda knew it was time to get him in line with her wife.

"How you feelin', *Papi?* Taking your meds?"

"Oh, *ja,* all good," he said as he took a slurping sip of his hot drink.

"You know, I'm glad you're here—the kids are really glad you're here," Magda said.

Raoul nodded. "Hmmm."

"Especially with Ma gone. The kids miss her a lot." Magda's mother, Raoul's wife, before she passed away had snuck off at least twice a year to spend time with Magda and her family. All that time, all those years, Raoul was not talking to his daughter.

"You know that I knew," he said.

"You knew what?"

"That she was seeing you."

"Hmmm." Magda nodded. She didn't see a reason to follow down that road of conversation. He'd say he knew and Magda would say, *why didn't you say anything,* and then he'd remind her that he didn't agree with her lifestyle, etc., etc. She knew the script already. No point.

"So, now you're here," she said. "And I know why you

didn't talk to me or see me all those years, but now you're here, with us."

Raoul placed his cup down on the counter, waiting for where Magda was leading.

"And I'm so glad that you've gotten past things and can share my life, my family." She paused while her father took a slurping sip of his coffee. "But Pa, I can't welcome you in my home and have you treat my wife any less than anyone else important in my life."

"I'm not treating Cherokee badly," he said, not looking Magda in the face.

Magda narrowed her eyes. "You've never liked gay people, you've never liked black people, and that's some old bullshit that I won't have brought into my house."

Raoul took another sip of his coffee, his fluffy robe tied tight around his T-shirt and lounge pants. Magda was very understanding of his need to retire for a while, to step back after such a health scare, to heal and cope with the fall of his business. Like her, to cope with addictions, pain, and their mutual loss. "What's with you and *negritas* anyway?" he asked. Magda bristled. She knew this could end badly. Her job was to keep the peace, to be the real grown-up.

"You know, Pa, I'm not a deprogrammer. I can't remove the code in your brain that—without any intelligence—deems some people lower than others. See, *Mami* never had that. She knew we were all human beings, worthy of love and respect. What surprises me about you, *doctor,* is that for someone so intellectually smart, you are so un-self-aware of the holes in your own thinking." It was a small victory—two in one morning—that Magda wasn't yelling and her father wasn't, either. He seemed to be listening. "Am I not your flesh and blood? Did you not create me, eh? So to reject something that comes from you—and is good—is the greatest sin. And those *niños,* those beautiful babies with their blackness and their beautiful curls and smiles, those babies you are now getting to know and love, they're black. Their mother is black. My wife is black. So is the president. So, if you're in the running for David Duke's spot, you can take your racist shit out of my house or go to one of your other children who are more likely to share your narrow, small, tiny mind." Magda straightened herself up. "*Doc-TOR.*"

Chapter 20

Whoa. Gabi stepped back from the curb as a cab making a left turn nearly swiped her. She berated herself for looking at her phone while Magda texted her madly. As Gabi looked around herself for the first time in blocks of walking, she spun directly into a bus stop; the face on the poster felt like a bad joke on Gabi that morning.

Maxwell Dane's face loomed over her. Very much in character, he glowered handsomely in his period garb. His show's new season was about to start. Gabi winced at seeing his face blown up large. She should have been seeing his flesh and blood face. His face in her hands, buried in her breasts, between her legs. *Snap out of it, Gabs!* After what she thought was a stellar date, the now fairly famous Maxwell had decided, Gabi assumed, that she was not someone he'd like to pursue. *Goddamn it. I'm sick of being alone. Sick of it.*

Though her phone continued to buzz with texts from Magda, Gabi assumed, she didn't look at it now. Instead she walked and walked, several blocks past her train stop. She wrapped her head in self-pity. As a mental health practitioner she knew exactly what she was doing in that moment. She also knew what she could do to turn it around (a bit of cognitive behavioral therapy, "attitude of gratitude"), but she also knew that for now, wallowing in her own muck felt good. She gave herself another block to sit in it. After that, it would be time to crack out of it. Spend too much time in the muck, end up trapped. She wasn't going to let that happen.

One block.

You were too needy. You talked too much. You offered to help too much. You know too much about him and his family now that he's famous. He doesn't need you. He met some slammin', younger gal. He just used you for information and advice. He got what he needed. They always use you, don't they? And you let them. Gotta get out of this cycle. Who did I think I was that he'd go out with me? I'm on TV, he's on TV, but . . . Being a single mom sucks. Who's gonna want this? This stretched-out, baby-making body. Who's gonna be able to cope with the mess in my head? How will I resist these assholes? How will I make sure to never be hurt like this again?

Next block.

You can't. You can't make sure of anything. The only thing you have control over is your internal state—your mind—and even that is subject to hormones and genetics. Do what you can. Do it for Max. You'll be fine with him as your focus for a while. Focus on Max. Focus on work. Help Magda, and no more going it on your own. Too dangerous. That was messed up. . . . Wait! Be kind to yourself, Gabi. You're human. You did it because you cared. Oh, Magda.

Gabi picked up her cell.

"Hey, girl, I'm hearing you," Gabi said.

"Gabs, I came too, too close last night."

"But you didn't do it—I am so proud of you. That's huge." Gabi talked as she walked more carefully this time, looking both ways before crossing, keeping her son in mind every moment, as it made her more careful. Single-mom alert.

"Yeah." Magda sighed into her phone. "And separately from all this shit, Cherokee's on her last nerve—Raoul is treating her like shit so I had to give him an ultimatum this morning."

"Whaaa?!"

"He's gotta shape up with her and his fuckin' prejudices or he's out," Magda said.

Gabi noted that cutting him out was a reflection of what he did to Magda years ago. Like father like daughter. "Mags, his being racist in your house while you're helping him is inexcusable. But just keep in mind that just as you won him over eventually, you can win him over when it comes to Cherokee, too—it may take some time and some finagling."

"Finagle . . . I don't wanna finagle!"

Gabi chuckled. "I know, hon, but setting boundaries was smart. Sounds like you made him think. Just try not to push him away again. I think he'll come around. Look at how he was hangin' with the Tuckers! I mean, shoot. He may just turn because he can't escape all the color . . . and the gay!"

"Ha! Good one," Magda said. They both paused. Gabi felt the weight of her secret visit to Sharon weighing on her. She felt dishonest with her friend.

"Mags. I gotta tell you something."

"Uh. Whaaat?"

"Mags. Don't be mad," Gabi said, but got no response. "I went to see Sharon."

"*What?!*" Magda yelled into the phone.

"Okay, yes, I know, I know, I shouldn't have done it without talking to you," Gabi said.

"What the fuck, Gabs? Where was she?"

"I found out she hosts at a restaurant downtown. I just wanted to warn her to take it down—that you're not alone in this. That you have people who love you—"

"Gabriella Adriana Gomez, I do not need you to take care of me here."

"Mags, I know. I'm sorry. I get protective, you know that."

Magda sighed. "I know all too well."

"I honestly did it out of love, so please, just go ahead and be mad at me."

"I am," Magda replied. And they both paused as a wailing ambulance went by. In that break of a few seconds, Magda softened. "So, what happened?"

"I just told her to back off. She was nasty. Of course. But I can tell that she's just off—even a bit scared." Gabi wondered if she should say anything about finding out the woman blackmailing her friend and former lover had also seen her ex-husband. The connection made Gabi nauseous. She felt guilty not telling Magda about Sharon's threats to her, too, but she needed to talk to Bert first. Then, maybe then, she'd share. She was so embarrassed by his behavior.

"Well. That's something," Magda said.

"But I still think you should stick to your plan. Don't engage. Don't pay. Better you pay lawyers and even hackers to take down the video than pay her."

"You're right. That's money better spent," Magda said. Gabi breathed in relief. "Okay, Gabs, I have to run. Let's talk tonight, okay?"

"Yeah. Love you."

"Love you too." And Magda hung up.

It was off to the next ex in her life. Gabi was halfway through her coffee, only barely miffed about Bert being twenty minutes late and not texting. She had trained herself to manage her expectations. She knew he was always late, a passive-aggressive tactic, so she expected him to be late, always. In that way, she never got upset at him being late. In her mind, he was right on time.

"Oh, hey, sorry." Bert swung onto the seat in front of her with a *whoosh*. Gabi didn't answer his apology or say, "Oh, that's okay." Another bit of her training. She knew him as someone who didn't exist unless he elicited or manipulated a reaction out of someone. *We are all mirrors to him—what can he get reflected back?*

His coffee was delivered and Gabi took him in. These days she only saw him briefly when she had to hand off Max for his visits, but she had managed not to have to look directly at his face, focusing always on her son. But now, Max wasn't here this time, and she was curious as to what had happened to this man she once loved so dearly. She was not without fault in their marriage. Overbearing, too scolding, always fixing. But she didn't deserve what he had done to her. The cheating was beyond anything she could have imagined, even after years of working with adults and all their predilections. Now that she thought about it, of course Sharon knew him. He had been hooking up with random women on Craigslist, women on dating sites, and women he worked with. Women she had known and met over the years when she'd shown up and supported him at his events before Max was born. Then, she ended up supporting her husband as he couldn't pick himself up after a restaurant failed, ergo supporting these women, as she also found he'd taken them out on the household credit card. And this was what she got in return. What made her throw up so much the morning she discovered evidence of all the cheating was the thought that he could easily have been inside one woman in the morning when he was "getting coffee and reading the paper" and then inside her that night. Not that much sex was happening at that point in their marriage. Once Max was born and Gabi's practice and media career took off, Bert crumpled and pulled away. So painful. So deceitful and unnecessary.

And, in the spirit of the ugliness of deception, their split wasn't amicable. He blamed her for all his flaws, a full-blown alcohol abuser by the end, on top of smoking too much weed. Gabi would chuckle sometimes, thinking, "How does he do it? The drinking, the smoking, the women—exhausting!" What a charade. And Gabi had to acknowledge her role in all this. Her codependent leanings. Her excusing his behavior for years. Not wanting to see all the lies so clearly in front of her. Wanting to preserve her narrative, her story, that they were such a cool, happy family.

"Well, I'm glad Max is doing better in school," Bert responded to Gabi making small talk about their son.

Might as well get that out of the way. Warm things up.

"So. I met someone who knows you the other day," Gabi said.

Bert's face tensed up. He seemed to have earned some wrinkles and gray hairs plus ten pounds of belly fat since the split. Gabi also noted he looked scraggly, unkempt. Much more than usual.

"Who?" he asked.

"Sharon."

Bert shrugged. "Sharon who? I don't know a Sharon."

Gabi sensed that he knew exactly who she was talking about. From courtship to marriage to Bert, she had subconsciously turned down, or off, her powers of perception. Like fiddling with the volume on a stereo, the noise was loud and present but Gabi would just move the dial, turning the truth down to a whisper. A whisper that kept her up at night until she found evidence that she could no longer ignore. It was a scream.

This time, Gabi kept the volume high. She didn't adjust it. She heard it loud and clear. She didn't respond to his question, because after all, he knew the answer and he knew who she was talking about. "Sharon threatened me with telling everyone in the press and social media about you and . . . the things you do, with her. Together."

Bert straightened up in his chair abruptly, the wooden legs making a loud scraping sound on the floor. "I don't know what the fuck this is about. What are you accusing me of? And why are you ambushing me with this?!" His voice went from a three to a ten within half a second. *Truth talks while guilt screams. Why didn't he ever realize that?*

"Either way, I don't need this affecting my business." Gabi remained calm and again ignored Bert's denials and tone.

"Need what?! Need what affecting your business?! And what about my business, huh? Like, I don't even know what this person is threatening. I maybe, maybe . . ." He leaned back, weakened. "Maybe I met her at a party, but she's full of shit!" He went back to yelling. Gabi was grateful the coffee shop was mostly empty. She worked to stay composed. It wasn't a simple skill. It was natural to fight or flee. The response was in her genes, in all human genes. She had to work hard at tamping the fire down.

"She may be full of shit, but whatever it is she's threatening, if it affects me, it affects Max, and I can't have that."

"Oh, right, you, you can't have that—you on your fucking high horse—"

"Did you not hear what I just said?! Your son, our son, Max, is affected by this. If I lose business, Max suffers!" Gabi's Achilles' heel, her son, her baby, her favorite person in the world. She couldn't keep her cool too much now.

"That's bullshit—she's full of shit."

"Like all those other women were full of shit, right?!" Gabi decided that as being nice was off the table, ineffective, it was time to amp it up.

"You're jealous! You're just jealous—always have been!"

"Bert. If it weren't for Maximo, I would very happily never, ever, see you again or give you a second thought." Gabi regretted those words as soon as they left her mouth. He was still Max's father. That was low. Not necessary. It was obvious that Bert was going to most likely end up alone through old age, or with some very sad, very low-self-esteem female. Gabi did have a high horse. Though when they first met, Bert put her up on that pedestal. And he was the one who decided to turn it into a high horse. From marble to mane. Either way, delusion.

"That's a real shitty thing to say," he said.

Gabi shrugged. She wasn't going to let him know that she regretted stooping that low. She owed him no apologies.

"Your ego is fucking insane!" The look in Bert's eyes was the only thing insane in that moment.

Gabi realized that she was going to get nowhere. *Deny 'til you die* was Bert's motto. Or, *deny until your wife finds dozens of explicit e-mails from other women on your computer, plus your twisted search history and your online dating profiles, while you're married to her.* In this case, Gabi didn't have a smoking gun. Just Sharon's threat.

Gabi was done. She got up, Bert still staring at her with wild, raging eyes. She recognized them as the eyes of a very sad, lonely, unloved child. That was all Bert ever was and ever would be. Gabi had produced lectures on narcissistic personality disorder in the past and helped people understand the idea that these folks were more than just the pop-culture definition of narcissism, in love with themselves. Instead, they were the loneliest people of all because they looked out into the world and only saw mirrors in people's eyes, mirrors reflecting back only themselves. They saw no one else's existence or personhood. And if you reflected back to them some truth that they didn't like about themselves, well, beware. You became the villain in their life and they needed to either destroy you or win you over. In the past couple of years since the separation, Gabi had been the object of both kinds of attempts. But her mirror held strong with its reflection of Bert. His truth.

However, there was no need for her to sit around and take the abuse anymore. He yelled after her as she walked toward the door, patrons and staff in the shop frozen in place, staring at this screaming, out-of-control grown man. Gabi kept walking right into the street. As she made her way down the subway steps, having not looked back once, her phone rang from Bert. She didn't answer.

But she did ask herself a question. *Why did I talk to him at all about this? I knew I wasn't going to accomplish anything because he'll never admit to anything. He can never be at fault. So why did I do it?*

As the train pulled up, billowing her brown curls, she remembered once being home on a college break so she could make some money waiting tables when she stumbled on her mother finishing up an emotional conversation with her younger sister. As Gabi turned to lock the door behind her, their mother disappeared into her room.

"What happened?" Gabi asked her sister, Millie.

Millie shrugged as she would if someone forgot to get the mail. "Mom followed Pops to some lady's house."

"Um, what?!" Gabi was shocked. She wasn't surprised so much that their father was at a woman's house—he was a Latin man, after all—but that their mother would do something so, well, so dramatically telenovela.

Millie dropped onto the couch and reached for the remote. Gabi intercepted it. "Mills, what the fuck?"

"All right, fine, so you know *Papi*'s been working late like all the time lately. . . ." Millie began.

"Yeah, but the economy sucks right now, right? And he's afraid he's gonna lose his job. . . ."

Millie gave her older sister a look of patience and a silent nod of agreement that yes, she, too, wished she could believe that that was all it was, his work. "Look, Mom followed him and he ended up at this stranger's house, so Mom banged on the door and made a big scene, and the woman—*una gringa,* mind you—threatened to call the police."

Gabi had no response. The scene was vibrant. She could imagine the whole thing. Millie gave her one last look and turned on the television. The spoon in the teenager's late-night bowl of cereal clanked loudly against the chipped ceramic.

"Stand clear of the closing doors."

The subway announcement drew Gabi out of the memory. She had always made excuses for her father. Just as she made excuses for her ex-husband. *We always want to master in adulthood what we couldn't master in childhood. I married my father. And before that was Magda, who did the same.*

Gabi realized that it was time for her to grow up. Responsible Dr. Fixer Gabi, known all around the country, was like a doctor who smoked. Or worse, a doctor dipping into her own prescription stash, always thinking that status and education meant being in control. No more. *Time to turn those powers onto yourself. It's gonna hurt, but for Max's sake, it's time to sober up.*

Chapter 21

"Hon, you here?" Luz called out to her husband, Chris, her voice echoing through their cavernous apartment. Her trailing call was met with the rumble of her kids' running feet and their playful yelling back and forth. The words didn't matter, the tone was what Luz took a moment to savor. It was joyful. She needed that. Her kids' happy play slipped her a dose of spiritual aspirin. "*Ay*, my babies!" Nina and 'Fina, dressed in jazzy sports gear, ran around Luz's legs, playing tag in warm-up for what looked like a soccer session in the park.

"Hey, Mama." Luz's husband, Chris, had snuck up behind the distraction of Luz trying to catch and plant kisses and hugs on her brood. He kissed her instead. "Just taking them out for some ball. Are you okay?" He had an uncanny, symbiotic ability to hone in on his wife. Seemed like a dream to many women, but at times, Luz wished he couldn't see inside her so well. Not this time.

"Boo—" she started, but was interrupted by a slight knock on the door.

"Oh, hey, Diego! So glad you're here," Chris said to the family's resident part-time coach. A Colombian graduate student and former semipro *fútbol* player, Diego was happy to answer the ad to help coach a couple of twins in the most worldwide of sports a couple times a week. Chris had taken to him, enjoying mentoring a bright, young student. "Hey, D, do you mind going ahead with the kids and I'll meet up with you in a bit, okay?"

"Sure, happy to do so. *Vámonos, chiquita* bananas!" The children slipped out the door before Luz had a chance to hug them. They were charmed by Diego's energy and good looks. Luz yelled after them, sending them her love, telling them to be careful crossing the street. She closed the front door.

"He calls them *chiquita* bananas?" she asked.

Chris shrugged. "Yeah. Got that from me." He smiled.

"I know. Funny." Her voice dropped as she remembered where she'd just come from. Chris took her arm and led her out of the foyer into the kitchen. Sandwiching her between him and the island, he held her arms gently and kissed her forehead.

"What happened, Mama?" he asked.

"I went to see Ben Quinton."

"No shit."

"Yup." Luz sighed.

"Mama, why didn't you tell me? I would have gone with you." Luz shrugged in response. Chris continued, "Dare I ask how it went?"

"Well, let's just say we may have to spend some money on lawyers soon."

"Shit! Are you kidding me?" Chris asked.

Luz slowly shook her head. "I wish I was, Papa."

"Goddamn it. From zero to sixty like that."

"Yup."

Chris knew better than to grill his wife just yet. Luz needed a minute. It would all come out. Plus, needing lawyers kind of explained itself.

"Where's Emelie?" Luz asked.

"She went out after you left this morning. She was heading to Ailey for class."

Luz wondered for a moment, protectively, if a pregnant teenager should be jerking around and jumping in hip hop class. *That's silly. If any pregnant female could handle strenuous exercise, it would be a teenager. Plus, she's not that far along—*

Luz's thoughts, and undoubtedly her husband's, were interrupted by the slamming front door. It was an oversized metal loft door overlaid with a natural wood, ornate carving imported from Mexico. Luz hated anyone slamming the door, as each time she'd envision cracks forming in the hundred-year-old dry lumber.

It was Emelie. Uncharacteristically, she passed Luz and Chris quickly, mumbled a "Hi," and jogged to her bedroom, slamming that door as well. Chris locked eyes with Luz—*Uh-oh,* they thought. He then nodded as his wife broke from him swiftly and followed her sister. As Luz made it to Emelie's door, she noted that Chris left them alone, walking out to meet the kids and Diego. She was grateful for his tact.

"Em? Emelie? Are you okay?" Luz asked, through the door. She knocked. "Can I come in?" She knocked again. Not getting a response, she was surprised, turning the knob, that it wasn't locked. She gently opened the door, not sure what she was going to encounter.

The teen was curled up on her bed on top of her bedspread. The tasteful ruffles mirrored the waves in Emelie's long ponytail. *I don't think I've ever seen Em with a ponytail.* The girl looked stunned, as pale as her skin tone would allow, her eyes frozen open, staring at the opposing wall. Luz sat down near her legs.

"Em. Em, are you okay?"

"Yeah," Emelie answered hoarsely.

"Sweetie, what happened? Are you sick?"

"It's gone."

Luz's stomach instantly knotted. "What's gone, Em?"

"It's gone. You don't have to worry anymore."

"Wha . . . ?" Luz froze this time. Her eyes, too, wouldn't close. They remained wide open in a kind of horror. *Nooooooooooo.* She was aware that a grunt of some sort came out of her. She couldn't speak just yet. Not for a moment had she thought that Emelie would do this or even consider it for a while, without talking to her first, without coming to her for help or advice. There was a baby. Now there wasn't a baby?

"I . . ." Luz tried to speak as a tear let loose from her right eye. The sensation of it surprised her into blinking.

"It's okay," Emelie said in a monotone.

"Why"—Luz's voice cracked—"why did you go alone? You didn't have to go alone."

"Eunice went with me." Luz vaguely remembered Emelie mentioning a twenty-something distant cousin from the Heights she kept in touch with. Of course she wouldn't take a friend from school. *Her other family.*

"Eunice? Okay. Let me get you something." Luz made a brisk walk to the master bath and pulled out her heating pad with a knitted cover. It was a silly cover, a funny dog's face with its tongue hanging out. Luz figured that the aftermath of an abortion probably felt like the worst cramping of your life. Not childbirth, of course. But something like it, especially for a teenager only a few years into painful periods. She grabbed two giant pain relievers and a can of Emelie's favorite flavored seltzer, cherry. Luz didn't allow soda in the house, much to Emelie's shock. The girl was raised on soda. Hence, Emelie's several-thousand-dollar dentist and orthodontist bill her first year with them. Cherry seltzer was a solid wean.

Luz set everything down by Emelie's bed on her side table. She handed her the heating pad, close to her belly but not directly on top, letting the girl place it herself. Luz thought she saw a slight release in the tension in Emelie's face when the girl saw the funny dog face on the knitting.

"Are you in a lot of pain?" Luz asked.

"Nah. I'll be okay. It's just cramping."

Luz stroked Emelie's hip. They both had so much to tell each other. What felt like months had passed in the space of a day. That morning, Emelie, Luz's teenage sister, who she'd just met two years ago and legally adopted, a Dominican-American girl from the 'hood, now educated in the most expensive, exclusive private school in the city, was pregnant. Her future completely headed down one road. And Luz was readying herself for lawyers and paparazzi and all the drama that came with getting knocked up by not just some stupid kid but the stupid son of a mega movie star. *That's this town for you. And now . . .*

"Did Eunice sign for you and . . . everything?" Luz asked.

"She didn't need to. Don't need that in New York."

"Oh. Wow. Okay." Luz was impressed with Emelie's resourcefulness and even her independence, though of course Emelie hadn't had a choice, spending years without a mother around. But Luz was skating around the question she really wanted to ask.

Emelie kept one hand on the water bottle on her belly and placed her other hand on Luz's. She squeezed. Luz took that as permission.

"Em. Why did you . . . why did you choose . . ."

Emelie sniffed, and as she breathed back out, she let the tears fall, as if there were tiny sponges behind her eyes being squeezed and wrung with the rhythm of her blinking. "I just couldn't, you know?" Luz reached over to her nightstand and pulled a wad of tissues out from a box, handing them to her sister. "You know, I kind of miss *Papi,* but I was kinda glad he went away."

This turn of focus surprised Luz. "You were?"

"Yeah."

"Was he bad to you?"

"No, no. It wasn't that." Emelie wiped her runny nose, sliding her tissue-wrapped hand up her face, like a kid. "It was just like, I didn't realize that being in that kind of life was a trap, you know?" Luz raised her brow. "Like, it was its own prison for me. Felt like I had no options." The girl paused, and Luz was still in enough shock that her silence was helpful, a kind of patience that wasn't her usual state. Emelie continued, "I really didn't want to go back to that. No options. Or, like, few options. When I came here, I saw just how big the world is, you know?" Luz nodded. She knew. "Like, I didn't have to be trapped in one world because that's how I was born. That I could escape and move into other worlds. That I could really do things. You showed me that."

"And," Luz chose her words very carefully, "you thought that this, um . . ." She gestured to Emelie's stomach. ". . . would have trapped you again?"

"Yeah."

"I would have helped you, though hon. And the family— we're all here for you." Luz took her sister's hand again. Why was Luz so pained by Emelie's decision? Why did this feel like the loss of a child, another child, when Luz knew full well that at only ten weeks they were many decisions away from changing diapers? With her panic at the Quinton fiasco earlier in the day, why didn't Luz feel relief? Instead, she felt like someone had carved out a piece of her, too. A chunk. It wasn't her pregnancy. But she had been ready to claim it. Claim it as family. That was on her.

"I know. You guys are great. I know. But Peter's family would never have let me do what I want to do once they found out, and Luz . . . I've seen it now, the other way I can go. The other direction. And I want to be able to do that, to go there. Not to end up like some of the girls back home."

"I see." Luz understood. That desire not to be a statistic. Gabi talked about that. About how she'd had a feeling that her relationship, her marriage, Bert wasn't going to last but that her clock was ticking and she wasn't going to be another unmarried Latina having a baby, professionally successful or not. She'd rather be a divorced, single mother. At least she'd been married when she had her baby. It was admittedly antiquated thinking, so Luz was surprised that Emelie felt that, too. She wasn't sure why. "Oh, Em. Your father."

Emelie sat up a bit at the mention of her imprisoned father. "You know. Too bad. I'm not going to have a baby just so I can get famous or so he can be famous—like what, famous in jail? I'm going to have a baby when I want one." Luz looked surprised, and Emelie smiled at her face. Luz smiled back.

"Well. I have to say, I am impressed by your maturity here, but, I mean, I think he was thinking about you being taken care of," Luz said.

"Yeah, well, about that. I'm a feminist, okay, and he may not like that, but I don't need to have some rich kid's baby to, like, 'secure' my future." She was enthusiastic with her air quotes on *secure*.

"Damn straight, honey." Luz patted her sister's salt-streaked cheek. "But, did you tell Peter, though?" In all this, Luz had been too selfish to even ask again if the baby's father knew. She had instead stomped off to his father's place—well, they were teenagers, right?—possibly making a much bigger mess of this than had been necessary.

"No."

"No?" Luz was slightly panicked.

"Nope. And now there's nothing to tell him." Emelie blew her nose loudly.

Luz patted her sister's leg and said, "Let me grab you some more tissues." She walked out and went toward the pantry and let loose, chastising herself.

There's nothing to tell him?! You stupid cow. Stupid, meddling cow. Thinking you had to "mom" your way out of this. Messed it up.

"Lu?" She heard Emelie call after her. "Lu, nobody else knows, right?"

Right.

Chapter 22

It was finally starting to get cold for the winter, and Gabi felt the brisk wind pull at her oversprayed curls. She'd just wrapped another late-morning television segment on celebrity divorces; the tarted-up host had been clueless as to Gabi's own marital status. The hosts of Gabi's other regular spots knew what she'd been through and all chatted amicably with her about how she was doing and what was next on her horizon. *Oh, the usual! Another book, lots of speaking dates, and of course, my practice, which is now primarily divorcées, or women looking to divorce eventually.* Gabi's practice was taking up much more of her time and bringing in much more money than just a few years ago, and she felt good about that. It wasn't the easy money that speaking engagements were, as the sessions sometimes left her drained, but it kept her from having to travel and be away from her darling boy, Maximo. *Priorities, priorities.*

"*Hola,* Mama!" Gabi mouthed. Magda stood on the other side of the glass window where Gabi was sitting. She'd texted Gabi to meet up after her television appearance, her "hit," as it was called in TV lingo. *Important,* she'd written. Though there were half a dozen items in their lives that were important. Gabi's stomach was in knots as she chewed on her guilt, suspecting one "important" thing in particular.

"Hey, girl." Magda rose to give Gabi a peck on the cheek. The French bistro was warm, and Gabi was relieved to shed some layers and order coffee. As she did so, she noted her friend's tight brow.

"Gabs. What did you do?" Magda asked, unsmiling.

"Oh, Mags." Gabi could only sigh and take a deep breath. She had to fess up to sticking her long nose far into Magda's business. "I'm sorry," was all she could manage. Magda looked out the window, leaned forward, and clasped her hands in front of her chin. The irises of her eyes were tiny in the sunlight. Gabi continued. "Magda. I am so, so sorry. I . . . I just felt like I had to do something. I should know better. It was messed up and could have gotten us both into deeper trouble." Magda looked down at the tiny, circular round table between them, seeming to study the veins in the cream marble, mini rivers they needed to cross.

"Gabi. I know you wanted to help. I know your intentions were good. But. But this . . . It just didn't help." Rarely was their speech together so stilted, parsed out. Former lovers and longtime friends, Gabi and Magda had a banter that was staccato and playful. Normally, they jostled and toyed with their words, Gabi usually scolding, mothering, guiding, and Magda enjoying being chastised, kept in check. An id and a superego.

"I know," Gabi said. "What did she tell you?"

"Sharon?" Magda asked. Gabi nodded. Magda pulled out her cell phone. "Well. Let me tell you." She started reading from her phone. "She said: 'Sending your old lady to scare me? Doesn't work. Time to double it.' "

"Double it?!" Gabi was surprised. She had made it much worse than she thought. "Double how much money she wants?"

"Yup," Magda answered.

Gabi put her head in her hands. From there she mumbled, "Mags, I am so sorry."

"Okay. Look. Enough. It is what it is. I know you . . . meant well."

"If it makes you feel better, I fucked myself over, too," Gabi said.

Magda turned her eyes directly to Gabi's. "What? What do you mean?"

"Well. Our lovely Sharon, *puta* . . . Seems she knows Bert."

"What the fuck?!" Magda's turn at surprise. Her face turned from shock to sorrow. She knew what that meant. "Gabi . . . *Dios*. I'm sorry."

Their closeness, their history, and comfort flipped a switch in Gabi from her always-present fortitude to permission to break down, just a little, and her eyes teared up. "Yeah, and again, stupid me, I go and confront him about it—"

"Oh, Gabs, you knew that wasn't going to go well."

"I know! I know."

"Sorry. Keep going," Magda said. Bert was not well known for his maturity or ability to rein himself in. He was a notorious hothead, not only in their marriage but in his kitchens. He'd gotten bad enough in a few instances that his colleagues were alarmed at how he went from zero to sixty with his temper. It wasn't normal. Gabi, unfortunately, found out, and cared enough to do something about it, too late.

"I just had to talk to him, you know? I mean, she says to me that she knows him, hints that of course it's professionally, which was totally creepy, mind you . . . and she threatened to go public with him, too."

"Public with him?!" Magda was on the edge of her seat. At six feet tall and solid in her suit, she was intense. "Wow. She's really crossed the line now." Magda sat back in her seat, her legs splayed before her, a power pose, as she looked into space.

As Gabi saw her dear friend's eyes glaze over with thought, she knew what that meant. With Magda's money, she had power. That face of concentration was the same face Gabi would see when Magda was preparing to take someone on in business. She'd only seen it maybe twice before, but both times she'd taken a big risk to wipe out a competitor, and had won. Eye of the tiger.

"Magdalena?" Gabi queried. She didn't answer. Gabi let her sit and think for a moment as their coffees were refilled. Abruptly, Magda pulled herself up in her chair and leaned in toward Gabi.

"I didn't want to have to do this, hon, but it's time."

Gabi felt her skin tingle. "Time for what?"

As Magda turned to stir her coffee, she kept within close earshot of Gabi, now both of them acting relaxed to not call too much attention to themselves.

"I've got someone who can fix this," Magda said.

"Fix this? Who?"

"Look, what Sharon does, in general, is illegal."

"Wait, is it, though? I thought she was just a dominatrix or something?"

"She's that. And other things. The drugs alone . . ."

"Drugs too? Prostitution? Shit." Gabi was simultaneously impressed and horrified. How did she end up one degree of separation from this element of society? "You gonna call the police?"

"Oh, and get us all into trouble?"

"Well, would we get into trouble?" Gabi asked. Magda rolled her eyes at her friend's lack of savvy.

"Of course. Don't you remember every time a madam gets busted the client list somehow makes it out? Or, the names of a few folks who will make headlines?"

"Oh." Gabi was chastised. "Right."

Magda sucked on her teeth. "The key is her online life."

"Her computer?"

"Her phone."

Gabi marveled a bit at Magda's turn from victim to aggressor. "You're going to steal her phone and hack into it?"

"Better. No need to steal the phone. Just hack in."

"But Mags, hacking is illegal!" Gabi whispered with a punitive hiss. "You'll get us in even more trouble!"

"Gabriella Gomez. Girl, I am not going to let us get caught—"

"Oh, don't say us, Mama . . . I can't afford to be taken away from my baby—you have an actual competent parent or two to take care of those kids. I've got an irresponsible, verbally abusive douchebag for an ex, and I'm not going to do one thing that would harm my baby. You can go ahead. I'm out."

Magda nodded. She knew that Gabi was right. Beyond money was the safety net of family, responsible adults to lean back on. Gabi was bereft in that department.

"Okay then. You're not hearing me say that I'm going to get someone on this. I'm not in tech for nothing. I'll have to pay him big but I'm sure she has some weak password spots or drops into public wireless sometimes—probably at her restaurant job—and even if it's just a switch of her SIM card while she's working, it can be done. And no. I'm not going to get caught. My guy will make sure to tip off the cops anonymously. That's what they do."

Gabi couldn't look at Magda. She was absolutely nervous but also reassured. She knew that Magda would take a fall for them both, protecting Gabi in this whole process. She also knew that Magda had little choice. This woman could not only be a sinkhole of money but a threat to Magda's business. If a hack protected them both and ended the blackmail, well, so be it. *But goddamn it, she—we—can't get caught.*

"Trust me, Mama." Magda put her hand on Gabi's. She squeezed, looking at her friend through the blond fall of her short hair. "Trust me."

Gabi blinked slowly and turned her eyes to Magda's. "Just take care of this, okay?"

"I will, *mujer*. She won't know what hit her."

Chapter 23

"Um, Ms. Rivera . . . hello? Excuse me!" The receptionist might as well have been yelling into the wind. Cat paid her no mind as she walked straight into August Tilly's office, her focus clear. As she opened and closed the oversized wooden door behind her, she saw him with his back turned to the door, on the phone. The executive at first mistook the sounds of Cat's arrival for those of his assistant. He then swung around to face her slowly, only to jolt himself forward as he saw who his interloper really was.

"Uh, gotta go." He hung up the phone and stared at Cat, unblinking, misconstruing her intensity for something more positive. "Hello!"

Cat stood over him, leaning on his desk, her eyes fiery despite her promise to herself to remain as civil and calm as possible. After all, pissing off someone with this much money and possibly this much unhinged could mean a bad outcome. But he'd already crossed many lines with her. Now it was her turn.

"What the *fuck* were you thinking?" Cat said to August. As she swore, her fingers balled into fists of frustration, except for the one she used to point at him, accusing.

August smiled at first, but his eyes turned away a moment.

Cat noted that this meant he thought she was actually coming in to say something happy to him. *Prick.*

He raised his hands in a gesture of surrender. "Hey, c'mon . . . What's a man to do?" Now, a smirk.

"Not fucking send a diamond ring and flowers to the home I share with my partner and my child."

August stood up lazily. Cat stepped back from the desk as he made his way around it to get closer to her. She backed away a step in response, yet held enough ground to let him know that her feet were planted firmly not only on his floor, but on her take on his shenanigans.

"Listen. Big feelings need grand gestures," he said.

"Big feelings?! What the fuck do you know about big feelings? What you did was all about *your* feelings—that's all you know! Your feelings! You have no idea what feelings between people are—none."

August did his I'm-such-a-bad-boy shrug again, his palms facing up to the ceiling like a supplicant. "C'mon," he whined. "I want to be with you, Cat. Don't you want this? All this?" He gestured at his office, his view of the city below them. His heavy, expensive watch glistened in the sunlight.

Cat felt a tug. The tug and pull of something she'd always wanted. Money. Power. But not money for money's sake. Money equaled safety and security for her. It was a way out of the barrio for good, a way to help support her mother even if she didn't talk to her much.

Maybe, Cat thought, *maybe I've always wanted money just to say to Ma,* See? *See what I can do? Did I mean,* See what you couldn't do? *Competing with her? Or was I impressing her? Either way, nice to see you again, old friend. You're so familiar. You pushed and pushed me through to my own television show. To national fame. You pushed me into waiting too long to have a life—giving up dating or love or children until getting canceled forced me to face the control you've had over my life . . . the pursuit of money. But you can't be my only motivation anymore. You can't control me. Money. Power. I see you!*

Cat hesitated, looking around the room. She wanted to be very clear not only with August, but with herself as to why she chose a moderately successful (in her circles) but hardworking and loving younger man to be her partner, the father of her child, rather than someone who could take care of her and her daughter—and yes, her mother—for the rest of their lives. Even if they got sick. *Medical bills. What if another show is canceled? You're so seductive, aren't you? Tempting me with all the things that could go wrong. The things that could bankrupt me. Take everything away that I've worked so hard for. But no. I may be bankrupt but I won't be bankrupt of soul. I have dear friends and family . . . I have love. The real thing. Someone who cares how I feel.*

"Cat . . ." August saw an in and leaned closer. She put up her ringless hand to stop him from approaching.

"Here's what you don't understand, August," she began, calmly this time, her voice shifting in cadence, "I've got plenty. As a matter of fact, I have all I need."

He flinched. "How can you have all you need? No one has all they need! I mean, what, you have an Internet show? And some mid-level corporate guy?" Cat didn't answer him. She wanted to hear what he had to dish up next. Where did he see the holes in her life? "There's a lot more out there, Cat! A lot more, and I can give it to you."

"You going to buy it for me, August?" she asked.

He seemed to know that she was looking for another answer, but he couldn't help responding in the only way he knew how. "Yes. I'm going to buy it for you."

Cat scoffed politely, though with taunting conviction. "You can't buy love, August. You can't buy people." He shifted the weight on his feet. "See, what you don't understand is that I have a family, a big, wide family now, not just me and my mother. And this family, Tomas, our child, her family and his, is mine too now, and that can't be bought. Their love—his love—is all I need and something that can't compete in the slightest with what you're offering me." As Cat's resolve sank into the CEO, his body language changed. He crossed his arms and narrowed his eyes.

"Then why haven't you married him?" To August, this was a challenge more than a question needing an answer.

"Good question," Cat said. "And standing here, I'm realizing that every reason I gave myself for not marrying him has just dropped away. Because I was scared. Because I didn't have a model as to what a healthy relationship was. Because I was too career-focused and worried about losing my identity." Cat turned toward the window and continued, looking out, talking more to herself than to August. "I don't owe you an explanation. I only owe myself honesty, and so, I guess I have to thank you." She turned back toward him. "Because your grand gesture made me realize a very grand thing. That I love Tomas and want to spend the rest of my life with him. And I'm going to be his wife." August remained tightly wound, his lips pulled together.

"I'll give you a day to reconsider," August said. "Let's talk tomorrow."

"Seriously?!" Cat blurted. "There's nothing to reconsider because there was nothing to consider!"

"No one says no to me." August cut her off.

His voice took on a tone so abruptly different it turned Cat's skin cold. It was psychotic, nearly. Flat affect, close to threatening. Any question Cat had as to her decision to reject him flew out the window so fast, it nearly ruffled her hair. Now Cat saw who August truly was. It was as if a screen had been pulled away from him, or a skin had been shed. What she saw was dark. She was grateful they were in a fairly public place. His office, his employees, but still. He wouldn't risk throwing her out the window of his own building, though he looked that angry.

"Well," Cat responded. "Allow me to be the first. Though I doubt I am, but I'll take the honor." The threat honed Cat's verbal knives. Before her current incarnation as an online host, she'd hosted a business show, with male guests ninety percent of the time, many thinking that she was small and weak due to her femininity and ethnicity. But she so relished taking them down with the brain between her ears and the sharp tongue in her mouth. Relished.

"I knew from the start that your women-focused policies were bullshit, and I was right." Cat picked up the purse that she'd dropped on a chair on her way in. "If you had really meant it, really knew and believed in what you were doing, you'd know just how offensive it was to shove yourself into my family and think that you could buy me. You buy people, August. You buy them to serve you and say yes to you and build the world you want to build. But not everyone can be bought, and you made a big misjudgment when you pegged me as a mark." She got within a few steps of him, both with their arms now crossed. "Now, do us both a favor and stay away from me and my family. Go find yourself a 'yes' girl. There are so many fish in that sea."

Cat didn't wait for a retort from August. She didn't even wait for a visual reaction. He took it as she dealt it with his stern face; Cat tingled with the rage she felt coming from him. She jumped slightly at the *bam* of his fist coming down on his desk once she crossed his office threshold. She was startled, but she smiled with accomplishment.

It was a powerful thing to be wanted by someone so wealthy and influential. But she was now realizing that the power had come from herself—it was hers all along. All August did was confirm something that Cat realized she had buried deep inside, packaged up like a storage box. The idea that she deserved a good relationship—that she deserved to be loved. That her mother's rejection of a relationship with any man since her father meant Cat grew up with an odd sense that they weren't worthy of one. That they both weren't worthy of someone to share their lives with. It was out of their reach, a holy grail. Not something made for them. And simply by birth, Cat had thought. Tomas was a wonderful person. On the surface, Cat's reticence was nothing more than a pile of excuses. *He's too young. Marriages end in divorce. But what if . . .* Below that was: *I don't trust men. I don't know what a healthy relationship is.* But now she knew more.

And now that she'd rejected someone other women would have killed to be with, she felt that there was one thing August had been right about. That she was a catch. As Cat left the building and walked toward traffic, instead of hailing a car right away, she kept her stride, the cool wind tickling her face. She felt like she'd just thrown off a heavy cloak that had been obstructing her view. She was free, she could see, and she wanted to revel in it a bit longer.

Cat had always been a "no" girl. No to drinking and drugs in high school (messes with your grades, after all). No to settling down or dating the dozens of guys who showed interest in her over the years, especially the yahoo male guests on her show. No to colleagues who asked her out. No to listening to herself, her needs, her wants, instead following a path set out for her by her mother. She liked saying yes now. Yes to her wants and hopes and voice, which led to her current show and all its success. Yes to authenticity. To having the baby she'd always wanted.

And now she was going to say yes to one very big thing.

Yes, Tomas. Yes.

Chapter 24

Luz had driven to the prison now several times. Never alone, though. She had turned off the music in her car at least a mile away from the parking lot, driving in silence. She wasn't sure if it was reverence of some sort, as if she were entering a cemetery or more of a purgatory, or, was it her nerves? This was going to be a hard conversation, or a hard announcement. Luz had always liked to sit in quiet before a big meeting. In her former post as an SVP at an agency, her team knew she needed to step away for a few minutes, no matter where in the world they were, even if it was a bathroom break, sitting in a stall, the metal walls blocking out the world. With her current business, she was the boss, so she had her assistant always bake into the schedule her time of solace. But there was also something about approaching a compound of cement surrounded by gate after gate and men with guns. So many male souls inside. Difficult, frightening souls. Luz had reverence for the situation.

Her wheels crunched on the sloppy potholes someone had attempted to fill, the tar now crumbling out and around them like black popcorn. As she turned the car off in its parking spot, she sighed. How did she end up here? She had led such a charmed life. She had really raked it in, with bonuses, nearly a million a year by thirty-two. Married to a self-made multi-millionaire. Beautiful children. Shoot, Luz was pretty cute, looking sexy for her years. *Life is so strange. I never thought I'd be here. And to think . . . I used to look down on the people who end up here. I did. Admit it, girl. You thought you were better. You thought that your upbringing was so far away from the rest of folks with the color of your skin that you were immune to the narrative of this country and its history. How closely tied we all are. All of us.*

Thinking of the connection, of family and the essence of its obligation, made Luz feel fortified. She made her way to the first gate of the prison grounds. The sound of other visitors flowed around her in the air, rubbing at her ears. Every sound, heightened. Even the colors and textures around her seemed to pulse in her eyes. As she walked through each checkpoint, shuffling along with other families, feeling even more alone, Luz's mind wandered to the thought of the baby that could have been. Emelie was her connection to this world, with its clanging sounds and pervasiveness of metal. But if she'd had that boy's baby, the connection between this world and an even more rarified one would have been sealed. *I bet this would never happen in any other part of the world. No other country or place. Only here. American history. American legacies. Opportunity and punishment. Hand in hand.*

"Tucker Lee." Luz's name called, she entered the common room. Eugenio was already sitting at their usual table, his hands clasped in front of him as he worked to appear nonchalant, though Luz knew that he looked forward to these visits tremendously and wished they'd come more. She could only imagine what his fellow felons thought of the two ladies who visited him. What they thought of her, in particular. Though she took off all her jewelry and wore her most drab, shapeless clothes, her face with only enough makeup to hide the bags under her eyes, she wondered. *Probably not fair, but real.*

Eugenio looked up when Luz's name was called. His face fell as he only saw Luz, and his eyes darted behind her, looking for his daughter. His hands unfurled and lay flat on the table as if he could grip the surface in anxiety. "Where's my daughter?" His voice cracked.

"Hi, Eugenio. She couldn't make it."

"What do you mean, couldn't make it?! She sick?"

"Sort of," Luz answered.

Eugenio searched Luz's face for an answer, the answer she might have been trying to hide with her words but that he could see in the tiny movements of her eyes and mouth. "What happened, Luz?" His voice went flat.

"Emelie decided to have an abortion."

"An abortion?!"

"Yes. I'm sorry." Luz apologized only to deflect the anger from Emelie's father she was primed for. She wasn't sorry for Emelie's decision. It was hers to make. She made it, and for her own good reasons. Luz only wished that as the girl's legal parent, she didn't feel strongly that she had to be here at all—he'd handed over his rights, yes?—but she knew it was the right thing to do. He was Emelie's father and had raised her up until two years ago. And, he technically was Luz's family, too.

Eugenio put his head in his hands, his tattooed fingers braided together on his shaved skull. His head rose again to meet Luz's eyes; his hands moved behind his own neck, pulling. "Why? Why would she do that, huh?"

"She just wasn't ready, Eugenio. She—"

"I mean, did she go by herself?! Did you do this?!" He was whispering now, but his voice cut through the air like a blade, hissing into Luz's sensitive ears.

"She did do this on her own. I was not there, and she didn't tell me she was going to do it."

"Isn't that illegal? I mean, she's only sixteen." His eyes for the first time seemed more hurt than shocked. They pleaded with Luz to tell him that his life wasn't true. That he wasn't behind bars because he made a stupid decision to try to make more money by dealing. That he wasn't sitting here instead of his own home, away from his daughter, who he knew had to be in some kind of pain, even if it wasn't a pain he understood. That he could get up and get in the car with Luz to see his child.

"No. In New York it's not."

"Was it the father? Did he force her to do this?"

"No. He didn't even know."

"What?!"

Luz shook her head.

"But . . . this was a ticket, right? I mean, a famous guy's son. Hollywood."

"Eugenio. I know it's hard for you to believe, I mean, you haven't seen my place or my life, but I can assure you that Emelie will never lack anything for the rest of her life."

He looked at Luz incredulously. He took in her brown skin, darker than his, her tightly curled hair. "Why? What are you, famous too?"

"I'm not famous, but I own a successful company. My husband has done very well, too." That's all Luz wanted Eugenio to know. She didn't want him telling anyone inside with him any more about her or her life. She didn't need to invite trouble into her life or take him or more family in. She wasn't stupid. He might not mean to blab, but he seemed the type to brag first, think of consequences later.

"*Humph.*" He scoffed a bit. "I know your moms did good with marrying that guy, but I didn't realize that you did even better."

"I have. Emelie never has to marry for money or fame or anything but getting married because she wants to."

"And not without a prenup, riiiight?" Eugenio joked.

"Yeah. A prenup for sure." Luz had to smile. She grew up noting that her Dominican family, though so much similar in skin color and genetic heritage to her father's family, was dozens of degrees warmer.

"It's not that she didn't want to be here," Luz continued,

"but she knew how much it seemed like you wanted her to have this baby and she wasn't ready to face your disappointment." Eugenio looked downward, his eyes brimming. "Look." Luz leaned in. "Emelie felt like, well, coming to live with us, that she's been opened to a new world, and she wants to continue in that world and not fall behind. She's so young, so much ahead of her. She didn't want to be trapped."

"Trapped?" Eugenio snapped. "Trapped," he said again, acceptingly.

"Sorry." Luz mumbled an apology for the reference as she looked around them. Emelie had used the word "prison," and Luz knew that Eugenio was a smart man, too, at least intellectually. He knew what she meant by that, and she felt guilty for delivering the message that his daughter, her sister, said essentially that she felt that her life with him was a trap. That she also didn't want to end up like him, trapped. Luz watched it all sink in to her father. He was handsome, Luz thought. *What if he'd been born to parents like mine? How far would he have gone? Where would he be? Famous?*

"I don't agree with it, Luz. Abortion is a sin." Eugenio's back was straight and the two of them remained a bubble of intense conversation, all the noises and hugs and tears around them, the nagging from wives and mothers left behind by their men on the other side of the law, falling into a low hum. "But, you've done a good job, you know, *m'ija?* You've done so much for my girl." He choked on emotion. "I miss her so much." He flicked away tears. "You good. You good."

Luz nodded, her head bowed. She didn't want to meet his eyes, embarrass him any further than he might have been.

"If her mother was here," Eugenio pointed at the table, "she'd be so grateful to you. And you'd like her, you know?" Luz smiled. "She'd like you. . . . She would. And she'd be so grateful to you."

Luz didn't know what to say besides mouthing a "thank

you." They sat in silence for a moment, allowing the outside world in slightly.

Eugenio mumbled something Luz couldn't make out over the din of noise they'd suddenly let into their space.

"What?"

"*Familia,*" he said.

"Yes," Luz agreed.

As she walked back out to her car her mind began preparing itself for her next difficult conversation. Ben Quinton. This was going to be quite another kind of presentation. Considering how things went before, lawyers and all, she was ready to approach him directly in the spirit of what Eugenio just reminded her of, family. No, an unrealized pregnancy did not qualify the Quintons, but it did put Luz's heart in an open place. *I pray he's civilized.*

She fiddled with the tuner on her console, looking for music, but then thought twice.

Silence.

"Em, why didn't you tell me?" Peter Quinton was a more beautiful version of his famous father. He was five inches taller already at eighteen years old, and the addition of his mother's Nordic genes gave his features room to breathe compared to his father's harder, pointed, yet expressive, face.

"I was going to . . . when I made a decision about it," Emelie answered.

They leaned against the railing on the west side of Central Park, their school several blocks away. This was where the upper school kids were able to escape during "community time." The coffee shop on the corner had amazing croissants, and the burger shop on the opposite one had the most popular fries in school.

"But, man, why did I have to find out from my father like that?" The teen wasn't hostile so much as insulted and embarrassed.

Emelie was wise enough to pick up on where his concern came in. It came from and was about him. He wasn't a bad kid. He was gorgeous and smart but the product of his upbringing, just as Emelie was of hers.

"Look, I'm sorry, okay? I didn't know my sister was going to tell your dad like that, and she didn't mean to cause problems. She was just trying to help me."

Peter sat sullenly.

Classmates wandered by them, close enough for Peter and Emelie to nod or smile, but not within earshot.

"Are you okay? I mean, are you feeling okay?" Peter asked.

"Yeah. I'm okay."

Emelie patted his hand resting next to hers. "Look, it was stupid of us anyway. Like, really stupid." Peter bowed his head further. "And you know, it was my decision. I needed to make the decision, so I did. I need my life, Peter. I need to wait until I'm ready."

"I get it." A double-long bus drove by noisily. Peter waited until it went past to continue. "So, is that it? I mean . . ."

"Yeah, Peter. That's it." Emelie might have been worlds behind Peter in social status and family breeding, but she was miles ahead in maturity. It would serve her so well in her adult life. She had a gut feeling it would. "You know, I'm kinda grateful this happened."

"Wha . . . ?" he asked.

"Yeah. Life lesson, right?"

"I . . . I guess."

"Life lesson. Thanks for that, Peter." Emelie patted his hand and walked away smiling. She was going to be more than okay. She was going to be great.

Chapter 25

"Follow me," directed Sharon. Sashaying in her usual snug black garb today, only the top half of her equally inky hair was piled on her head in a fashionably messy topknot, the rest flowing down her back, silky and expensive. As she brought the party to their table, a middle-aged couple on what looked like an early date—Sharon could always tell by how gussied up they were; longtime couples tended to fall into complacency, not making an effort, after years together—she missed out on the next couple who came through the four-star doors.

"We're looking for Sharon Chin." The officer was plain-clothes, small and compact. His eyes deep and big, his face that of a handsome father and husband with a small house in the Rockaways in Queens. Good-looking, cleaned-up, and innocuous enough to be successful in his department, which required a kind of self-marketing: Vice. He wore his badge on a lanyard; it glinted in the eyes of the second host, a twenty-something light-skinned model with blond dreads and blue eyes, stunned into silence by the badge. He looked over at the other cop. This one was built like an ox, hirsute and bearish. He was unsmiling, his jacket not as on-trend as his partner's. The muscle.

The Adonis-looking host number two pointed behind the officers, not a sound leaving his mouth though it was dropped open. Sharon's head was down, focused on the menus she was organizing in her hands. As she rose toward them on the shallow but wide stone staircase separating the main dining room from the entryway, the officers created a mini phalanx at the top landing. They waited with their hands folded at their fronts, their faces slack, smirking satisfaction at her unknowing approach. Now they just hoped she didn't try to turn and run. Though with her stacked ankle booties and narrow skirt, she'd be lucky to make it as far as the bar.

Sharon finally looked up. She froze as her eyes took in the badges hanging on the officers' chests. In that moment the men saw several looks cross her face as she ran through every option she could think of: *Run. Maybe they're here for someone else. Nope, it's me. My lawyer. My cat. Mom. Run?*

"Sharon Chin," the smaller officer with his pleasant features said. "Come with us."

"What? What is this about?" Sharon did her best to feign her usual snootiness. She was above it all, even this. Her model cohost had shrunk back from the host stand. A few patrons looking to enter worked around the officers, thinking they were only in line. But as they absorbed the air of the scene, they stood back and watched it unfold.

"Come with us." The burlier officer remained silent as his partner continued to patiently nod at their target and tried to wave her along.

"Just let me get my coat," Sharon said as she turned and attempted to make it back down the stairs. Deftly, the handsome officer snatched her thin, CrossFit arm and gripped tight.

"You're coming with us now, okay?"

Sharon looked at him, then his partner, who looked ready to carry her out while leaving bruises on her most valuable asset, her body. But it was the scene she was more concerned about, making a scene. The gravity of her situation sank in. She realized now that it had all caught up to her, and she genuinely wasn't sure who had finally gotten it done.

The officers led her out the door of the restaurant, leaving a buzz of chatter behind them, the management doing damage control, the patrons mostly feeling odd excitement at witnessing a probable arrest, and Adonis still wide-eyed as he was questioned by his manager.

"Sharon Chin, you are under arrest for solicitation and extortion." The handsome officer continued with her Miranda rights as he discreetly handcuffed her, making sure the cuffs did their job despite the tiny wrists they were responsible for holding.

The air was cold and Sharon was sleeveless. She shivered yet burned at the same time. And as she folded herself into the back of the police vehicle for the first time in her life, she kept her head down.

Magda picked up her cell. The number wasn't programmed into her phone for a reason. It was a number that changed every time, yet was always the same person.

"Yeah?" she asked.

"It's done," said a male voice, young and clear.

Magda fell into her office chair. "Are you sure?"

"Arrested at 12:05 p.m. today, taken to midtown precinct and booked. No trace."

"You're sure, no trace?"

"Mags. C'mon. You've just bought me my retirement cabana in Cabo. You're clear. And, you're welcome."

"Thank you." She hung up and dropped the device on her desk, her head falling into her hands. *Thank you, thank you, thank you.* She spoke to herself, to God, to the universe, even to her mother. Her mother, so devoted to Magda despite her culture, her family, her husband telling her to cut her firstborn out of her life because she was gay, who risked the wrath of all to maintain their relationship. They were so close. Magda missed her so much. But Carolina never knew about Magda's illicit activities. She knew about her alcohol troubles, her woman troubles, even, a bit. There was always a rotating band of attractive and intelligent women in and out of Magda's life for stretches of time, her ex-wife included. And as Carolina accepted that her beloved, self-made daughter was all too much like her own husband, Magda's father, a hardworking, alcoholic womanizer, she simply tried to be there for her. Enabling, yes. But it was the string that held Magda's frame together. She didn't know what she would have done without her, how far or not she would have risen or fallen. And now, here, she somehow managed to do it on her own. To not lose herself in the drama. *I'm so sorry, Mami. So sorry for messing up. For risking so much, and the kids, their safety. I miss you.*

And Gabi. Magda thought of her dear friend, who she would always love, though now without the romance. *Poor Gabi.* Magda forgave her quickly for confronting Sharon. That was a move well outside of Gabi's usual rational and professional self, but it spoke to her most irrational and big-hearted self. It felt gallant and ride-or-die. Who could resist that? And then for her to find out that this woman had been somehow connected to her own life? Had been with her ex-husband? *Ay, Dios.* What a mess. Gabi deserved better. She just didn't know it yet. Magda picked up her phone and dialed.

"Gabs? Yeah. It's done. . . . Done. Like, over." Magda paused and sighed. "Gabs . . . Gabriella! We are not going to get into trouble. Okay, stop talking, someone is going to hear you, okay? Let's talk in person, but please, just know that I would never try to fix something by throwing shit on it. You trust me, right? On this, I mean." Magda nodded. "Trust me, Mama. It's over, for good."

What Magda didn't expect was the incredible download of data that her guy managed to pull off Sharon's cache. Before he tipped off the cops, anonymously and untraceably, of course, he swung by to give Magda evidence of just how deep this girl had gotten herself. She had an international billionaire, some big sports stars, and a celebrity or three all tied up in the same situation as Magda. And in comparison to them, Magda was the least interesting of the bunch. And Bert, Gabi's ex, was so low on the hierarchy, he was barely a blip. The odds of the list being leaked to the press were low, as a high-ranking city official was listed as well as a sitting judge. Magda had to admire Sharon's reach and her business savvy in keeping her restaurant job as a cover for her cash deposits. No one knew she wasn't a server in a big-tipping restaurant. And she'd worked out a deal with the manager—who took his cut—to make her bigger blackmail deposits a separate part of the restaurant books. *Smart girl.*

But one thing that all these fellow former clients didn't have was Magda's connections in tech. Magda's hacker pool was small but devoted, and not even her wife or Gabi knew just how deep her reach was, or that they even existed. *Have to make sure things stay that way.*

There was a knock at her office door.

"Hey, Mags. Did that connect work out for you, with getting that information?" A handsome, twenty-something black man with coiffed facial hair, a ubiquitous knit cap, and oversized Run DMC glasses popped his head in.

"Yeah, G, all good. Thanks, man."

"Cool. Cool . . ." He lingered for a moment. "Thanks for taking care of my moms."

Magda smiled. "You're welcome, man. We're solid." *A favor for a favor. Getting rid of one woman, then helping another.*

He smiled back and respectfully closed her door.

We're solid.

Chapter 26

"I do," Cat said, her face radiant, open, and as relaxed as it had ever been.

"By the power vested in me by the state of New York, I now pronounce you man and wife."

Tomas and Cat drew together and kissed. His parents, Roger and Altagracia, clapped and whooped, Altagracia blotting her eyes with tissues as baby Alma began to cry, losing her pacifier. Her grandmother picked it up, stuck it in her mouth to "clean" it off, as *abuelas* tended to do, and then right back in Alma's in between both their sobs.

"Ma! Don't do that!" Tomas broke his focus from his now-wife after catching the unsanitary exchange between his mother and daughter.

"Today, it's okay," Cat said to her husband, the father of her child. She took his face, reaching up to bridge the several inches between them, and squeezed with an "Oooooo!" of excitement. They were both dressed in white, Tomas in a trendy, fitted suit, his smooth, dark brown skin a gorgeous contrast, and Cat had fitted her hair into a messy ponytail, a white feathered hair clip behind her right ear. Her dress was off the rack, spotted in a magazine just a week before. She had arrived with an old white suit jacket hanging off her now-exposed shoulders.

141 Worth Street was a jumble of blended families, couples

waiting to be married in the easiest possible way in the city. The building loomed across the street from City Hall, just off the entrance to the Brooklyn Bridge. The carpet was worn, the halls cold and civilian, the chairs, if swabbed, would be petri dishes of flora left by the people from all places flowing in and out nearly every weekday of the year.

But to Cat, that day it was the Sistine Chapel. She meant it when she said to herself after leaving August's office that she was going to say yes to Tomas. Yes to him, to making a commitment, to marriage. Her mother's backstory had been like a lid on the box in her mind that held the potential for love. Love that was about giving, putting someone else's needs in front of your own sometimes. The lid had felt like it was made of lead, but now that the weight was off, Cat felt clearer than ever. Clear to confront and accept just how much she'd wanted to be married, have a family. To not live in fear of it all going away. Fear that she didn't deserve it. She did deserve it. Not that the universe was fair, or anyone truly deserved anything, but damn it if she was going to look the gift horse of the universe in the mouth anymore. She'd hit a jackpot in her new husband and child and their extended family. You didn't say *no thanks* to a jackpot.

And yes, it stung just a bit that Tomas's parents were there and not her own family. Her mother had been there for every school play, every graduation; she'd even asked to come on the set to witness her first show (however, Cat knew better than to add to the stress of that situation, instead having her there about six months into her run), and those were all accomplishments of some sort. Times in her life when Cat felt like she'd won something. Today was winning, too, but the taste of it, the feeling in Cat's head, was not of any kind of competition or keeping score, it was more meeting her destiny. Being where she was supposed to be and with who she was supposed to be with.

So for the first time, the consistent loneliness of her life felt more like an echo rather than a wet, musty shawl worn day in and day out. That was it. She had a new family. A stable, loving, expansive, multicolored family. Cat looked at her baby girl, Alma, now in her *abuela*'s arms, babbling and gnawing on a teether, her slobber soaking into the front of her white sateen dress. As they moved as a group out of the main room back into the waiting area, Tomas took Alma from his mother's arms, kissed all three of his beloved women, his wife, his baby, and his mother, then hugged his father, Roger, squarely. In that moment, Altagracia took Cat's arm in hers, held her eyes with her own, and said, "*M'ija,* my daughter, you are and always will be a part of this family, and I can't tell you how happy we are to have you and be here for you and have our little Almita!"

"*Ay, gracias,* Alta. It means so much to me." Cat teared up again, radiant with a hint of sadness.

"Family, *nena.* Family." The older woman took Cat's face in her hands and gave her two strong pecks, one on each cheek. "Now, let's get out of here and celebrate—*vámonos!*"

As Tomas, Cat, baby Alma, Roger, and Altagracia walked out of the marble entryway onto the open landing of the building, just before the sidewalk, they spotted more revelers in between the double-wide columns.

"Luuuu!" Cat yelled out to Tomas's sister, now her sister-in-law. Cat's hands were high in the air, one holding her orchid bouquet. Luz came right into her arms.

"You did it! You did it. I love you." She gave Cat celebratory kisses.

Behind Luz, Cat could see her longtime friend's whole family—her kids, her sister, Emelie, and husband, Chris—all grinning and hugging Tomas and trading spaces around Alma, each waiting for their chance to congratulate the bride.

She felt Luz squeeze her shoulder in between hugging Luz's kids. "Cat, there's someone else here to celebrate with you." Cat was confused, and her mind went fuzzy for a moment. She looked in the direction of Luz's nod. A slight, older woman, dressed in a pristine navy skirt suit and white, frilly blouse, hair done—not just done at home in the bathroom mirror, but salon-done—had gotten out of a livery cab. Dolores always was put together and sharp. But what shocked Cat was the combination of extra care plus the look on her mother's face. Instead of her usual pursed, unsatisfied lips and stern, judging brow, she saw a relaxed, grinning face coming toward her.

"Ma," Cat said as her mother came into the celebratory family scrum to embrace her daughter. "Ma." Catalina could hold back no longer as she felt her mother's chest heave in and out with a happy sob. The group around them fell respectfully quiet and formed an unchoreographed circle, with mother and daughter in the middle. They held each other in what felt like a new way, as if the first time again; all the noise of life and the baggage and expectations that lay between them fell aside as their bodies held each other. They were two women who had been through so much, who loved each other so dearly, who they almost never dared to really know for fear of seeing each other's pain.

Dolores pulled herself away just enough to see her daughter's wedding day face. "*M'ija,* I'm so happy for you. Please forgive me." With those words, Cat felt the ground shift. Her mother never apologized. Never admitted a wrong. But Cat knew why now. Her mother had always been protecting herself, too. Born on the defensive, born in the fight mode of fight or flight. Her life in a new country had taught her and rewarded her for keeping her chin up and plowing ahead. She didn't have the luxury of vulnerability that her daughter, the next generation, had and maybe took for granted.

Cat forgot any vanity and let her tears flow. "Mama, always. Always. *Te amo, Mami.*"

"Okay, you two! We still have pictures to take!" Luz interjected gently.

"I know! But, Ma, I have to introduce you to my new husband." Cat reached out and pulled Tomas toward them, her groom sporting a tentative smile. He'd listened for hours to Cat's stories about growing up with Dolores and how and why she needed not to speak to her mother for a while. That was a hard pill for him to swallow, as he couldn't imagine ever doing something like that in his family, but then again, his mother wasn't Dolores—the woman who lost her mind when she found out her daughter was going to have a baby with a black man. This black man.

"*Hola, Señora,*" he said as he held out his hand.

Dolores blinked through her made-up lashes, her eyeliner already smudged from crying and hugging. She took Tomas in, and his family stood in awkward silence. They too knew of Dolores's old-fashioned racism, but Luz had primed them for this surprise of her being there that day. Key now, in terms of how and if they took her in, would be how she would act in this very moment to their son, brother, uncle, husband.

"*Mi yerno,*" Dolores said as she ignored Tomas's hand and went right in for an honest, warm hug. She'd called him son-in-law. The group exhaled, and Luz and Chris clapped with "Yay!" as the children, who had no idea what just happened, joined in.

Tomas was twice the size of Dolores, the petite *Mexicana*. Luz called out, "Wait! Turn around, Dolores! We gotta take *un* photo!" And rather than letting Tomas go completely, Dolores kept her feet firm, just turning to face Luz as Tomas did, with one of his arms still draped across her chest. She smiled broadly. Cat had to laugh. She saw her mother enjoying a handsome man's arms wrapped around her, a family man, her man, and she loved it.

"*Y ahora,* where is *mi nieta?*" Altagracia handed baby Alma to Dolores. Alma with her large, black curls and cocoa skin. The baby cried and they all laughed.

"Okay, people! Let's head to Magda's! We've got a lot more celebrating to do and she's got the space for it—*vamonos!*" Luz waved her arms as if directing a large plane out of a gate. Cat appreciated her taking the lead on all this.

"Thank you, friend. Thank you so much," Cat told her as she shuttled kids into waiting cars.

"Cat, I'm so glad you're happy I did that—I wasn't sure if you would want to kill me, surprising you like this on your big day, but I bumped into her at the market and she asked about you, Mama. She teared up so fast. She missed you so much, and I think seeing me, knowing Tomas is my brother, well, she melted and we were in the frozen food aisle!" The women chuckled. "So we talked for a bit and then she mentioned that you had visited and she'd hoped she'd see you again soon. And silly me, I then go and invite her to this, but Cat, I can't even explain to you, her face was like beatific, went all touched by the Holy Spirit of joy and shit—but I made her promise that she would behave and be nothing but a positive part of this day. And she swore to me—I made her swear on Our Lady of Guadalupe, for reals!"

Cat laughed. "Well, that'll work."

"It did. Are you mad?"

Cat smiled. "Nah. Thank you."

"Whew! I'm so relieved. Okay, now, let's see how the rest of the day goes. In the meantime, congratulations, sister. Welcome— officially—to the family."

Chapter 27

Magda watched her father warmly embrace his newest friends, Altagracia and Roger. She had to chuckle to herself. *The old racist bastard. How much you're enjoying living in my world now.* She felt a slight touch of told-you-so as she nudged her righteousness to the side to keep room in her heart, now filled with the joy of the day. Cat and Tomas's mini reception was just coming together, and though Magda had a few agendas for the next couple of hours, she wanted to first fill everyone's bellies, and then their hearts with happiness.

"Chaos! Happy chaos!" Gabi hollered as she came down the hall with her dapper Max. The boy was outfitted in full Brooklyn-dandy gear, his bow tie just right and his mass of light curls piled high.

"Is that gel in your hair, Maxi?! What's your mama doin' to you, *precioso?*" Magda scooped him up and gave him a big smooch.

"*Tía* Mags, I got my first progress report!" he told her as he held her face in his small hands.

"Oh, really? And how did you do, *hombre?*"

"Nailed it!" Max pumped his fist.

"That's my boy! Love you, munchkin." Magda beamed as she sat him down. He ran away quickly to see his cousins. Gabi decided early on that her closest friends, particularly Magda, were all *tías,* and their kids were therefore Max's cousins. As a single mom with family scattered afar over the country, it gave her the ability to cocoon her son with the feeling of close family. This was the family that Gabi chose, for her and for Max.

"*Hola, chica,*" Gabi said as she greeted Magda. The women held a lot between them that everyone else in the room didn't know about. "So, it's real?"

"It's real, hon. She's gone for a very long time." Magda spoke quietly, though not quietly enough to raise any suspicions that they were trading secrets. She'd catch someone's eye every minute or so and smile.

"You okay?" Gabi asked.

"Of course. Now, much better than okay," Magda said. "And you should be okay, too, right?"

"I am. Just nervous about things getting out."

"Look, I couldn't tell you anywhere but offline, but trust me—the people on her lists ran so high and deep that you and I don't even register."

Gabi paused a moment, her basest side wanting to dish on who those folks were, but as someone who was paid to keep secrets and trust, she knew that wasn't going to happen. "And what about all this getting traced back to you? The illegality of it?"

Magda sighed, praying for patience with a nontech. "Hon. Not. Happening." She put her fingers together in a pyramid. "Only the best, Gabs. I deal with only the best. Plus, money sometimes takes care of things."

"Well, you've got a lot of that." Gabi looked at the apartment's expansive view. "I'm so relieved." She had to trust her friend. "And you forgive me, right?"

"More than forgiven." Magda smiled. "Can we party now?" Gabi nodded. "Gabs, get your ass over there and hang with my wife and our lovely newlyweds, okay?"

"Done." Gabi moved right into the scrum.

"Speaking of money . . ." Cat approached Magda, catching the last part of their conversation over the din of the party.

"Okay, girl, you are uncanny with your abilities," Magda teased.

"I know, so don't mess with the master."

"You mean, the Mrs.—am I right?!"

"Ugh. That was bad."

"So why are you blushing?"

Cat smiled as Luz joined in. "So, I don't even get to hear from my friend about this whole shebang, I have to hear it from my brother!"

"Well, it was kind of quick!" Cat defended herself.

"Humph. Not on my watch," Luz said.

"Yeah. Yeah," Cat demurred.

"So, Catalina. What happened with the tech bro rollin' in dough?" Magda asked.

Luz made a face of distaste. "Ugh. Do I have to be here for this? I don't wanna."

"Stay here! Stay here!" Cat held Luz's arm and pulled her back around. Gabi caught the gathering and pulled herself away from the milling family to join her friends gathered close to the kitchen island.

"Quick, before we get separated," Gabi said.

"Well, you guys know about the ring, right?" Cat asked.

"That's some fucked up shit right there," Magda said as she took a sip of her soda water and the other ladies nodded in agreement.

"I went to his office and told him off and told him to stay away," Cat explained.

"How'd that go?" Gabi asked.

"Um, not so well. He actually showed me a side of him that, well . . . Let's just say that I dodged a bullet."

"Oh, he cray? *Un loco?*" Magda cut through to the heart of the matter. Gabi squirmed at Magda's use of psychological labels.

"You mean, like violent? Or threatening?" Gabi asked.

"I'll tell you more later," Cat said. "Let's just leave it at I chose the right guy." She looked over at Tomas, covered with children climbing over his lanky frame like a jungle gym. "There's not enough money in the world to replace this."

"No. No, there isn't," Gabi agreed, slightly envious of Cat's situation. She wanted a husband badly, always had, if only to have a family with, not for any reason regarding support or fitting into society. She had just wanted a family, that's all, one of her own. A family that stayed together. A partner who was a real partner, 'til the end. She had chosen the wrong person. One day, she hoped for the opportunity to choose the right one. There was no malice toward her celebrating friend, just a pang of hope. Gabi focused on that hope. Cat had gone years with no one, and here she was, with a young husband and beautiful baby girl. *Life is good. And one day it will be good for me again.* Gabi looked at her Max, as she stroked baby Alma's face lovingly. *Oh, my heart. Maybe one day.*

"What changed your mind, *chica?*" Magda asked. Cat looked at her a bit quizzically. "I mean, we know you love him dearly. We can see that." Magda gestured toward Cat's glowing face. "But you were always so scared of this."

"Yeah, well, coming from you, Ms. Not Ever Scared!" Cat had to dig at Magda's love of marital commitment if not actual sexual commitment.

"Ha, ha," Magda deadpanned. Gabi and Luz chuckled.

The women watched Cat look over at her mother, Dolores. The sixty-something *abuela* was talking with Emelie and seemed engaged with the teen. Luz had to give Emelie credit for being a teenager who could smile and have polite conversation with a senior citizen she'd just met. Both Luz and Cat were feeling the same sentiment about the conversation: *Bravo.* Bravo to Dolores for engaging with her new family. Bravo to Emelie for holding her own with her new family.

"I had a big conversation with Ma," Cat said. Her friends waited for more, but Cat gave them nothing.

"That must have been a big conversation, since you're not exactly brimming forth with details," Magda said.

"Yeah." Cat dropped her head modestly. "It was so hard to do it, but it really cleared up a lot for me. And look, I'll admit it—Luz, cover your ears here." Her friend pretended to do just that but rolled her eyes in defiance. "Hearing Dolores talk about why we ended up alone for so long and then all that stuff with August, well, everything became just crystal. And really, I just became so grateful for what I have. Kind of like when the show went away and I had to face myself—what did I really want to do? That August stuff and talking with my moms, I faced the question of who do I want around me? What do I value and frankly, who values—truly values—me." The women stood silent, smiling. Cat shrugged.

"And here you are, *nena,* here you are!" Magda outstretched her arms to encompass the big, wide room filled with love and music. The couple of young servers helping out with food and drink were even smiling as they eavesdropped. Then Altagracia and Roger starting bringing the staff into their conversations, asking about where they were going to school, what their life plans were, brightening their workday immeasurably.

In the hallway bathroom, Cherokee, Magda's wife, tapped her shiny nose with a piece of tissue paper and took one last look at herself in the mirror, pulling out a few of her twists for balance. The big family picture was coming up next and she wanted to look her best. Assured that at least she looked presentable, she looked down at her simple but fitted olive green halter-top dress, the same color as the cargo pants she wore when she first met her wife, then opened the door without looking.

Cherokee's forehead met with Raoul's chin, as he was standing just outside the door.

"*Oof!*"

"Oh! Oh my God, *Señor!* Are you okay?" she cried out.

"Oh, *ay, sí,* I'm okay. I think." Raoul held his chin. He'd been coming down the hall to use the bathroom himself, but both had their attention fixed elsewhere.

"I'm sorry, so sorry," she said.

"No, no that's okay. I was looking at the kids."

Cherokee was concerned as Raoul patted his chin gently and then looked at Cherokee's head to make sure she was fine as well.

"You are good, Cherokee?"

Magda's wife was taken aback by her father-in-law's concern. She'd spent months trying to get him to give her the time of day. She worked regular hours with her studies, but as Magda sometimes clocked sixty-plus hours a week, Cherokee often found herself alone in the apartment with him. He mostly went out during the day and spent his nights watching shows in his room or talking on the phone to his other kids and friends back in Miami. Or, at least that was what Cherokee assumed from his tone and Spanish. She didn't speak it, but she was learning.

"Yes. I'm good, Raoul. Thanks for asking."

They stood awkwardly for a beat. It seemed to her that he wanted to say something. Instead of looking toward the bathroom, where he'd been headed, he kept looking down the hall anxiously.

"Um, you're good, Raoul?" she asked after him again.

At last he looked toward her, his handsome face now less tan than before but more regal, with a well-coiffed silver beard. His eyes brightened.

"Cherokee." His accent made her name sound much more like *dere-OH-kee.* "I . . . I just want to say that I'm sorry."

She looked at him, questioning. Didn't they just exchange apologies? What was this about? "*Señor?*"

"You're my child's wife, yes?"

"Um, yes."

"Well, I don't think I've treated you as well as I should . . . considering we are family."

"Oh!"

"Look." He cleared his throat and looked back down the hall at the happy hubbub of three generations. "This time here, with Magdalena, with you and, well, all these people," he gestured down the hall, "I'm realizing a lot of things."

"Okay." Cherokee was still a bit on guard. He'd hurt her feelings deeply, particularly the first few months. She knew the stories Magda would tell her about how he'd treated her after she came out and the many times Magda's mother would cry into her arms about another infidelity.

"I know I'm an old man—"

"Now, *Señor*—"

"Yes, yes, I'm an old man!"

Cherokee nodded and let him finish.

"But, I'm learning. I'm learning. I just hope it's not too late." His eyes seemed sincere, and Cherokee was satisfied by his admission to the process of change. He had been humbled by all that had hit him late in life, the loss of his wife, his practice, his home. Admitting that he was doing something about his old ways boded much better to Cherokee than just an apology. It meant that he knew he had work to do. That was heavy.

"Raoul, that's the great thing about life. It's never too late."

Simultaneously, the two of them who both loved Magda embraced for a moment, warmly. Cherokee pulled back a bit, not wanting to linger too much on this happy time lest it run away from them, and asked, "Didn't you need to use this bathroom?"

"Ah! Yes, yes. Thank you," he said, and walked in.

As the door closed, Cherokee reminded him, "*Señor*, be quick! They're setting everyone up for the family picture!"

★ ★ ★

"C'mon people! C'mon!" Back in the living room in front of the six-foot-wide fireplace, all white marble and modernist, Luz was doing her usual wrangling of the clans. Her children, as they did, listened and calmly fixed each other's hair. Little Max was a bit more of a struggle.

"Maxi! Stay still! Stop playing with her bow," Gabi scolded. Max was tweaking baby Alma's bow and bopping her nose like she was his own personal doll.

"I'm coming! We're coming!" Cherokee assured the family and the photographer, a quiet sort gently holding folks by their arms to guide them closer for the shot.

"Where's *Papi?*" Magda called out.

"Oh, he's just coming from—"

"*Aquí!* Here," Raoul muttered as the photographer pointed where he should stand. He smiled broadly and proudly between his daughter, her children, and her wife. He put one arm each around Magda and Cherokee.

The rainbow of friends and family, Cat and Tomas in the middle with Alma, did not need to be told to smile. Each and every one seemed to feel the power of the day. The bonds that had long been present had been made stronger, and the new ones formed were treasured.

The photographer was ready. "Family, let's do this! Say cheese!"

The Tucker, Lee, Gomez, Reveron, and Rivera families had something else in mind:

"*Queso!*"

NEVER TOO LATE

Carmen Rita

About This Guide

The suggested questions are included
to enhance your group's reading of
Carmen Rita's *Never Too Late*.

Discussion Questions

1. What do you think about Cat's fears of getting married to Tomas? Are they justified?

2. Would you have made the same decision Magda does, to take in her father and help him after he'd disowned her? If no, why not?

3. Do you see disadvantages to Gabi's tendency to always want to help? How does her role as a "caretaker" to her friends and fans possibly get in the way? Or does it not?

4. What is your take on Cat's impressions of August Tilly? Does she have a chip on her shoulder, and if so, do you think it's warranted?

5. If you had been in Luz's place, how would you feel about the discovery of her sister's secret? Would anger have played a bigger role in your feelings?

6. What would you have done in Cat's place when she meets August in his office for the first time? How would your response to him differ from hers?

7. How is meeting Maxwell useful for Gabi? Do you think he is genuine? Or is he just using her for advice?

8. How does Magda's father, Raoul, make such a turnaround in his relationship with his daughter? If you were one of Magda's siblings, how would you feel about it?

9. Luz seems patient with Cat's refusal to commit to Tomas. How would your relationship with a close friend change if she had a child or was in a relationship with a brother or sister of yours?

10. Have you experienced a parent being severely disappointed with your choice of a romantic partner because of race or ethnicity, like Dolores is with Cat or in the way Raoul struggles with Magda's wife? How did you manage it compared to Cat and Magda?

11. Is Magda correct in potentially breaking the law by arranging for Sharon to be hacked? Do you think she weighs the risks well, or do you think she is able to play by a different set of rules because of her wealth?

12. What do you think of Emelie's decision in the end? What would you have done if you had been Luz?

If you enjoyed *Never Too Late,*
be sure not to miss Carmen Rita's

NEVER TOO REAL

Cat, Magda, Gabi, and Luz: They've helped each other up the ladder with unshakable encouragement—and raw honesty—since forever. But lately, trouble is throwing everything these formidable women thought they knew into doubt.

When outspoken Cat's high-flying TV career crashes and burns, she's got to figure out which dream she wants to keep alive the most—her own, or someone else's.

Gorgeous venture capitalist Magda defied her traditional family to make her own way—in her personal life and her career—but an unexpected crisis could finally shatter her chance to resolve the past.

As a therapist, sensitive, supportive Gabi has all the answers. But when her own world falls apart, can she turn her compassion—and her trademark tough love—on herself?

And proud, wealthy Luz thought she knew everything about her upper-class family background—until a revelation she never saw coming threatens to be the one legacy she can't afford.

Now all four women will have to face the truths that make them vulnerable and the failings that give them strength to discover who they really are—and what real happiness means.

Keep reading for a special look!
A Kensington trade paperback and e-book on sale now!

Chapter 1

Never forget how far you've come.

This was Catalina Rosa Rivera's mantra, one she whispered to herself for the hundredth time as she made her way through the behind-the-scenes maze on the set of her television show. The stomp of her faux-lizard heels echoed against the walls of particle board surrounding her, an embrace of corners and wiring. Catalina's pace was more brisk and the grip on her blue-card notes tighter today. She was ready. At least she looked ready, war paint and all. Just an hour earlier the show's makeup artist, sensing bad juju, gave her extra body armor with a full strip of fake lashes, crimson lips, and hair sprayed into architecture.

Turning the bend into the hot spotlight on her desk, Cat, as she was known to her national viewing audience, ran fingers across her teeth to remove any stray lipstick. As she came into view of the show's staff and her guests, she instinctively replaced her clomping elephant gait with a more appropriate, professional stride.

The one-hour show was mapped out, no big changes in format or topic. But the tension on set was viscous. Usually self-assured, Cat's hands began to tremble in a combination of anxiety and relief. As her wide, dark eyes shifted from commanding her hands to be still to looking up at her set with the broad-smiling mask of a professional national television host, she was now 100 percent sure that the end of her time as the captain of this TV news ship was on the horizon. Despite solid ratings, the signs were stark—the shakiness of the economy, the migration of eyeballs from TV to the Web, the loss of nearly half the usual advertising revenue. All business reasons, money reasons. And she had heard and seen the buzz around the halls and blogs, the mass layoffs and cancellations at other networks.

It's just a matter of time. And it's not my fault . . . Right?

Painfully, the strongest confirmation of her cancellation instincts was personal. The once-enthusiastic head of her department had stopped returning her calls, or picking them up at all. And just two days ago, she had received the most passive-aggressive form of communication of all, a sin of omission. Cat was left off the invitation to a regular staff meeting, changed from its usual time without her knowledge. She was *always* in her staff meetings. She was not only the host of the show, but the co-creator. Nail in coffin.

Stab me in the front, people. I can take it. I prefer it.

"Hey, baaaybays!" She greeted her set crew as if all were well.

These were guys you'd see at the local pub, biker tees, baseball caps, and, for the most part, warm smiles. Only one didn't smile. The steady-cam guy. A burly, military-cut, late-thirties, bearded blond, he erased his grin in response to Cat's. All had been well with the whole on-set team of sound and camera crew, and there was a solid teasing camaraderie among a bunch of fairly macho males and Cat's big-sister persona. That was until the new steady-cam guy arrived. At first, he folded in nicely. Then he made an amateur mistake—he took Cat's kindness and joviality during commercial breaks for weakness. He began to talk over her and disregard her need for quiet when time got tight—this was a live show, where one second could mean the camera catching an errant gesture or expression that could mar a career. Or, she'd just be thrown off and mess up. Cat may not have been the boss behind the scenes, but damn well she was the boss on the set. It was her face, her name, her career on the line. She needed some deference, some respect. After gently asking the new guy to cool it a few times on set, and receiving no compliance in return, Cat had turned to his boss, her director. Since he spoke to the yapper, all Cat got from behind the steady-cam that trailed her every move was a steely glare.

Fuck him.

"Hey, girl . . . Sup," the rest of the crew replied with a bit less enthusiasm these days.

Hip-hop thumped through the speakers at Cat's request. It helped her gear up just before going live. Out of respect for her usually non-urban guests, it was usually the clean, radio version, but sometimes words leaked through that jarred James Taylor–trained ears.

"I'm young, bitches . . ." Jay-Z's voice threw out over the speakers.

"Ayyy yay yay, guys! Shhhhhhh . . ." Cat's blue-manicured hand gestured her sound team to turn the music down as she shimmied onto her stool, skirt tight, bottom round. She aligned her Spanxed navel up to the ragged snip of black duct tape stuck to the glass desk's edge, marking her spot. The rap faded quickly.

"We're gonna scare our guests . . ." She threw a diplomatic, soothing smile toward her anxious desk companions, her head swinging back to the script notes set down swiftly in front of her by an intern seconds before. "Thanks, hon—can you snag me an extra water, too, please? I'm parched." Cat could usually make it through a show on one network-logoed mug of water, but tonight her mouth was as dry as a bag of saltines. *I wish this was tequila.* She smacked her lips quietly thinking of the sour, strong, mind-numbing taste she'd rather have in her mouth.

The show's guests shifted; Cat watched them out of the corner of her eye. For every show she noted like an interrogator which one seemed eager or excited, which was potentially hostile, and which was just shitting his pants because it was his first time on live television. She knew their bios, but they were all newbies to her set. Bringing in fresh talent after so long seemed also ominous, rather than bringing in her regular superstars or potential new hosts. Maybe they were trying to kill some ratings so they could blame Cat for the show's demise. Or, maybe they just didn't give a crap anymore and they were saving their energy for what's next.

I'll go with option two.

Cat winked at her floor crew, ignoring the steady cam. She then turned to her three suited, very pale, and very male guests sitting to her left. Knowing that jittery guests don't make the best guests, Cat considered it her job as host of this fiesta of folly to put everyone at ease.

"Sorry about the music, guys. Gotta go with the PG version, right?"

"Yeah, I'm more of a James Taylor kind of guy myself," said the rosacea-faced fund manager directly to her right, as he tightened his tie.

Cat narrowed her eyes and took a moment to discern if he was being antagonistic and condescending or was simply an uncomfortable Boomer.

Boomer.

"I think I've heard of him," she responded, within her sweet grin a teenager's eye roll at a dorky father.

The men and crew smiled while Mr. Red Face blushed further, charmed. Cat was charismatic and beautiful, powerful weapons in her day-to-day battles, particularly in the finance industry she covered, where an attractive woman's presence had the power to throw men off their game. Her black hair glistened in the robust lights, its glossiness brushing her shoulders and her skin just bronze enough to make clear her non-Anglo-Saxon heritage. As news television dictated, she was "dressed as a crayon," encased in a cerulean blue dress assigned with the job of making her "pop" on screen, while also making her gender clear.

Now, it was time to make some TV.

In rare form, Cat barreled through the first half of the show. Not one to reveal what was behind her eyes, her anger at all that was going unspoken between her higher-ups and their host had a way of focusing Cat, giving her a buzz—it was fuel. Anger and self-righteousness had always been something for her to run on. The pattern was set when her drunk, absentee father left her and her mother broke and on their own when she was six. She'd show him. She'd show them. Cat knew her bosses were watching—thousands were watching. She channeled ire into spunk.

"I'm sorry, what?" Cat asked sharply during a commercial break.

She was speaking into the air, not to her guests. Cat received feedback from the control room directly into her ear, plus notes on upcoming segments. Her producers and director watched her through the cameras facing her, as the audience did, but from the control room on another floor. In many ways, hosting a show was like driving a fast, expensive car. There were pricy parts and pieces, and all had to work smoothly. But in the end, the host worked the clutch, gearing up, gearing down.

Cat worked hard to focus, to package up the ugly feelings caught in her throat, to not let them see. As no one on the set with her, including her guests, could hear what she was hearing in her earpiece when the control room was speaking to her, it appeared to newbies as if she was just lost in thought, silent during the break. So, she was often interrupted.

"Cat, so, are you really Spanish?" It was the Red Boomer again, directly to Cat's left, whispering to her. She drew a deep breath and straightened her back as she remembered that this one had flown himself in his own plane from Salt Lake City to be on the show.

Mr. Carbon Footprint, James Taylor–listening, old man . . . I'll give you a Utah pass on this one.

Without moving her eyes from her script, Cat responded

coolly, albeit politely. " 'Spanish?' Do you mean, am I Hispanic?" She offered up a side-eye.

He nodded. "Yeah."

She nodded back, now looking at him head-on. "Yes, Bob. I'm Hispanic. Not Spanish."

Even though she answered his question, his expression became confused.

"Wow. You're so smart!"

I can't even . . .

Cat's executive producer came into her ear and teased her about the ad-libbed outro to the last segment, a ditty she made up about the LIBOR, the most boring yet important interest rate in town.

She busted his chops back through her mic, then ran through some time cues with him. "Yup . . . okay . . . sure." She was grateful he was such a good guy.

"Hey, guys?" She decided to take advantage of her guests yabbering among themselves to talk directly to her control room team and riff off the un-PC item they'd just heard. "Um, so, is Rich really a Canadian?" Cat envisioned the room chuckling. "Rich, seriously. I mean, I heard the rumors, but I had no idea!" She gestured to the plug in her ear. "Like, there's a Canadian in my ear . . . and he's so smart!"

Rich opened her ear feed so she could hear the laughter wrapped in relief from behind the scenes in the control room. This "Are you Spanish/Hispanic?" comment was the second one that week alone, and it made everyone uncomfortable. Cat was proudly her brown self and for the most part, her staff was young and savvy and her Canadian head was, well, Canadian. He knew what was up. Her first year they made it a mock drinking game. Every time a guest (usually male, usually white, over forty) asked her to confirm or not "what" she was, Cat would look into camera one, her main communiqué to her team in the control room, point, and say, "Drink!" The guest doing the asking had no idea why she was responding that way. Unfortunately, it happened so often, the joke got old, so Cat found new ways to play off of it. To remove the sting.

Twelve minutes and twenty-one seconds later, the show was done. Cat shimmied off her stool, attempting to keep her mummy-band dress in one piece. Curvy girls and high stools: a challenge.

"Bye, guys. Thanks for coming. You were great." The host gave an adept smile to each guest, made solid eye contact, and shook their hands with an authoritative grip, even one for Mr. Utah. Cat thought each time she encountered someone like him, maybe she'd opened some minds today, solved some problems. Maybe.

"Hey, Cat . . ." Rich, her head producer, was back in her earpiece.

Cat sighed. "Whassup?"

A female sound engineer worked to unhook Cat's mic from inside her dress without flashing anyone, turning her into a brief contortionist.

Rich's pause in response lasted a beat too long. "You . . . uh, you gotta head up to Heather's office. Now."

"Oh, hi. Hi. Come in, come in. Sit down." Heather Kraven, the head of the division, Cat's top boss who didn't answer her calls anymore, was in hyper mode, squawking like a caged macaw. Her boho blouse sleeves fluttered with her arms like wilted, feeble wings. Cat noted the usual presence of a pink Pepto bottle on her desk. Heather had built a hit show for the network five years earlier and had tried and failed ever since to recreate that same magic. She took out all her impotence on the staff, particularly the on-air talent.

"Hi." Cat seated herself, keeping Heather in the corner of

her eye as the producer passed behind her to close the door. Cat imagined she caught a whiff of sulfur and sickness behind the musk oil.

"Well, so . . ." Heather sat hunched forward across her desktop, clasping her aged hands punctuated with short, unpolished, chewed nails. She forced a Cheshire smile but offered no eye contact, her skin lacking maintenance and revealing too many late nights, long days, and bad food choices. "We really wanted to tell you before it hit the *Post* in the morning . . ."

"The *New York Post*?" Cat tendered a false grin, her eyes thinned in suspicion.

"Well . . ."

In Heather's two-second pause, Cat quickly summed up her hunches: *She's already leaked whatever she's about to tell me to the* Post. *Jesus Christ.* Cat sucked her teeth, raised her brows.

"Yah?" she prompted.

Heather, a normally intense, in-your-face boss, couldn't meet her eyes. "We've had to cancel the show." She put her thumb to her mouth, taking her nail between her front teeth, making a sucking sound as she then pulled it away.

Yuck.

"Really?" Cat continued to grin, this time bizarrely, honestly. A bubbly feeling brewed inside of her; she felt her forehead relaxing for the first time in, well, a long time. It was a sensation Cat would have to work out, because it was surprising her.

She locked her eyes on Heather, moving away from the pleasant feelings inside, toward sealing the deal of the business. "But wait, didn't you say just a couple of months ago that I saved your contract—your job?" Heather pursed her lips like a politician—*I can neither confirm nor deny* . . . Cat continued. "You were thanking me for that. And we beat Joe's show twice a week." A blowhard who resembled a hobbit, Joe was the "star" Heather took credit for having created years earlier. He'd taken a hit in the ratings lately—but then again, everyone had, as

TV continued to bleed revenue like a lanced sow. "So how's this happening?" Cat asked.

Heather nodded, mulling her response, still not looking Cat in the eye. She absentmindedly rubbed her stomach and glanced at the constant bottle of pink elixir in front of her. Looked like she needed some.

"We took a big chance on you, and we gave you a lot of time. And it was good! We did good!" Heather's arms fluttered again.

She looks like a crow about to steal my lunch.

"So, then . . . what was it?" Cat aimed her focus on leaving the office with answers and she was determined not to allow even a glimpse of feisty stereotype into the room.

"Listen, we probably overestimated what kind of audience you could bring." Heather shrugged.

"What do you mean?"

"Y'know, the numbers were there and we really had hoped for a new—more—demographic . . ." This reveal turned Heather into a babbling faucet. "And the whole, y'know, AltaVision thing was something we really needed." AltaVision was the network's Spanish-language partner and one of the only spots where business growth was happening.

"AltaVision? Listen, I never once said I would go on TV speaking Spanish. You didn't even bring it up in negotiations."

"Well, y'know, we tried, we tried with the show. But, well, it's in the paper tomorrow so . . ." Heather was done. She threw up her hands in surrender.

The abrupt end caught up to Cat. Maybe four minutes had passed since she'd sat down. "Wait—so that's it? We're dark? That show—the one we just taped—was my last one?"

Cat could not believe her eyes as she watched the once-fawning Heather, the Heather who'd wanted to hang out and gossip about who's-dating-who or who would slap Cat's back with joy about their ratings, instead end their relationship by standing up and stepping forward from behind her desk, toward the door. Cat was being ushered out.

Business is business.

"I'm afraid so. It's done," Heather said coldly as she lumbered behind Cat and opened the office door. Heather's two research minions stood waiting on the other side. Armed with new reports, surely, on what people wanted to see next, or whom.

Wow. Great choreography, Cat thought.

These two were also Cat's enthusiastic allies only months ago, but now the two small men mumbled hellos and couldn't meet her eyes. She was tempted to turn back toward the office and yell with pointed finger at Heather, to remind her how recently she had been the one crying gratefully to Cat as the show's numbers had saved her job. But that was then. This was now. And now, as humiliated and steamed as Cat was, she was all too curious about the feeling of joy ruffling her feathers inside, beckoning her to come closer and away from these people.

Numbly, Cat walked back to her desk, back straight. As the only brown girl in her private school growing up, the scholarship girl, she had learned how to silo herself in, to protect herself with a psychic bubble. And she was not going to let this be a walk of shame. In her head, she fell onto another mantra that helped her when she was ostracized as a kid: "Fuck 'em."

It took fifteen years post-college for Cat to scale her way up from intern to local news producer to, with little on-air experience, host of a national cable news show on screens big and small, five days a week. With this network she'd also packed in hundreds of supporting appearances on its highest-rated national morning show, the local news outlet, online post-show shows, blogs, vlogs, and evenings hosting philanthropic events—a thousand smiles delivered, one after another. She'd been featured in dozens of magazines and even had an Ivy League degree. Internally, as she walked with concentration, Cat recited her accomplishments, the lines in her bio, one with each stride. Reviewing all she'd come through, all she'd accomplished functioned like a vaccine. It stopped her from feeling small. From letting her circumstances determine her self-worth.

But as Cat got to the back elevator, stepping in, rather than taking the main staircase in view of the whole newsroom, other thoughts began to seep in, dark thoughts. She was alone. She'd had no other life. No child. No spouse. No siblings. Just a suffocating, overbearing mother. So focused on accomplishing, building herself and her career, she hadn't slept in years—hadn't gotten laid in at least two. What had she done? What was she going to do? What was next?

Though Cat knew it was only an excuse, Heather said that the cancellation of her show had depended on one thing: Cat hadn't brought in the hoped-for Hispanic demographic. Sure, Cat wished she were fully bilingual, but an absent father and a mother obsessed with her daughter being as "American" as possible, aka Anglo, white—add that to a New England education and the odds had been stacked against her. But no Latina whom Cat knew in the business was fully bilingual either. Which meant that you were either AltaVision material or SBC network material. The network had assumed that Cat, a gesticulating second-generation Mexican-American, would appear on their sibling network in Spanish. They hadn't even mentioned it to her agent two years previous when they'd plucked her from her brief correspondent gig at a rival network. What, did they think she'd crossed the border yesterday? Stereotyping was just too easy for these people. This mistake had been costly for everyone.

Cat's English-only policy came through the first week of taping when she was asked to appear on AltaVision to promote her new show.

"I don't speak Spanish on air."

"What do you meeeeean you don't speak Spanish on air?" Heather had wailed, grabbing at her parched hair as she paced her office.

"But—but you're Hispanic!" From the couch along one wall of Heather's office, the muscled, miniature research director croaked.

"And?" Cat replied with a smile, doing her best to make light of what she realized was a lose-lose situation. "We don't all speak Spanish that well, you know. More than half of us don't. I was born here, just like you." She turned to the bald research director with an Italian last name. "Can you speak Italian?" He averted his eyes. She continued. "I can talk to relatives and give people directions on the subway, but I'm certainly not going on TV with it."

The room went silent. One side was panicking at their mistake. The other, recalling many mistakes along the way, including being forced to take eight years of French in school.

Approaching her pod of cubicles, after what felt like a long walk through the desert, Cat found her staff quiet. She realized that they were probably all out of work, too—or, hopefully, just reassigned. She wouldn't be. She was now an embarrassment to the network. The Great Brown Hope who failed them. She kept her head down, maintaining face.

Rich, the Canadian, popped up by her side as she dropped into her chair, the cubicle walls shielding her from sight. "Cat, I'm so sorry."

Without looking up, Cat replied, "I'm sorry, too."

She hustled phone chargers into her bag and grabbed a favorite coffee mug. Behind her hung a poster made of a national full-page ad created for the show, Cat's face and body taking up two-thirds of the space, her arms folded for authority. Heather said that poster was to go up in Times Square. Well, that wasn't happening. The image already felt nostalgic. "I gotta go. Can we talk later?" Cat needed to clear her head. She wasn't close to breaking down, she was just roiling inside, still baffled by the murmuring of glee vibrating in her gut. She couldn't meet his eyes.

"Yeah, yeah, sure . . ." He sidestepped her gently. "Just call me, okay?" Rich was legitimately concerned for Cat, but he also had to deal with the rest of their staff, and his own future.

"Yup, I'll call ya." Cat, shifting a packed bag onto her shoulders, put out her hand for a shake.

Rich took it and sighed.

One more walk down the halls. At least for today.

She'd come back for everything else, her clothes, her handwritten notes from grateful guests. Cat still had time on her contract, and they'd surely find a way to make their money off of her once the fog cleared. She'd be back in some capacity, she hoped. But as Cat strolled out, lighter this time, not one person looked up—she was an instant nobody. Folks who always had time to throw out a "Hey, C!" her way kept their heads down, watching her out of the sides of their eyes. Protective bubble in place, all Cat could think was, *Everyone knew but me.*

Chapter 2

"No POTUS today? Not even FLOTUS?" The deep voice belonged to a tall, slim woman with a Leonardo DiCaprio haircut circa *Basketball Diaries,* standing ardently dapper in a custom-fitted, designer pantsuit. Magdalena Sofia Carolina Reveron de Soto not only cut a sharp, gender-bending figure in the room—contrasting with the handful of women around her who glistened in colorful dresses and jewelry—she was the only blue-eyed blonde, male or female, in a sea of brown and black faces.

Magda, as she preferred, was mingling among the bustle of handpicked business-owning insiders jammed into the concrete meeting room in the Executive Building of the White House. The president's head of minority investment, a *dulce de leche* thirty-something who matched Magda in height, gave her a macho backslap in greeting. "Sorry, girl. Ghanaian president was here and the meeting took too long."

Magda leaned back at his "girl" but patted his arm with affection. She needed him on her side for some pending deals. "African-American president pushes blacks and Latinos off the sched for an African president . . . Ha! Funny. How've you been, man?" As she asked, Magda scanned the room, everyone on break between the day's sessions, looking for opportunities. Always lookin'.

"Y'know, good. All good. And how about this thing, right?" He swept his hand across the chamber in which, rumor had it, Thomas Jefferson preferred to hold his summer meetings thanks to the room's concrete coolness. "We cannot go wrong with the people in this room."

The White House's chief technology officer, communications director, and chef had just left the stage. Gathered for the full day, among rows of red velvet chairs, were fifty well-groomed bodies, nearly all of color. One-third of the room was female—black, Latina, and a smattering of Asian. The men were the same mix, including a stately turbaned Sikh. And then there was Magda.

Magda's appearance was a natural calling card in the room. She was a sunny-haired, butch, self-made multimillionaire lesbian with an enviable effect: She glowed with money, success, and charisma. Groomed by her Miami-based Venezuelan family to be a beauty queen, Magda was instead the irresistibly handsome king of her domain. Her face model-like, with makeup and a dress she would have slain the straight male half of the room. But that would be wearing a costume. Magda had much more swagger sans feminine packaging because she presented herself as herself. Besides, she was a devoted lady-killer.

"Magda! Hey, guuurl. Have you met Dev yet?" Kristina Jo, her face framed with a lion's mane of curly, ebony Caribbean hair, her pantsuit fighting her curves, was the chattiest master-connector presidential appointee in D.C. Hustle skills honed in the Bronx, Kristina spent the next several minutes swinging her friend and ally, Magda, around, showing her off to the room.

Nearly everyone present knew Magda's name, if not the face of the richest, independent, minority venture capitalist in the United States, possibly the world. She purposefully had no press, all the knowledge mostly built word of mouth. Having been in the closet until college, Magda was in the habit of conducting business close to the vest—all business. Everyone was thrilled to be introduced to Magda, from the African head of Facebook global, the Latina officer at Twitter . . . she'd make their follow-up lists at a ninety percent rate. The other ten percent would miss a gravy train. Magda had made much of her money early on, wrangling wise, front-end moves in social media and green energy. Her mind raced at a quantum rate and she preferred to operate without waste—every minute had a reason, every hour something to be done.

"Kristina, hon, I've got to check this e-mail." Magda squinted at her cell. "What's with the lack of service down here? It's like a bunker in eighteen fifty. Shit."

Kristina's face dropped, but relit quickly. "Okay, listen, just ooooone small favor. The White House press corps is interviewing folks here on the event. Can you *por favor* do one in Spanish, too? There's one other person in this room who speaks—"

"Fine, fine. But it's gotta be real quick, all right?" *Man,* Magda thought, *this girl is so good she's got even me doing press. Be careful.*

The stage bustled with handheld audio sticks, phones set on "mic," and one guy with a video camera.

"Here's our guy!" Kristina waved Magda through and set her up directly in front of the young, Euro-styled videographer.

"Okay . . . Magdalena?"

Magda gave him a look that set his back straight. There were many ways in which she was absolutely untraditional, but when it came to addressing someone, someone older and accomplished, she'd never shake what her mama taught her.

He corrected himself. "*Señora Soto.* Can you tell us why this meeting of minority small business leaders is so important?"

Magda switched into "on" mode, a function of years of pageant training. She also had the rare ability to fuse conviction and concision. The few within earshot hushed to listen, then stifled the urge to applaud when she was done.

Magda's Spanish wasn't perfect, but it was authoritative. The greatest gift her parents had given her was neither her swimmer's body nor her gorgeous face, computer-like brain, or work ethic, but the superpower of being multilingual. Multilingual meant global. And global meant powerful. Global meant money.

"*Muchisimas gracias, Señora Soto.* So happy you could be here and help us!"

Magda nodded a good-bye and looked around to note where everyone else was headed. Like cattle to feed, most were moving toward the door that opened on lunch. Magda's stomach commanded her to follow.

"Excuse me, Ms. Soto?" called a dulcet voice.

"Yessss." With polite exasperation, Magda turned around, then looked a bit downward, toward the much smaller person speaking to her.

"Hi, I'm Paloma Sala."

It was the fortieth hand of the day offered in greeting. Magda took it while she also drew in the woman before her with her eyes. Beautiful skin. Umber. *Her mouth could be in a toothpaste ad.* This had to be the most attractive woman here, well, to her taste—and she was in a red dress. Magda's groin awoke, silencing her hungry stomach.

"Paloma." She rolled the name in her mouth. "That's my *tía*'s name."

A quiet three seconds moved like glue as their hands remained together as Magda took Paloma in and Paloma lay in her gaze, hypnotized by her striking figure and noted power.

"Hey, kids! You've met." It was Kristina. "Paloma, this is Magda. Magda, Paloma."

"Yeah, hon, we just got that done." Magda snickered gently while continuing to gaze into Paloma's full, blushed face.

Kristina caught on as Paloma looked away, suddenly a bit shy. "Good! Okay, so . . . Paloma runs an amaaazing education firm that specializes in financial curriculum for schools."

This mention of her work, her passion, woke Paloma up

and she chimed in. "Yes, and we're doing great so far. But we're always in need of more funding, so . . ."

Magda let go of her hand and snapped back into business mode. "Listen, I've gotta nab the CTO during this break, but are you in town for the night?" she asked her new acquaintance in the fitted red dress.

Kristina put on a knowing smile as she watched the two women.

"*Yes.*" Paloma nearly jumped on Magda, most likely excited about the source of "funding" she was about to spend time with, mildly unaware of Magda's possible intentions. "I'm staying just a few blocks down. Here's my card—feel free to text me. And can I have yours?"

"Sure." Magda handed it over like something precious. "Just keep it close, okay?"

"Absolutely. See you soon." Paloma bowed slightly and made her way to the door with her fellow lingering networkers.

Kristina followed Magda's covetous gaze. "Maaagdaaa . . ." Her head tilted in a here-you-go-again.

"She wants to talk. So, we'll talk!" *We'll do a lot of talking,* Magda thought as she ran her fingers through the front flop of her blond do.

"Shit, girl . . . *coño.* Listen, she's straight. Coming out of a bad marriage—husband cheated, yada yada—so the last thing she needs is for you to screw her over."

"Sounds like what she needs is some lovin', ya heard?" Magda threw on her urban-vanilla persona when she could, for fun. She was no crasser than her closest straight female friends. Shoot, only Cat held it all too tight in—she was nearly a novitiate, and mostly because she was a workaholic. Luz could catcall a man like nobody's business and Gabi, damn. Gabi had been one of Magda's first post-closet conquests but now was simply a dear friend who knew her all too well. And shit, that girl could talk about pleasuring men in graphic detail, without a stutter. Not that Magda ever wanted to hear about that.

"Ugh." Kristina knew her warnings fell on deaf ears. Magda, just like many of the men in the room, thought with what was between her legs. She savored her plan to text Paloma later, wrapped her arm around her friend, and led her to the door. "C'mon. Let's eat."

Connect with U_s

Visit us online at
KensingtonBooks.com
to read more from your favorite authors, see books
by series, view reading group guides, and more.

Join us on social media
for sneak peeks, chances to win books and prize packs,
and to share your thoughts with other readers.

facebook.com/kensingtonpublishing
twitter.com/kensingtonbooks

Tell us what you think!
To share your thoughts, submit a review,
or sign up for our eNewsletters, please visit:
KensingtonBooks.com/TellUs.